Barefoot Memories

The Tradewinds Series

Porch Swing Girl
Sand Castle Dreams
Mele Kalikimaka
Barefoot Memories

Barefoot Memories

Book four in the Tradewinds series

By Taylor Bennett

Barefoot Memories
Published by Mountain Brook Ink
White Salmon, WA U.S.A.

The website addresses shown in this book are not intended in any way to be or imply an endorsement on the part of Mountain Brook Ink, nor do we vouch for their content.

This story is a work of fiction. All characters and events are the product of the author's imagination. Any resemblance to any person, living or dead, is coincidental.

Scriptures taken from the Holy Bible, New International Version®, NIV®. Copyright © 1973, 1978, 1984, 2011 by Biblica, Inc.™ Used by permission of Zondervan. All rights reserved worldwide. www.zondervan.com The "NIV" and "New International Version" are trademarks registered in the United States Patent and Trademark Office by Biblica, Inc.™

ISBN 978-1-943959-79-2
© 2020 Taylor Bennett

The Team: Miralee Ferrell, Nikki Wright, Cindy Jackson
Cover Design: Indie Cover Design, Lynnette Bonner Designer

Mountain Brook Ink is an inspirational publisher offering fiction you can believe in.
Printed in the United States of America

Dedication

To Aunt Janice and Dr. Freeh—
Without you, the world of *Tradewinds* wouldn't exist.
Thank you both for everything.

Acknowledgments

"Acknowledgments are hard," I lamented to my mom. "It's hard to thank the same people over and over again."

And it's true.

It's almost impossible to put into words the depth with which I appreciate the people who have helped me in my writing journey. It's even harder to do it twice—let alone three, four times!! I'm beyond-words thankful for every single one of you who have come alongside me in my writing journey and offered help, encouragement, and virtual cake as I walk through creative dry spells/celebrate accomplishments/etc.

But beyond-words-thankfulness means exactly what you'd think. It goes beyond words. Which means that the words I have with which to thank you all feel ridiculously inadequate.

Yet still I will try:

Miralee Ferrell, you're the best editor/publisher/boss a person could ever ask for. Thank you for taking a chance on me all those years ago, for falling just as in love with Olive and Brander and Jazz as I did, and for believing in me even when I can't believe in myself. You have no idea how much your support means to me, and I only hope that one day I can put into words how grateful I am to know you. You're a star!

Sonya Downing and Jenny Mertes—you two are the most incredible editors/proofreaders I've ever met, and I'm so thankful to God for bringing us together. This book would not be half of what it is without your expert help. Thank you!!

Sara Ella, Nadine Brandes, Jim Rubart, Stephanie Morrill, Jill Williamson, and all the other "real writers" out there who have offered me priceless advice and support over the years—I wouldn't be writing these words right now if not for all of you. Thank you for helping me believe that I actually *can* write the stories my heart yearns to tell.

Virtual shave ice to all of my Porch Swing Girls—those special members of my street team who would literally drop anything and everything to help me celebrate a cover reveal/book launch/epic giveaway, etc. I have no idea how I got so blessed as to have found you, but I'm *so* grateful that I did. You're the best!

Mom and Dad, thank you for putting up with a crazy-writer type of daughter. Most people are smart enough to at least move out before they decide to become entrepreneurs/college students/authors—all at the same time! Thanks for putting up with my crazy schedule, writerly ramblings, and late nights spent bent over the keyboard. If writing books ever makes me rich and famous, I'll buy you both a condo in Maui—you deserve it.

And finally, thank you Jesus for this story. When I look back over it, I see so much that comes from You. Not me! Readers—if you find any part of this book wise, witty, or wonderful, rest assured that those words come from Him. And to Him be the glory for ever and ever. Amen.

Chapter One

New Year's Eve

"HAPPY NEW YEAR!" MY LITTLE SISTER Macie reaches over me on the couch to grab a stray party horn, then blows it—right in my ear.

I yelp and jump off the couch before winking across the room at my best friend, Jazz, then ruffle Macie's topsy-turvy ponytail. "Back-atcha, squirt." I smile—it *is* New Year's Eve after all. Why let something like a burst eardrum spoil the evening?

Macie giggles and hops off the couch to stand next to me, nearly colliding with Gramma, who steps into the room with a platter piled high with goodies sure to give Macie even more of a sugar rush than she has already.

Jazz's gaze finds my own, and we wind up on either side of Gramma as she places her treat tray on the coffee table. "Thanks for having me over, *Tutu* Bonnie." Jazz grins at Grams as she reaches for a pineapple upside-down cupcake, and I do the same. When Macie and I first came to live with Grams in Maui, it seemed weird for Jazz to call Grams *Tutu*, the Hawaiian word for Grandma. Now it seems natural. After all, we're all one big *ohana*—a family, connected by love if not by blood.

Strange, the things a person gets used to.

My gaze strays to the framed photo of Mom hanging in the hall. All things considered, I've adjusted to life on the islands pretty well over the past months. But will I ever get used to celebrating the holidays without Mom?

Footsteps sound from the stairwell before I can ride my runaway train of thought right down the line to a pity party. Dad appears in the doorway wearing a garish sequined tie over his usual weekend uniform of dark-wash jeans and Harvard University t-shirt. He's practically lived in that getup—minus the tie, of course—since he surprised us all by showing up on Gramma's doorstep a couple of weeks before Christmas.

"Who got the party started without me?" He crosses the room to grab a handful of Gramma's famous macadamia nut caramel corn.

"Nice look, Dad." I snort at his disco-ball tie and pretend to cover my eyes. "At least now we don't have to bother staying up to watch the ball drop—you *are* the ball."

Dad laughs. "Speaking of letting things drop..." He flashes a grin that makes the hair on the base of my neck prickle. The last time Dad let something drop, Macie and I were the *something* in question.

A bubble of resentment forms in my chest, and suddenly I'm stuck in my head, watching Dad dump me and Macie here. Watching him transform into a monster before my very eyes. Watching him run home to put our house on the market without even asking us how we might feel about it.

Now that I know Dad can do all of that without a backward glance...who knows what else he has planned that will rock my world?

As if she can sense my nerves, Jazz sidesteps closer to me, her prosthetic leg clunking against Gramma's polished floors. I open my mouth to whisper to her, but Dad clears his throat and cuts me off. "I believe I can speak for all of us when I say that the last year has been the most challenging one we've ever faced. Now that the New Year is—"

"Sorry to interrupt." Jazz reaches out to squeeze my hand. "But do you want me to leave? This sounds kind of personal."

"No way." I return the squeeze so hard Jazz's fingers twitch. "You're family. You're *ohana*. You're my other sister. Whatever Dad has to say, you should hear it too." Besides, whether I'm willing to admit it or not, I'd roll over and croak without Jazz here to support me right now.

"Continuing on then." Dad brushes his hands together and squares his shoulders, looking every inch the esteemed Harvard professor—sequined tie and all. "I'd like to attempt to make up for some small portion of where I went wrong this last year. But to do that, we need to spend more time together. As a family."

Goosebumps tug at my arms, despite the warmth and coziness of Gramma's living room. Family togetherness is a good thing, right? Unless Dad plans on dragging me and Macie to Boston with him when he goes back to work.

"That's why I've decided to stay here, if that's all right with you, Bonnie." Dad delivers this zinger in a tone similar to one he might use to discuss the weather.

Too bad I can't respond in the same way.

"What?" My mouth falls open, but thankfully a quick scan of the living room assures me that everyone else reacted to Dad's news in the same way.

"Of course you can stay, Alex. But—you're leaving Harvard?" Gramma's eyes goggle like fishing lures in the choppy waves at the Lahaina Breakwall. "You just got your tenure."

Dad shakes his head and takes a breath. "Not leaving permanently but going on sabbatical."

"You're staying?" Macie bounces on her toes and clasps her hands over her chest, then gives another toot on her horn. "Then this is gonna be the best-est New Year ever."

A smile replaces Gramma's gaping, gasping mouth, and her gaze flickers with warmth. "How long will you be able to stay?"

"I'm not exactly sure yet. I'll admit, this was a bit of a

last-minute decision." Dad's eyes meet my own, and I flash a smile his way, even though my stomach is churning beneath the surface of my New Year's cheer.

Since Dad showed up for Christmas, we've been getting along about as well as I get along with my friend Brander's dog Rosco. That is to say, *barely*.

It's not Dad's fault he tries too hard to patch over the holes that got torn in our family when Mom died, but still...

I sigh.

"Right, *Olive*?" Jazz elbows me straight in the ribs.

I wince, refocusing on the festive scene before me. Macie is still dancing around with her horn, Gramma is on her way to the kitchen—probably for more snacks—and...something tells me Dad's waiting for an answer. From me.

"Uh, right." I smile wider and shrug, then pull Jazz aside the second Dad steps over to waltz down the hall with Macie. "What exactly did I agree to?"

"That you'll chip in to help get Macie a puppy for her birthday." Jazz's voice is deadpan, but the light in her eyes dances like the flames of a late-summer bonfire.

I laugh, though a tiny bit of my stomach twists at the thought. "You *are* kidding. Right?"

Jazz snickers. "Of course, I'm kidding. We made sure your dad knew he wouldn't disturb us while we did school is all."

"Gotcha." When Jazz lost her leg to cancer this summer, she decided to do her junior year of high school online. Since she needed help catching up her grades—and I wasn't exactly itching to be the new girl at a new school—I joined her in her homeschooling efforts. "I can't believe we're going back to school already. It seems like we barely started Christmas vacation."

"Tell me about it." Jazz opens her mouth, as if to say more, but then my phone blares its jaunty ringtone—a certain hit single by a certain new Christian music star.

"It must be Brander." I reach into my pocket. "He said he'd try to call in between sets."

I never could have dreamed that Brander Delacroix, the island's most music-loving, God-fearing teenager, would have headed off to Nashville last fall, but viral videos have a strange way of throwing a monkey wrench in people's lives. A freak encounter with the right viewers sent a clip of Brander's singing into the national spotlight, and now it seems he's stuck there.

But for how long?

"Are you going to answer that?" Jazz motions toward my pocket, and I withdraw the phone, moving a little slower than normal. There must be unusually high melancholy levels in the air tonight—a byproduct of all of the verses of "Auld Lang Syne" being sung around the world?

I blink hard a couple of times and answer the call—a video chat, actually. Within seconds, Brander's face flashes on the screen, and I turn the phone so he can see both me and Jazz. "Happy New Year!"

"Not for us." Jazz beams, then checks the time on her phone. "Not for another...six hours."

"Oh. Right." Brander shrugs, and his trademark ebony cowlick bobs atop his head. "I've gotta go onstage pretty soon, but I wanted to make sure and catch you guys."

"Thanks for doing that." I quirk an eyebrow at the phone's camera. "This is your last show, right?"

Brander nods. "Yep. The midnight spectacular." He yawns.

Jazz claps her hands together. "Does that mean you're coming home soon?"

"Not exactly." Brander's almond-shaped eyes grow even narrower than usual, and he hangs his head. "It sounds like I've got some loose ends to tie up in Nashville with Mike and the label."

"For real?" Jazz groans. "We're supposed to go down the

road to Hana this weekend. Olive's calendar says so."

Before he left, Brander got me a calendar with a smattering of weekend dates filled in with pre-planned adventures for the three of us to go on after he comes home from his tour. My stomach sinks at the thought of having to throw all those plans into the bay because of something as silly as *loose ends*.

"I'm sorry." Brander's gaze darkens. "I wasn't too thrilled about it either when Mike told me. But I'll try to make it home soon."

Thankfully Jazz is quick to change the subject, and we chat for a few precious minutes before Brander peers into the phone, as though trying to see farther into the house. "Is that one of *Tutu* Bonnie's famous treat trays?"

I nod and pan toward the spread laid out on the coffee table. "Bet you wish you were here, huh?"

A cloud passes over Brander's face, obscuring his smile for a moment, but he's quick to regain his usual laid-back expression. "Speaking of Bonnie, is she around?"

Grams must've been listening from her spot in the kitchen, because she's quick to come over and say hi to Brander. They spend a couple minutes catching up—sounds like something about a mutual friend on both of their prayer lists—before a commotion rises on Brander's end of the phone.

"Sorry. Gotta go. That's the intro music for my set." Brander's eyebrows twist, and he peers into the phone to wave at the three of us. "Have a great rest of your night. And happy New Year."

"Happy New Year!" Jazz, Gramma, and I say it at the same time as the screen goes black and Macie and Dad dash into the room, both of them headed straight for Gramma's treat tray.

Jazz and I join them in their quest for sugar, then we all head for a stroll along the beach before returning and congregating around the coffee table for a board game marathon. Even though Dad seems a little uncomfortable amongst us girls, he manages to beat us in a game of Life.

After a while, though, we're yawning more than talking. One by one, we fall silent—sucked into the age-old void of sleepiness mingled with nostalgia. Soon the only sound is the echo of Gramma's wall clock, every tick moving us closer and closer toward midnight. Toward a new year—a fresh start?

A cluster of candles on an end table flicker, and the darkness beyond the window seeps in to the living room, wrapping each of us—except Macie, who's snoring like a model train engine in Dad's lap—in our own velvet curtain of memories.

As if drawn by invisible strings, I slip out of the living room and creep upstairs, where I grab a half-full notebook from my desk. Before Mom died and the world as I knew it erupted, I used to keep a semi-consistent journal. Maybe I'll start writing again this year.

But until then...

I flip it open and skim through the pages until I find it:

December 31st

Funny how last year at this time life was normal. And now...

A wave of tears builds deep in my chest, but I swallow it down and read:

I'm not usually a New Year's Resolution kind of person, but this year is different. I'm almost sixteen—time for me to start planning for the future. What better time than now?

To be Completed This Year
1. Get my driver's license
2. Read Jane Eyre. All of it.
3. Get an Instagram account. (But what would I post?)
4. Look into Harvard undergrad admissions—start with

Dad

    5. Volunteer somewhere?

    6. Come up with something cool to get Mom for her big 4-0 B-Day

There are more items on the list, but I slam the journal cover closed before I can read any more. Here I am, a year later, and I can't check a single thing off my bucket list—minus that Instagram account. And my few random posts never got more than a handful of likes.

But taking driver's ed?

Reading Jane Eyre?

Nope.

Mom barely made it to her fortieth birthday, and it was a pretty pathetic affair, spent in a sterile hospital room with a handful of saggy balloons and an overly sweet bakery cake. *You deserved so much better, Mom.*

"Olive!" A commotion sounds from the living room, and I check the time—only five minutes until midnight. "Where are you? Come on!"

Footsteps pitter-patter up the stairs, and I shove the journal into my desk drawer as Macie barges into the room. "You're going to miss the New Year!"

A smile overtakes my wavering frown as I let Macie take me by the arm and drag me downstairs, where Jazz snaps a party hat onto my head and Gramma hands me a horn.

We stand clustered together, watching on Grams' staticky TV screen as the Times Square ball makes its descent. As the ball reaches the ground, the ancient television speakers crackle as the crowd onscreen lets out an earsplitting cheer.

Another wave of tears wells up, nearly choking me, and I close my eyes—alone for a precious moment amid the clamor of cheers and Happy-New-Year wishes.

God, I don't have time to write out any New Year's

resolutions right now, but I know You're listening. And this year, I only have one goal.

I'm going to do whatever it takes to get life back to normal—old normal, new normal, doesn't matter. All I know is I'm ready to stop hurting and start healing. Amen.

And then, despite everything that's happened in this last year, I throw up my hands, blow into my party horn, and give Gramma a smooch on the cheek.

It's January first, after all—a fresh start after the most painful year of my life.

Things can only go up from here.

Chapter Two

DAD DROPS ONTO THE STOOL NEXT to me at the breakfast bar as I bite into one of Gramma's famous coconut muffins early Monday morning. "Are you ready to get back to the books?"

A coconut crumb slides down the wrong side of my throat, and I cough before answering. "No. Jazz and I both wish it was still vacation." I cast a wary eye at Dad before taking another bite of muffin. Dad and I don't do small talk. At least, not anymore. Most likely, the play-pretend friendliness he's exhibited ever since he showed up last month will wear off all too soon.

Dad huffs and grabs a muffin for himself before slathering it all over with butter and taking a bite. He doesn't even warm it up first. "Well I hope you've prepared yourself. It's almost time for your final exams."

"Right. In fact—" I shove half the muffin in my mouth and jump from the stool. "Now that you say that, I can't even remember where my bio textbook is. I'd better find my stuff before Jazz gets here." A handful of steps later, I'm halfway upstairs, having escaped what would no doubt have been a painfully awkward conversation. If only Gramma hadn't had to work an early shift at the art gallery where she sells her handmade jewelry. She's the perfect buffer, and it always helps to have reinforcements around when it comes to conversing with Dad.

In the room I share with Macie, I root around for my biology textbook as I finish my breakfast. But the richness of Gramma's pineapple-glazed coconut muffin does little to sweeten my mood.

Why is it that I clam up every time Dad tries to have a normal conversation with me? I should be glad he's trying. I slam my new literature book—*Animal Farm*—onto my desk and stack a few notebooks on top of it.

It's not like I was ever Dad's best bud. That's always been Macie's role. But ever since Dad stepped into the hospital room that night to find me standing stock still as Mom breathed her last...

Things have never been the same.

And I doubt they ever will be, either.

I grab another notebook and shudder as the roar of ocean waves seeps through my ears, ending up deep in my mind. There, the steady crashing morphs into a different rhythm. One that eerily mirrors the echoing beep of a heart monitor.

And then suddenly I'm saying goodbye...again. The cacophony of hospital noises, plus the pounding of my pulse, mixes with the hum of Gramma's ceiling fan, the noise building within me in a dramatic crescendo. I drop the book I'm holding and clap my hands over my ears.

Something to stop the noise.

Anything.

"Olive?"

Rats. Guess my hands aren't soundproof after all.

"What?" I whirl toward the door and drop my hands to keep from looking like a total idiot in front of my little sister.

"I don't wanna go to school." Macie scowls and scuffs her foot along the floor. "I miss Christmas. And the cookies. And the *presents*."

A half-smile pulls at my lips, washing away the lingering sourness of my mood. If only I could be as innocent as Macie—only worried about the next time my house would receive a visit from the big man in red. I cross the room and give Macie's chubby arm a squeeze. "I get it, squirt. But we'll survive. Plus," I lower my voice to a conspiratorial whisper,

"I heard Gramma say something about ordering in Pirate Pete's tonight."

"You mean the bad news pizza?" Macie's eyes grow wide. "The last time we ate Pirate Pete's was when Jazzie—"

"Oh, yeah." Macie's right. The one and only time Gramma ever served us Pirate Pete's famous pineapple pizza was the night Jazz told us about her cancer. And the consequential amputation of her leg. I've had it a few times since—it's a favorite at youth group—but Macie hasn't. "You know there's no such thing as bad news pizza, right?"

Macie just stares.

"If it makes you feel any better, I'll make sure Grams gets something besides pineapple. Okay?"

"I *do* like pizza." Macie sets her mouth in a hard line and nods. Temper tantrum averted. "I guess I'll survive."

"I knew I could count on you." I brush a clump of muffin crumbs from Macie's chin and lend her a smile that's as much for my benefit as it is for her own. "Now come on. We'd better get you ready for the bus stop. Jazz'll be here any minute, and I still have a biology book to find."

By the time Jazz shows up, Macie's face is crumb free, I've successfully located my bio textbook, and Dad has made himself comfortable in the living room—AKA the schoolroom. And he's sitting on *my* side of the couch.

"You girls won't mind if I'm in here, will you?" Dad adjusts his wire-rimmed glasses and lifts his latest reading material—a book of essays on some wacky-quacky psychological condition. "I like to stretch out when I read, and I'm not sure the porch swing will tolerate that."

"No problem, Mr. Galloway." Jazz doesn't give Dad a second glance as she flops onto the loveseat and wrestles her math book out of her backpack.

I, on the other hand, keep an eye on Dad as I squeeze onto the loveseat next to Jazz. I know he's into books and all that, but he's never been the laze-around-and-read-all-day type. Cozy bookish days were always more Mom's thing.

Either Dad's changed a lot in the last six months, or he's got something up his sleeve. Like spying on me and Jazz. Emphasis on *me*.

Grams has been wary about school all year, convinced that I can't keep up with my own schoolwork while helping Jazz with hers. Maybe they're in on this plot together.

Maybe there isn't a plot and I'm way overthinking this.

All I know is I'm not too fond of the idea of Dad crashing my school days with Jazz. Because, even though we get a lot of work done, we definitely talk too. I'm sure not about to have a heart-to-heart with my best friend in front of a Harvard psychology professor. Especially when said professor also happens to be my father.

So instead, it's business as usual—or *un*usual, as the case may be. I never get through my work this fast, and even Jazz is going along at a faster clip than normal.

By the time Dad rouses himself from the couch and pads into the kitchen in search of lunch, I'm done for the day. All Jazz has left is a bio quiz and a math worksheet.

Usually that means free time, but when I tell Dad as much over a meal of haphazardly constructed PB&J sandwiches with *way* too much peanut butter, he frowns. "You two haven't been working very long. Olive, perhaps you should start on your next day's workload. I never have liked the notion of homeschooling. It breeds laziness and fosters a neglect of responsibility."

I open my mouth with a counterargument—no matter what he wants to say about homeschool, I know for a fact that "real school" breeds bullying and insecurity. Even my private school in Boston was full of drama queens and snobs. Besides, my "advanced" classes moved through things at a snail's pace.

Unfortunately, Dad's pocket dings before I can make my point. Holding a finger in the air, he digs out his phone, ducking his head to read the illuminated screen.

If Gramma was here right now, that phone would be back in his pocket in two seconds flat. She croaked the first—and last—time I tried to read a text at the table. But Gramma's still at the gallery, so Dad pecks on the device for several long, silent minutes before pocketing it and looking up with a smile. "You two are awfully quiet today. I hope I haven't been disturbing you."

"Not at all." Jazz beams and returns Dad's smile. "It's nice to have another body in the house." I resist the urge to roll my eyes. Doesn't Jazz get that Dad is totally ruining our time together? Or does she honestly not care?

Both of those possibilities seem absolutely absurd, yet Jazz seems genuinely fine with how the day is going. Even so, I keep a close eye on Jazz during the rest of the afternoon, while I knock out half of tomorrow's assignments.

By the time Jazz is done with her quiz and Dad seems appropriately satisfied by my slaving over two extra pages of trigonometry equations, it's almost time for Grams and Macie to come home.

Which means that if I want to enjoy a bit of time with my best friend, I need to act fast.

"Wanna go check on the papayas out back? Grams said there are a few almost ready to pick." I lead the way to the door, and Jazz is close behind. A few blissful moments later, we're alone on the deck that hovers above Gramma's lush garden.

"Come on." I jog down the steps, setting a course for the papaya tree at the farthest corner of the overgrown lawn.

Sure enough, several of the strange-looking tropical fruits are ripe and ready to eat, but that's not why I'm out here. Jazz must know it too.

"What gives?" She plucks a clementine from a neighboring tree and peels it, then hands me half and pops a segment into her mouth.

"What *gives*? Are you kidding? Dad must be driving you nuts."

"Huh?" Jazz mumbles something else around another piece of clementine, and some of the fruit's orange nectar spurts onto her chin. She clears her throat and wipes her face before trying again. "Why would your dad bug me? He's sitting on the couch, doing his thing."

"He's not making you uncomfortable? I've felt like a bug under a microscope all day."

"Why? He's your *dad.* And a pretty cool one too." Jazz shrugs and rocks on her toes. If I didn't know better, I'd never guess that she had a prosthetic leg hiding under those denim overalls. "But...I guess I think having any kind of a dad would be cool. Especially one like yours."

"You're serious?"

"Totally."

"Good for you then. I guess."

"What do you mean?" Jazz pops the last piece of fruit into her mouth before nodding at my untouched half. "You going to eat that?"

"Go ahead." I toss it to her. "Ever since Mom died, things with Dad have been...off."

"What do you mean?" Jazz plucks a jasmine blossom from one of Gramma's overgrown bushes and sticks it in her long, blonde braid.

"There's nothing for us to talk about. If we ever ended up talking about Mom, he'd give me a big laundry list of names for all the stages of grief I'm going through." I reach up to touch my necklace, worrying its smooth orange-and-pink shell pendant with my thumb. "Using his big, fancy psychology PhD to help parent his own daughter might make him feel better, but I don't want to be his next emotional guinea pig."

"What do you want to be then?"

"I want to be his *daughter*. But if he can't stand that…" I huff out a breath so hard it almost makes me cough. "The thing is, Dad and I never got along that great even when Mom *was* alive. Now after everything that's happened, I wish he'd leave us alone."

"Whoa." Jazz flinches, as though taking a verbal bullet for my dad. "That's harsh. He's hurting too, you know."

"That's why he thought it would be a good idea to treat me and Macie like a bag headed for the Goodwill last summer? Just another load of junk to get out of the house before it went on the market."

"I wouldn't say *Tutu* Bonnie's place is anything like Goodwill. And I would know. I've shopped there ever since I was a little kid."

"Fair enough."

"And fine—your dad messed up. But now he's here. Making things right." Jazz plucks another jasmine flower. "And from what I've seen, he's a great dad. Remember, some of us don't even get to *have* dads."

"I'd be more than happy to give you mine."

"Stop it." Jazz narrows her eyes so much that, if I didn't know better, I'd think she was glaring at me. Maybe she is. It's definitely an expression I've never seen her wear before. "You don't realize how lucky you are. I used to ask God for a daddy every single night when I was little. All I got was Mom dragging home some creepy boyfriend every few months." Jazz's voice cracks. Only a little, but I hear it. "Sorry to turn this all on me, but maybe you need to get a new perspective."

"Right. Because I'm a selfish, spoiled brat." I mutter the words to myself, but much as Jazz or anyone else might be inclined to think, I'm not being sarcastic. "I know I should be more grateful than I am most of the time, but it's tough."

"You know how many mornings I wake up wishing I didn't have to put on this leg?" Jazz bends to knock on her left knee, pressing the ragged white denim of her overalls against the pole of her prosthesis. "Gratitude isn't always easy. But if I didn't have this leg, I wouldn't be able to walk. And if I didn't *need* this leg, I'd be dead. Just because things are a pain sometimes doesn't mean they can't have a purpose."

I open my mouth, Jazz's words whirling too fast in my brain for me to formulate an appropriate response. And, as it turns out, I don't need to.

Jazz's pocket starts playing the chorus of Brander's single, and she's quick to step behind a hibiscus bush and answer the call. In a few minutes, she returns. "That was Aunt Ruby. She's waiting out front."

"Rats." I frown, then check the time. Macie and Grams should be home any minute, and something tells me I'll be instantly subjected to at least an hour's worth of Macie's back-to-school stories. "Can't you stay for dinner? Grams is ordering in Pirate Pete's."

"I wish, but Ruby's taking me to visit Mom."

"Oh. Have fun." I regret those words as soon as they leave my mouth. How much fun can visiting an alcohol rehab clinic be? "Sorry. I mean...you know what I mean, right?"

"I know. See ya." Jazz wiggles her wrist, thumb and pinky extended in a *shaka*, her silvery gaze steeled with the determination of a soldier going off to do battle. I return the Hawaiian-style wave as Jazz disappears around the side of the house, but I can't make myself walk out with her. Instead, I hang back and watch her go.

I've done a lot of watching since Mom died.

Maybe too much.

A breeze lifts my hair, and wind chimes ring in the distance as I take a step forward. If I hurry, I could make today my day to stop watching and start living. I could catch up with Jazz, ride out to the rehab center with her, and be the support I'm sure she needs.

I take another step toward the front yard, then another. I can do this. For Jazz. Even though the thought of it makes me miss my own mom so bad my heart throbs in my chest.

"Olive!" I haven't even reached the gate when Macie's voice echoes from the back porch. "Grammy wants you."

I hesitate, half of my heart begging me to stick with my original plan and catch up with Jazz, the rest of me ready to play coward and run inside. Grass tickles my bare feet, and I stand on tiptoe to peer into the front yard.

As I do, Ruby's dinged-up minivan pulls away from the curb with a sputter and cough. Guess my choice has been made for me.

Still, I can't keep from clenching my fist in resolve as I make my way inside.

The next time I have to make a decision like this, I won't back down so easily. This is my year to stop watching and start living, after all. So far, I haven't been doing a very good job.

A bird caws from a neighbor's hibiscus bush, as though reprimanding me. *Yeah, yeah. I hear you. I'm going to get started on it...soon.*

But the words still feel fake somehow. I pluck a piece of bougainvillea as I walk inside and twirl the stem around my little finger.

Will I actually be able to follow through with my resolution, or will I let another year go by without checking a single thing off my list of goals?

I won't know until I try.

Chapter Three

Guilt gnaws at my stomach off and on throughout the evening with nearly as much intensity as my hunger. By the time the Pirate Pete's delivery boy drops off a box of extra-large pizza—half barbecue chicken, half Hawaiian—I feel like I could eat the whole thing myself.

"Olive, did I tell you what Mr. Sanders had us do today?" Macie beams across the table at me and grabs a slice of barbecue pizza right after Dad prays for the food.

"No." I return Macie's smile, then ask the question I know she's waiting for. "What did Mr. Sanders have you do?"

"I thought you'd *never* ask." Macie throws one hand over her head with all the dramatics of a Hollywood starlet before launching into a play-by-play of her school day.

I keep one eye on her as I reach for a slice of pizza, hand hovering over the greasy box. A piece of Hawaiian, complete with smoky ham and fresh pineapple—not the fake canned stuff like on the mainland—calls to me, but I'm instantly swept back to that night last summer when Jazz...

Don't be ridiculous. I flex my fingers before grabbing the slice, a chunk of pineapple dangling from it by a long, cheesy string. There's no such thing as Bad News Pizza. There never was.

Halfway through my piece, I've almost convinced myself of that fact when Macie launches up from the table and scampers down the hall to dig in her backpack for a crumpled sheet of paper. "I almost forgot." She races over to the table and jumps into her seat. "Mr. Sanders told us about a black king who had big dreams. And then we drew pictures about our own dream. See?"

She brandishes her drawing, revealing a cartoony dog with floppy ears, a wagging tail, and a protruding tongue. Much as I dislike dogs, I can't help smiling. "Is that a picture of Koa?"

Last fall, Jazz and I joined a teen support group through the church, and we all played a part in training a puppy—Koa—to become an emotional support dog. The little mutt was a handful at first, but even I couldn't resist his scruffy-puppy ways for long. Which is saying something for a girl who watched a pit bull kill her one and only childhood pet.

"Yeah. I miss him a lot." Macie frowns, then passes the picture to Dad. "That's why I decided that my big dream is to get a doggy all for myself."

"Whoa, there." I nearly choke on a piece of pineapple. "You want a dog? But I hate—"

"Daddy, Olive said a bad word." Macie shoves half a piece of pizza in her mouth and cuts her eyes at me.

"Good grief, Macie. Hate isn't a *real* bad word."

"Then why do you always tell me not to say it?"

"Because—never mind. Koa and I were cool with each other and everything, but that doesn't mean I want to have a dog, like, living here. In the house. Permanently." My throat constricts, keeping me from taking another bite of pizza. "Besides. Dogs are expensive."

Macie's eyes water, and she shoves away her plate. "But Mr. Sanders said anything is possible if we dream big enough."

I open my mouth to argue with the validity of that statement when Gramma jumps in to rescue me. "Macie, I think Mr. Sanders might have been wrong. With *God*, all things are possible. But we aren't strong enough to do anything on our own. You know that, right?"

"But Mr. Sanders *said*." Macie snuffles and wipes away

a tear.

"Well." Dad clears his throat and dunks a slice of pizza in ranch dressing. "Even teachers can be wrong sometimes. Haven't I ever made a mistake before?"

The conversation goes back and forth for a while, Gramma cautioning Macie about different worldviews and how she shouldn't automatically believe everything her teacher tells her. Dad even tries to pull out some psychologist jargon, though his Latin-rooted, triple-syllable words cause Macie to stare at him like he's sprouted another head.

Unfortunately, by the time he's run out of life lessons, Dad hasn't managed to confuse Macie enough to get her to forget what lies at the true heart of this mess.

Macie wants a puppy.

That's even more abundantly clear when I help her with her homework after dinner. It's all she can do to get through a page of math drills before moving on to her art project. "We have to make a collage about our dream. So I need to find pictures of puppies to put on here." Macie waves a purple sheet of construction paper, empty except for the word "DOG" scrawled in the center of the page.

I nearly laugh at my misfortune as I help Macie paw through Gramma's towering stack of happy-homemaker-type magazines to find a handful of dog pictures—everything from snapshots of scruffy mutts to professional photos of pedigreed pooches.

By the time we've glued half a dozen clippings onto the paper, my heart is pounding a little harder than usual. And Macie is *still* talking about puppies. The second Dad distracts her with the promise of a bedtime story—one about a dog, of course—I make my escape to the front porch and collapse onto the swing.

The sun hovers above the waters of the bay across the street, and the clouds swirl around it in a tie-dye pattern of pinks and oranges as evening descends on the island. For a few moments, I sit, breathing in the calm serenity.

But all too soon, Macie's case of puppy love sweeps me back to reality. My little sister can be painfully persuasive when she wants to be, and I already know Grams has a soft spot for animals. If they get Dad on board, then it's three against one.

And, even though I love my little sister and want her to be happy, even though I'd thought I was ready to face my fears, dream big, and start living...well, I wasn't planning on starting with something quite so *big*.

"Hey, Brander." My throat swells with a million words when I call him before bed that evening. There are so many things I'd like to tell him—we've only texted since our video chat on New Year's Eve—but, unfortunately, he's not *really* on the other line. At least his answering machine is a good listener.

"You won't believe what Macie's got her knickers in a twist over." I cringe at the Gramma-inspired saying, then shrug it off. Brander never used to care how I talked. Why should he now? Even though he's a...a *celebrity*.

Whatever.

Clearing my throat, I keep going, telling him—or, at least, his voicemail—all about Macie's "big dream."

I could have called Jazz, and maybe I should have—this voicemail's getting pretty long— but Brander's the only one who knows the full story about my kitten, Peaches, and that big, nasty pit bull. Besides, Jazz shouldn't have to listen to me whine twice in one day, especially after I didn't even offer to keep her company on the drive to visit her mom in rehab.

"So. Anyway, yeah. I hope you're having fun in Nashville." I've got to end this message somewhat coherently, but how? "I miss you. I mean, we all do.

Hopefully we'll see you soon. I—*aloha*, Brander."

My cheeks heat as I hang up. The old Brander would have been more than happy to let me ramble on like I did, but what will the new Brander think of my message? After all, he has—I do a quick check on my phone—fifty thousand Instagram followers. When I lived in Boston, I didn't catch the attention of any of the guys at my school. Why would someone as cool as Brander want to bother staying friends with me?

Thankfully, before I can sink deeper into a well of what-ifs and why-bothers, Gramma beckons me inside for the night. She gives my arm a gentle squeeze as I step inside, leaving behind the front porch, the balmy evening breeze, and a million unanswered questions.

Chapter Four

EARLY THE NEXT MORNING, EVEN BEFORE the wild roosters have begun to crow, I'm chomping on a piece of toasted Hawaiian bread at the breakfast bar when Gramma emerges from her downstairs bedroom.

"You're up early." Gramma steps into the kitchen, sniffing the air as she walks. "Do I smell coffee?"

I shrug. "I thought I'd get it started for you."

"That's nice of you." Gramma steps over to the coffeepot to pour herself a cup. Her smile is appreciative enough, but something in her gaze tells me she knows I wouldn't make her coffee for the fun of it. "Want to tell me what you're thinking now, or should we wait until the caffeine kicks in?"

I can't help but smile. One of the best—and sometimes worst—parts about Grams is that she can read me almost as well as Mom could. The thought of Mom's incredible intuition wraps a thick, fuzzy layer around my throat, but I choke it down and offer a lopsided smile. "Guess I might as well get it over with." I take another bite of toast, grimacing as it scrapes my throat on the way down. Dad must've forgotten to turn the toaster down again.

"Olive?" Gramma peers at me over the rim of her coffee cup, early-morning sunshine highlighting the feathery smile lines around her eyes.

"Sorry." I shake my head, as though that could clear the thick fog suddenly encasing my thoughts. "Maybe I need some of that coffee too."

Gramma grabs a mug advertising the Maui Ocean Center and fills it with steaming black liquid before handing it to me. I sniff it suspiciously before taking a swallow.

Way too strong.

I set the chipped mug down and sputter into a napkin to hide my grimace. "Sorry. Mom used to make hers with a lot more sugar and"—I cough again—"cream."

The corners of Gramma's mouth tip up, and she takes a slurp from her own mug. "I know. But something tells me you don't want to spend the morning talking about coffee."

"Right." A yarn-ball of words tangles in my throat, none of them sounding quite right. But I spit them out anyway. I have to, or else they'll strangle me. "We can't get a dog. I mean, Koa was cute and everything, but...no. I know Macie's going to be giving you *that look*, but if you ignore her long enough, she'll move on to wanting something else." Hopefully something a lot less traumatic than a puppy—like a kitten. A kitten would be nice.

"You don't want another dog in the house."

"Not one little bit."

Gramma purses her lips. "Macie got very attached to Koa. I think it was harder for her to say goodbye than we both realized. After all that's happened, don't you think that Macie deserves to know that she doesn't have to say goodbye to everyone and everything? That sometimes the people—or animals—who come into her life are there to stay? A dog is the most loyal friend a girl could have."

"What about you and me and all her little friends at school? We're not going anywhere." I stand and toss my toast crust in the garbage. "I get that animals are different, but...maybe she could start with a goldfish?"

"Do you really think that having a dog around would be so bad?" Gramma reaches across the counter to squeeze my hand. "I know you and Koa got off to a rough start, but it seemed like you were coming around."

"That's different."

"How so?"

"It wasn't a forever thing, and I knew it. If we're talking a full-time pet, that's different. Way different."

"I know. But do me a favor and pray about it, okay? I will too."

"What should I pray? That God'll drop a litter of puppies into Macie's lap?" I scowl and scuff at the floor. I'm being ornery and I know it, but this morning I can't help myself.

"Pray for wisdom. Guidance. For all of us." Gramma takes a long drink from her mug. "And it might not hurt to ask God for a little courage, either."

By the time Jazz shows up for school, God and I have done some serious business, but I don't feel a bit better. Maybe I won't until I get a dose of that courage Grams was talking about. Because, whether I'll ever be brave enough to admit it aloud or not, dogs still do scare me.

Just a little.

"You're awfully quiet today. Shark got your tongue?" Jazz winks at me from her spot in the armchair as she opens her history textbook.

I stick out my tongue to show her that it is, in fact, shark-free. Thank goodness Dad decided to go off and explore the island today, leaving Jazz and me with the space and time to talk. "Macie wants a puppy. And before you start squealing and offering to help her pick one out, I'll have you know that I am *not* onboard."

"I thought you liked having Koa around."

"He was okay, but that doesn't mean I want to live with a puppy twenty-four-seven."

"Have you prayed about it?"

I nod. "But I don't know what God is saying."

"Sometimes it takes a while for Him to speak. And sometimes it takes even longer for us to listen."

"Why do you sound so much like Gramma?"

Jazz practically blushes. I should've known she'd take that as a compliment. "I guess 'cause I spent so many years in her Sunday school class. Speaking of which," she adds after a moment's hesitation, "wanna go to youth group tomorrow? It feels like we haven't been in forever."

"Sure." Youth group—and shave ice with Brander afterward—was a weekly tradition for Jazz even before I showed up. The three of us were pretty much a fixture there until Brander left for Nashville. "It has been a while. The holidays were crazy."

"Cool. I've got PT in Kahului tomorrow, but I should be there in time. Aunt Ruby could swing by and pick you up if you want." Jazz grimaces and knocks on her prosthesis. "I wish we could walk, but I'm already gearing up for a lecture from Doc Freeh. Hank feels fine, but Doc keeps saying I'm going to overdo it if I'm not careful."

"Hank?"

Jazz shrugs. "It's kind of awkward calling it my stump all the time. I'm trying to find a good name. Something a bit more personable."

I roll my eyes toward the ceiling in an attempt to keep from laughing, since Jazz seems to be dead serious. By the time I've collected myself, Jazz is already turning pages in her book—faster than she was at the beginning of the year, I note with a flicker of satisfaction.

"Hey…if you have therapy tomorrow, does that mean I'll be on my own for school?"

Jazz nods. "It's not until afternoon, but Aunt Ruby wants to go early and do some shopping. I would've said something earlier, but I totally forgot about it until Ruby reminded me this morning."

"No problem." I heft my algebra book into my lap and get to work, but some part of my mind is still hung up on Jazz's earlier words.

I know it takes God a while to speak sometimes, but I hope that, whenever He does, I'll be ready to listen.

Chapter Five

"DID YOU MAKE A NEW YEAR'S resolution?" Jazz turns toward me from her spot on the porch steps after school. Even sitting a stair above her, I'm barely tall enough to meet her gaze evenly.

"Doesn't everyone make a New Year's resolution?" I lean over and pluck a plumeria blossom from one of Gramma's bushes before lifting it to my nose and taking a whiff. The scent, reminiscent of Mom's favorite perfume, is a balm to my soul.

"I didn't ask about everyone. I asked about *you*."

"Yeah. Kind of."

"How do you 'kind of' make a New Year's resolution?" Jazz props herself up on the step and adjusts her position, her prosthesis glinting in the sunlight.

"I don't know. I had a bunch of goals from last year and stuff that I forgot about when Mom...you know. So I made it my resolution to start living again. Actually do a few of the things I wanted to last year."

"Like a bucket list?"

"Kind of, I guess. I don't know. Mostly I want to find my normal." I twirl the plumeria between my fingers. "Why the sudden fascination with New Years' resolutions?"

Jazz shrugs, but if she's planning on passing off her interrogation as a case of mere curiosity, she'll have to think again. "Seriously, Jazz. What gives?"

Jazz ducks her head and twists the tail of her braid around one long, lean finger. "Yesterday Mom said she made a resolution. To stay sober all year."

"That's good." I take another breath of plumeria-scented air before tucking the flower behind my ear. "Right?"

"It's the same resolution she made last year. And the year before."

"Maybe this time she means it and things will work out. Isn't the rehab place helping her get on track?"

"You don't know my mom." A bird cackles from its perch in a tree somewhere down the street. Jazz purses her lips. "She says this treatment center is great and all that, but who's to say it'll help her any more than the last program she tried? Sometimes I want to give up on her."

"Did something happen yesterday?"

"She's—I don't get it." Jazz squeezes her thigh, right above the place where her prosthesis attaches. "The people at the center say she does great during group therapy and stuff, but whenever I visit...she's so *moody*. She spends the whole time complaining. Like it's my fault she's there. Last I checked, she was the one who signed up for the program."

"Tell me about it."

"What do you mean? Your dad's not in rehab."

"No, but a couple nights ago he went nuts over the fact that I'm *only* one percent above an A in math." I sigh, long and loud, then deepen my voice to sound more like his. "You'd better ace that final, young lady, or else you could have a permanent blight on your report card."

Jazz snickers, but I'm not laughing. "I'm telling you. He's always been a report card Nazi."

"I think it's nice that he cares."

I guess. "But he seemed really worked up over it. Then later he acted like it never happened and asked me if I wanted to play cribbage with him. He hates cribbage." And I love it, but I didn't think he knew that.

"That's totally different than what's going on with my mom." Jazz studies her lap. "So what if he keeps an eye on your grades? That means he actually cares. I don't get what's so wrong with that."

Other than the fact that, until now, he's barely spoken to me after Mom died? That he dropped me and Macie on Grams' front stoop this summer without so much as an explanation? Not that coming here was bad—it was definitely the best thing that happened all last year—but still. I'm not about to unload all of that on Jazz though. "Forget it."

"I don't think so." Jazz jerks her chin back and forth and pins me under her gaze. "Don't think I'm trying to parent you—"

"Then don't."

"No, listen." Jazz brings a hand to her chest. "Take it from me. You have no idea how lucky you are to have a dad."

I open my mouth to interrupt, but Jazz cuts me off before I can begin. "I don't care if he made a major mistake. I don't care if he was an A-class jerk. He's still in your life. He wants a relationship with you." Jazz's gaze grows cloudy, and she drops her head. "That's more than some of us ever get."

I blow out a breath from between stiff lips, and I lean my chin on my hand. "But it's like, even though he's here at Gramma's, we still have this massive ocean between us."

"I feel the same way with Mom most of the time. I always wonder if I could get through to her if I tried a little harder. Did...better." Jazz sighs. "Maybe sometimes, if we want to cross the ocean, we have to have the courage to jump in the boat and start rowing." Jazz's eyes flicker—with warmth, this time, and something tells me this pep talk was as much for her as it was for me.

"Hey, Dad."

I step into the living room after dinner that night and sit

on the couch next to him, cribbage board tucked under my arm. "About that cribbage game…" I slide the board onto the coffee table, nudging aside a stack of Dad's favorite psychology journals. "Do you have time tonight?"

Dad nods and blinks at me, as though trying to psychoanalyze my sudden change of heart, but he doesn't say anything as I pull a deck of cards from my pocket and shuffle them.

We cut for the deal, and Dad goes first. I watch as he handles the cards with the ease of a seasoned cardsharp.

"Cribbage used to be my favorite. Did you know that?" He keeps his eyes down, the cards reflecting in his glasses as they snap against each other with lightning speed as he shuffles.

"Really? What changed?"

Dad deals, and I take my cards and smother a groan. My hand holds a lousy four points. But if I could get the queen of hearts to cut up…

I lean forward to place two cards in the crib, then straighten in time to catch the tail end of Dad's wry grin. "I met your mother."

"Huh?"

Dad chuckles. "She liked cribbage even more than I did—and she was a far better player than I. She let me win when we played for the first time on our honeymoon. After that, the daggers came out. She never went easy on me again."

Despite the wave of melancholy associated with Mom, I smile. She was nothing if not competitive. I run my hand along the remainder of the deck before cutting once more. Dad lifts the card on the top of the stack and lays it face-up.

The queen of hearts.

I lift my cards high enough to cover the smugness that's sure to show on my face. It's up to me to carry on Mom's tradition of creaming Dad, and with a hand like this, I might have a chance.

The rounds go fast and furious, Dad and I pegging like fools to reach the finish line first. Even with my killer first hand, Dad manages to stake out an early lead, which results in a smack-talk battle out of which I emerge victorious. Then, before I know it, Dad's hands run dry, and I'm winning.

But it isn't until I leave him in the dust with a lucky twenty-four-point hand that something clicks into place—and not only my peg in the last hole on the cribbage board, either.

Dad and I are having fun.

We're getting along—playing a game and even talking about Mom. But mostly I'm stuck on the fact that, for the first time in almost a year, Dad and I are actually having fun.

And while this is nothing compared to eating manna in the wilderness or watching a lame man walk, I can't help but call it what it is.

A miracle.

"Play again?" I ask, returning our pegs to their starting position.

"You want to kick a man while he's down?" Dad scoffs and blinks at me through his glasses, giving me what I'm sure is his best attempt at an insulted glare. But Dad has never been good at hiding things—I can see the grin shining beneath the surface of his mock scowl.

I shuffle the deck, cards snapping. "You'd better watch out or I'll skunk you this time."

A half-dozen rounds later, it seems as though I might do exactly that, when Dad deals me a hand that totals a whopping nineteen points—cribbage-speak for *zero*. I'm frantically rearranging my cards, as though I can somehow coax a few points to magically appear in my hand, when Dad clears his throat. "Olive, there's something we need to discuss."

"Yeah?" I shiver, despite the warm, sea-scented breeze wafting in through the front window. Whatever Dad has to say, something in his voice tells me my luck has run out in more ways than one.

"You've been extremely lax in your schoolwork." Dad eyes me over his hand of cards as I lay down an ace, then he doubles my card for two points. "You were liking posts from that boy—Brander—on Instagram today at one o'clock in the afternoon. That doesn't strike me as the most productive use of your daytime hours."

"What? You're spying on me now?" I gasp in a breath and throw down another ace, though my hand shakes as I peg the resulting six points. "I was on my lunch break, Dad. So what if I wanted to check my Instagram? Every kid does that during lunch hour."

"But after your last math test don't you think—"

"It was one test, Dad. One! I got *one* bad grade on *one* test that knocked my score down—and I still have an A in the class. Give me a break." I snap my trap shut and stare past Dad to the sunset sky beyond the front window. No better way to sound like a spoiled brat than by bragging about how easy school has been.

But still...

"Seriously, though. Why are you spying on me? Just because I went through the worst summer of my life, that doesn't mean I'm going to turn into one of your rebel-teenager psycho case studies." I jerk a chin at Dad's teetering stack of psychology journals and rearrange my cards.

"Hold it right there, young lady. I deeply dislike that tone. Things might be different than they were a year ago, but I am still your father." His words, though spoken at a normal volume, boom in my ears like a cannon shot. "I expect to be treated with respect."

"Then why didn't you treat me and Macie with any of that *respect* last summer? Didn't your shrink books ever tell you? It's give respect, get respect. Besides that, it's not very good for a teenage girl's mental health to dump them on their grandma's front stoop like a hunk of garbage."

"That is quite enough, young lady." Tension rolls off Dad in waves, and though a part of me is cowering inside, another part of me thinks he deserved to hear every single word I had to say.

Still, Gramma's old-school wall clock ticks a good three dozen times before I dare open my mouth.

"Sorry." The word is small, timid, and only half-true. But it's all I can squeak out between the lumps of shame gathering in my throat. After all, as much as Dad had it coming to him, it wasn't my place to scold him.

I clear my throat, then force out a few more words. "That was dumb. Forgive me?" My heart brims over with a much more eloquent apology, but the ache in my chest stirred up by the memory of last summer keeps me from saying anything else.

I'm surprised Dad doesn't call off the game right then and there, but instead he huffs his forgiveness, then lays down a card—another ace—and takes his resulting *twelve* points.

We finish the game in silence.

And even though I manage a come-behind win that leaves Dad scratching his head, my victory is overshadowed by a black cloud of guilt.

Jazz said we should be the ones to start rowing, but I sure wish we'd talked about what to do when we dropped the oars.

Chapter Six

"I sunk the boat." I keep my voice low as I drop next to Jazz in the back seat of Ruby's minivan the next day.

"What are you talking about?" Jazz squints at me.

"With Dad. You said we should jump in and start rowing." I twine a piece of hair around my finger as Ruby blazes down the road to church. "I did, and it backfired. Dad and I are, like, incompatible."

"I've been trying to connect with Mom for sixteen years, and I haven't given up yet."

"Well, you're a better daughter than I am." Light from the setting sun streams through my window as Ruby drives across town, finally pulling in front of the church's open-air pavilion. It's already overflowing with kids from youth group, and I catch a whiff of something greasy, yet strangely appealing, as Jazz opens her door and climbs down from the van.

Jazz clambers up the pavilion steps a little slower than usual—she probably pushed herself too hard during therapy, like always—and I hang back with her. By the time we reach the top step, worship has already started.

We find a spot near the back. The setting sun beyond the pavilion creates a brilliant backdrop against which the worship team makes an odd silhouette as they lead us in the first song. I close my eyes and do my best to sing along with the music, though today's appointed worship leader isn't half as good as Brander. Brander has *soul*.

Later, it's as if Jazz can read my mind, because she leans toward me as we load our plates from the buffet line after worship. "When's Brander coming back?"

"I wish I knew. I haven't heard anything from him in forever." He never even called me after I left that message a few days ago. Maybe all my rambling really did scare him off. "I think he's pretty swamped." At least, I can't think of any other reason why he wouldn't have called back.

"Oh, well." Jazz shrugs and loads her plate with three pieces of batter-coated cod and what must be three potatoes' worth of fries before splattering the whole pile with tartar sauce. "He'll be home soon enough. I sure hope he'll be willing to do worship for the little people."

"His head better not have gotten that big." I laugh at the idea of humble, down-to-earth Brander ever getting a big head, then add a scoop of coleslaw to my plate of fish and chips before following Jazz to sit next to...

Malia?

"Aloha, girls." The dark-skinned Hawaiian beauty brushes long, thin fingers through rippling black hair, then takes a delicate bite of what appears to be dry coleslaw. Of course, there wouldn't be any fried food or mayo weighing down this swim team champ's plate.

I blow out a breath and plop into an empty chair, but before I can offer a greeting, Malia turns to ask Jazz something swimming related.

When Jazz had both legs, she managed to stay one stroke ahead of Malia at their swim meets, winning herself the title of team captain. Now Malia has taken over Jazz's position and Jazz, being her usual supportive self, seems willing to give her all the advice in the world.

By the time the two of them wrap up their powwow about freestyle strokes and relay orders, my plate is empty, save for a few grease spots and a smear of tartar sauce. And I still haven't said a single word.

Jonah, the youth pastor, claps for attention, and Jazz and Malia finally break off their conversation. Malia smiles at me and waves her fist in a *shaka,* as though noticing me for the first time. I return the gesture, but not without feeling the nerves roiling my stomach.

Last year it was always Brander, me, and Jazz against the rest of the world. Now Brander's gone and—well, something about Malia's new and improved attitude makes me wonder if she wants to become the newest member of our group. But filling Brander's place with Malia is a less-than-fair trade in my book, even though we aren't mortal enemies anymore. And Brander's going to come back one of these days, right?

"I have a quick announcement." Jonah paces the stage, tugging at his rumpled surfer-man bun with one hand. "I talked on the phone with Brander Delacroix today, and he said to tell you all *aloha.*"

Malia perks up and I do the same, my heart giving a strange flutter—a minor heart attack from all that grease in tonight's dinner? Not likely, considering the way my mouth is also stretching into a smile. I was never one for celebrity crushes, but considering Brander kissed me on the forehead long before he became a celebrity...

Wait.

Now's not the time to obsess about whatever kind of a relationship Brander and I have or don't have. For all I know, he kisses all his friends on the forehead.

I breathe out a quick puff of breath before tuning in to Jonah.

"Brander's tying up some loose ends in Nashville this week, and I know he'd appreciate your prayers. He's meeting with his record label to discuss the success of his single and decide what his next step should be."

"His next step should be coming home. They'd better not send him out on another tour." I lean close to whisper to Jazz, but Malia must hear because she turns to give me a funky look.

"Why not?" She mouths, eyebrows pinched close together.

I shake my head at her like she's nuts before Jonah continues.

"Brander also mentioned that he'll be flying home at the end of this month. He didn't ask me to say this, but I know he'll appreciate it if you help him keep a low profile. No blasting about his homecoming on social media or texting neighbor islanders to tell them when the Hawaiian Heartthrob will be in town."

I cringe at that nickname. Some lady on a national-news talk show gave it to him after he went viral, and I want to gag every time I hear it.

I mean, Brander's amazing and all that. With his deep, almond-eyed gaze and that kooky cowlick, could probably even make a teen-queen-magazine list of adorable guys. But a heartthrob?

No way. He's...Brander.

And in barely over a month, he'll be here. With us. I reach over to grasp Jazz's hand as a breeze whips through the pavilion and Jonah begins his message.

I grab my Bible and flip to the evening's passage, my heart still skipping around like Macie did that time Mom and Dad told us we were going to Disney World for spring break. Except this news is even better than knowing I'll be able to take a picture with some random guy in a mouse suit. Once Brander is back where he belongs, maybe some part of this crazy life will settle down.

Hey, a girl can hope, right?

"You wanna go out for shave ice?"

Jazz pops the question after the service ends with a final worship song, and I nod reflexively. After working at the

Shave Ice Shack for all of last summer, I've definitely developed a taste for the island treat. But something in me sags a little when I realize she's addressing both me *and* Malia.

"You mean, like dessert? During swim season?" Malia squints at Jazz. "Does the Shack do sugar-free stuff?"

"You really like eating chemicals that much? Come on. Everyone deserves a cheat day." Jazz hooks one arm around me and the other around Malia. "If we hurry, we can beat the evening rush."

Even after physical therapy, Jazz somehow possesses the energy to half-drag me and Malia down the short path to the Shave Ice Shack. Behind Jazz's back, Malia and I share a smile. Something tells me Malia's thinking the same thing I am—*Jazz is unstoppable.*

She was right about beating the rush too. By the time we're walking away with our treats, there's a line of sunburned tourists snaking almost all the way back to the parking lot. Icy treats already in tow, we stroll toward the shoreline.

"Do you guys hear from Brander much?" Malia asks after a long, semi-awkward silence.

I nod. "Not a ton right now that he's busy in Nashville, but yeah. We usually talk a few times a week."

From there, the conversation picks up—guess Malia considers herself a bit of a pop music aficionado—but something keeps niggling at my brain.

Though Jazz and I have endured our fair share of silences together, they've never been awkward. With Malia here, it's like there's something hanging heavily in the air between us, keeping my shoulders a little tighter than normal.

Jazz doesn't seem to notice—or care—though, so I take a deep breath and keep a smile on my face, even when Malia stops halfway through a sentence to answer a text.

Something else that rarely happens when it's just me and Jazz. Grams has us both well-trained.

When she finally pockets her phone, she fixes her gaze directly on me. "So Olive, Kanani said your dad's moving here?" She tilts her head, her long mane of ebony hair swishing down her back.

"No." *Thank goodness.* I laugh, but a tinge of guilt tickles my stomach. What did Dad ever do to me anyway? *Plenty,* my brain whispers, but I push it away. "He's on sabbatical." I explain about his job at Harvard, and somehow talk turns to school.

"I'm totally hating English Lit." Malia groans, like being given an hour out of the school day to talk about books is something akin to torture.

I stand a little straighter, almost instinctively, and Jazz snickers. "Watch out, Malia. Olive's been known to get pretty defensive about her *Pride and Prejudice.*"

"*Pride and Prejudice?*" Malia mock-gags. "Why does anyone have to read that? It's not like it's anything special. Another stupid love story with stupid characters and—"

"Are you kidding? It's only the best book *ever.*" I take a bite of shave ice, dripping in mango syrup, and let the flavors pull at my taste buds a little longer than usual before continuing. Maybe the sweetness on my tongue will counteract the sourness of my tone. "My mom would throttle you right now if she was still—if she was here."

Jazz reaches over and squeezes my hand in a silent show of support, and I return the gesture.

Fortunately, my mention of Mom seems to sink in enough to convince Malia to drop the subject. At least she knows better than to diss a dead person's favorite book in the presence of said dead person's daughter.

Unfortunately, she changes the topic to the only other thing she seems to know how to talk about—swim team.

I kick off my shoes and wade farther into the bay as

Malia grills Jazz on flutter kicks and relay races. The inky water wraps around my feet in the evening twilight, and I stare out past the sea to the islands and the horizon beyond. I take another bite of shave ice, and for a moment, the sweetness soothes the sting in my chest. Then the flavor fades, and sour jealousy crops up.

I can't help it that Jazz and Malia share such a long history together, but something in me feels forgotten. Like all of a sudden, I've become the third wheel.

I know Malia's had a rough go of it lately. She needs friends. A support system. Someone she can count on. But why did she have to pick Jazz to latch onto?

And why should I care?

A wave splashes higher than the rest, soaking me clear up past my knees. The evening breeze wraps around my bare calves, and I shiver, retreating before another wave can launch itself at me.

Is this God's way of telling me to cool it? To give Malia a break and stop feeling sorry for myself? It wouldn't be the first time I heard something like that from Him.

But why now, when I'm trying to find my new normal, would He let another wave of change come crashing into my life? I turn to peer down the beach at Jazz and Malia, who still seem happily caught up in their swim-team discussion.

God, what do you want from me? Haven't I been through enough lately? Or have I not learned my lesson yet?

I stay quiet, the night wrapping around me, and wait for God to speak.

But the evening air is hushed—almost silent, save for the contented cooing of a few doves and the murmur of Jazz and Malia's chatter farther down the shore. Something deep in my soul tells me God won't hit me over the head with His answer tonight. Maybe not even tomorrow.

But even so, a small, still voice seems to whisper to me.

God will never leave you nor forsake you.

You sure about that, Jesus? The old Bible verse sits sourly in the back of my throat, and I clench my hand into a fist. "It's true," I whisper, my words dissolving into the inky black evening.

I know it's true.

But something tells me that, no matter how long I stand here telling myself that, I'm not quite ready to believe it.

Chapter Seven

"YOU KNOW THIS IS AN ALLEGORICAL work of social criticism, right?" Dad flicks through the pages of *Animal Farm* and sets it on the coffee table.

"I know." I nod, though at this point, I probably would've said yes even if I *didn't* know. Anything to get Dad off my case.

"Don't you usually start school at eight o'clock? It's nearly a quarter after."

"Yeah, but Jazz is running late. Unfortunately. I could seriously use some backup this morning. "Who made you the homeschool truancy officer anyway?" I try to keep my tone light but probably only succeed halfway as I join Dad by the coffee table and flop onto the couch. "You know you can get online and check on my progress anytime, right? You can even see my grades."

"I'm well aware of that, thank you." Dad runs a hand over his stubble. One of these days he's going to forget to shave altogether, and he'll end up like one of the guys from that old *Duck Dynasty* show. Ick. "This isn't about your grades."

"Then what is it about?" Not that I'm particularly interested in the answer but listening to anything Dad has to say is better than thinking about him growing a redneck beard.

"It's about your work ethic."

I open my mouth to remind him that my work ethic is just fine, thank you, when a knock sounds on the door. Footsteps crash overhead as Macie barrels down the stairs to let Jazz in, and Dad makes a move to leave. "We can talk about this later." He tosses the words over his shoulder, as if we were in the middle of a friendly chat about the weekend's tsunami-warning drill. Still, a seed of frustration plants itself in my chest—why doesn't Dad get it? I'm doing fine in school, and I don't need him nagging me.

Jazz's forehead creases as she joins me on the couch, and the screen door slams as Dad heads out front. "What was that about?"

"Dad's on me about my work ethic. Like I can help it that my classes are too easy and I'm done with them before lunchtime. What does he want me to do? Double up? They're not *that* easy."

Jazz bites her lip and lets her backpack drop to the floor. "If everything's so easy for you, why don't you help me out more? I might be a faster reader than I used to be, but my history assignment is still trying to kill me."

"That's fine." It's not like I have anything better to do than more school. "Maybe I should remind Dad that I'm helping you too. It's like he's convinced I'm not responsible enough because I've been poking around online after I finish my stuff. I want to start working at the Shave Ice Shack with Brander when he comes home, but Dad won't let me if he thinks I'm slacking."

"At least you can reason with your dad."

"Huh?" I bite my lip at the shadows flitting beneath Jazz's usually bright and shiny smile.

"It's like no one around me actually *listens* anymore."

"*I* listen to you." I sit up tall, straightening my spine and looking Jazz straight in the eye. *At least, I'm trying my best.*

"You're one person." Jazz puffs out a breath. "Mom's still a closed book. I think it's because of me."

"What? That's ridiculous."

"It might be, but it's true. She's such a bear right now. I called her last night and she asked me how swim team's going. Like she doesn't remember that I can't swim."

"That's kind of harsh."

Jazz blinks at me.

"Your mom, I mean. Does she seriously have that bad of a memory?"

"Who knows? Maybe she does it to be mean—to remind me that all Whitakers are born failures—or maybe all the drinking finally blitzed her brain. It doesn't matter. The point is, I *would* be on that team if I could."

"And who says you can't? Isn't your prosthesis waterproof?"

"It's the phantom pain. Even if I could relearn how to swim—with or without my prosthesis—there's no way I could ever be sure that Arnold won't start hurting in the middle of a lap and take me out." Jazz squeezes her stump— Arnold, I guess she's calling it today. "Malia said they have a real chance at making Nationals this year."

Malia.

"Were you two always close?" The question flies out before I can remind myself that this conversation *should* be about *Jazz.* Not my own stupid insecurities.

"We spent every afternoon together at practice, but we never talked much until support group. Why?"

"Curious, I guess." I dip my head and flip forward to find my place in my book. "You sure you aren't up for swimming? You wouldn't have to go out for the team right away, you know. But maybe by fall—"

"I'm good." Jazz holds up a hand. "I'm still trying to figure out what Malia has to do with any of this."

"Nothing. Never mind." I bury my nose in my book before slipping into a world filled with communism and pigs.

"I'm sorry about earlier." I reach for Jazz's arm to pull her back before she can head out to Ruby's waiting rig after the school day is over.

"Huh?" Jazz quirks a brow and stares at me like I've sprouted a pineapple crown. Knowing her, she probably forgot about the morning's weirdness hours ago.

"The Malia thing. I shouldn't have brought her up."

"Oh." Jazz's other brow swoops up too. "Why *did* you bring her up?"

"It's awkward, I guess." I shuffle my bare feet on Gramma's smooth, polished floor. "Don't you think it's kind of awkward—having her hang out with us when we were on the outs for so long?"

"It's a bit of a change, I guess. But she needs a friend, and I'm happy to be one to her."

Good grief. How can someone like Jazz, who's had such a tough life, be so *nice*?

Before either of us can offer another word, a horn honks from the street once. Then again.

"Sorry." Jazz hoists her backpack higher on her back as the horn blares in my ear for the third time. "Ruby has the patience of a two-year-old. See ya."

I echo Jazz's goodbye and hold the front door open for her, watching as she makes her way to the waiting van. Why do I keep trying to pick a fight over Malia? It's not like I'm not some petty, clingy best friend—or am I?

I shudder at the thought, then walk into the living room and wave out the window as Ruby's van roars away from the curb. I picture Jazz inside, waving back, her usual Cheshire-cat smile on her face. Except...

It's not.

I stop waving and let my hand fall to my side.

Jazz's grin, while wide and open, is stretched a little tighter than normal. Come to think of it, I haven't seen that catlike smile of Jazz's—the extra-big, extra-wide one—lately. And *that* realization makes the corners of my own mouth fall in an all-out frown.

"Did you have a productive day?" Dad's words reach my ears, and I turn as he steps into the living room. "I heard quite a bit of giggling around lunch hour...except it lasted longer than an hour."

I open my mouth to offer my defense—I was helping Jazz brainstorm a plot line for her required short story about the Russian Revolution and things got a little wacky—before changing tactics. "We got everything taken care of."

Dad smiles and nods.

"Why do you ask? You still haven't told me why you're keeping such a close eye on me."

Dad scrubs at his chin again—at least he must've remembered to shave at some point today, because now he looks less like a wannabe bushman and more like a professor again. "I'm worried about you. If these classes are as easy as you say they are, then you're not being properly challenged. What will happen when you go to college? The workload there will be ambitious, to say the least."

"Then I won't be bored?"

Dad narrows his eyes.

I wince. "Seriously though—I don't have to worry about college for another year and a half. You could cut me some slack."

Dad sticks his hands in his pockets and jingles his change, a bad habit he claims to have picked up from a doddery professor he studied under at Harvard. "Don't go getting old and stodgy on me now." I nod toward Dad's hands, then peer out the window as Macie's bus pulls up at the stop. "Macie needs a young, cool dad. Not a feeble old professor."

Dad reddens and removes his hands from his pockets as Macie hops off the bus and sprints up the front walk. I meet her at the door and take her backpack, hanging it on the hook before ushering her into the kitchen for a snack.

Dad stays close behind. "What did you learn today, Macie?" He takes a seat next to Macie as I reach into the freezer for the homemade ice cream sandwiches Gramma whipped up before heading to the gallery earlier.

"Alani told me during recess that her dog had puppies." Macie takes the sandwich I offer her. "I asked if her mommy would text you a picture. To show Grammy."

"Oh yeah?" A text buzzes in my pants pocket, and my leg grows shivery-cold. "Why would I do that?"

"So Grammy can buy me one for my birthday." Macie opens her mouth wide and promptly fills it with half her sandwich. "Did you get the picture?"

My hand moving at the speed of a sea turtle on land, I reach into my pocket and withdraw my phone. Sure enough, I have a text from a strange number. I tap to open it and am met with a full-sized picture of a hairy, scrawny puppy that's more rat than dog.

Biting down on my tongue so as not to burst out laughing, I slide the phone across the breakfast bar so Dad can see. "You want a puppy that looks like that?" I do my best to keep my tone even, but a hint of incredulity sneaks in anyway.

"Why not?" Macie grabs the phone from Dad and stares at the picture, her eyes practically transforming into little pink cartoon hearts. I groan.

My sister is suffering from a serious case of puppy love. Why couldn't she have gotten the cat-lover gene like me? "You'd better eat your sandwich, squirt. Don't want it to melt." I point at Macie's half-eaten sandwich, a drip of vanilla ice cream making its way down the side of her arm.

I bite into a sandwich of my own as a rumble from the driveway announces Gramma's arrival. Macie squeaks and shoves the rest of her sandwich into her mouth before tightening her grip on my phone and bolting down the hallway to the front door. Dad and I follow, reaching the entryway as Gramma comes inside, a brown paper bag loaded with groceries hooked over her elbow, a box trailing several strands of jeweler's twine tucked under her arm.

"Aloha." She makes her way into the kitchen and drops her bag on the counter, the rest of us following close behind. "What's this? A welcoming committee?" She bends to place the box on the floor before turning to empty her grocery bag.

"I found my dream." Macie stands on her tiptoes to shove my phone in Gramma's face, and I cringe. Gramma's got such a soft heart—she'll probably fall in love with that ugly puppy too.

"That's nice, Macie. Whose puppy is that?" Thankfully, though I catch a softening in Gramma's gaze, her tone doesn't reveal anything.

"She's going to be *mine*." Macie hugs my phone to her chest and pirouettes across the floor.

"Hold on there." Dad holds up a hand and launches into his pet-ownership-is-a-big-responsibility speech. The same one he gave me before I got my kitten, Peaches, all those years ago. His words ring familiarly in my ears as I make my escape and dash upstairs, where I shut the bedroom door behind me and reach for my—

Nope.

Macie still has the phone, which means there's no way for me to call Jazz or Brander and vent. Not that I should need to. That little puppy doesn't appear to be the vicious type.

Still, something doesn't sit quite right with me.

Whether it's all because of that puppy, or whatever it is that seems to be bugging Jazz, or the fact that Brander *still* hasn't returned my call, I don't know.

All I know is, when I pictured a new normal, this wasn't exactly what I had in mind.

Chapter Eight

WHEN MY PHONE BUZZES LATE THE next afternoon, I nearly drop the bracelet I've been helping Macie make with the scraps Gramma brought home from her workstation at the gallery yesterday. One peek at my screen shows me exactly what I've been waiting for—Brander's calling.

"Get Grams to help you from here, okay?" I scramble from my seat next to Macie on the porch swing. Without waiting for her to answer, I slip on a pair of *slippas*—or flip-flops, as I used to call them before I came here—and jog across the street to the beach.

"Hey, Brander." My breath comes out in a puff as I slow my pace, kick off my shoes, and head for the shoreline. My feet sink into the soft sand, and for a second, I get the strange feeling that I'm walking barefoot in a giant bowl of graham cracker crumbs. "How've you been?"

"Okay." His usually smooth voice is rough—almost gravely.

"Long day?" I pick up a broken shell and pitch it into the waves, watching as it disappears immediately into the rolling surf.

Brander's breath rustles the phone line, somewhere between a huff and a laugh. "They're all long." He clears his throat. "I mean, this is an awesome opportunity, but being in the business isn't as easy as it sounds. Today I had interviews with three different teen magazines, recorded a song for a TV show pilot, and did a photo shoot for the company that makes my guitar strings."

"Gee, sounds tough. It must stink to be so popular."

Brander laughs. "Sorry. I guess it sounds pretty dumb for me to complain about all that, huh?"

"Most people would die to be in your shoes."

"And sometimes I think I'd die to give them the chance. Part of me wants to tell my parents how tough and lonely it is out here. *Okaasan* would jump on a nonstop flight to Nashville and drag me home before I could even pack a suitcase."

I snicker at the thought of Brander's straight-laced Japanese mother marching him out of the recording studio in the middle of a take. "You are coming back soon though, right? That's what Jonah told everyone."

"Yep. I'll be home by the end of the month."

"Cool."

For a moment, I don't hear anything but the gentle rush of water and the scrape of sand beneath my feet as I amble further along the shoreline.

"You're awfully quiet." We say it at the same time and laugh, then lapse into the same strange silence. For someone who's been waiting for this call with bated breath, I'm suddenly at a loss for words.

Finally, Brander speaks. "What's new with you?"

"Other than the fact that Macie's spending every waking hour begging Grams for a puppy and Dad's convinced I'm slacking on my schoolwork? Not much."

"A puppy?" Brander's words are soft, edged with a note of concern.

"Didn't you get my voicemail? I told you all about it."

Brander makes a noise on the other line, one that's half-sigh and half-groan. "No. When was that? I'm sorry Olive, I—"

"It's no big deal. Don't sweat it."

"But—"

"Seriously. Forget about it. You're here now. Er, not here but at least on the other line." I clear my throat to stop my rambling, then get him up to speed on the puppy problem.

"I think Grams likes the idea," I finish, chewing on my lip. "And for what it's worth, all Macie wants is a scrubby little rat dog, not a pit bull, so I guess I'll survive."

"Really?" Something in Brander's tone tells me he doesn't quite believe me. "You're sure about that?"

"Of course, I'll *survive*." I let my next thought roll around in my brain for a moment before letting the words spill off my tongue. "But the thought of permanently sharing a house with any kind of dog makes me want to jump in a boat and row myself across the channel."

"That's sounds more like it." Brander laughs, but the sound is tinged with his trademark empathy. "Have you talked to *Tutu* about it?"

"She told me to pray—that an immediate *no* on the subject isn't fair to Macie. And I get it. It's not."

"That doesn't make things any easier for you, though." Brander *hmms* for a moment, long enough to make me wonder if he isn't only talking about me. "Doesn't God have a warped sense of humor?"

"What do you mean?"

"You get over your dog phobia in time for Macie to go puppy-crazy. I get a taste of what it's like to do music full-time, and..."

"And what?" I grip the phone tighter and kick at a clump of sand. "Is everything okay over there?"

Brander breathes out, long and slow. In that one breath, he sounds at least eighty years old. "I'll be better when I get home. I miss you—you guys."

"We miss you too." I open my mouth to say more, but off in the distance a door slams.

"Olive!" The voice is faint, buried under the sound of crashing waves, but it catches my ear enough for me to spin around and find Gramma standing on the edge of the front lawn.

I flash her a *shaka* and she returns the gesture, then raises her hands to cup them around her mouth. "Dinner's on the table!"

"Rats. I've gotta go—Gramma wants me."

"Oh." Brander's voice—the one that made him into one of pop music's rising stars—is unusually dull. Usually when we talk, his words are full of excitement and he has dozens of stories about life on the road or in Nashville.

Tonight, he sounds practically miserable.

Gramma's waving me toward the house, and a goodbye and "aloha" are both on the tip of my tongue, but something won't let me say them quite yet. "You know I'm praying for you, right? And I can't wait to talk with you more. In person."

"Thanks, Olive. I can't wait to see you too."

"I'll start counting the days. And until then...aloha, Brander." My heart catches at the words. I don't usually get this emotional over a phone call. We're only friends, after all. Friends who have been through a whole lot together in the six months we've known each other. I'm about to take the phone away from my ear and hang up when Brander's voice sounds from the speaker one last time.

"Hey, Olive—one last thing. Give yourself a hug from me. Okay?"

I can almost hear a hint of a smile in his words before the line goes dead.

After dinner, I find myself back on the beach, bare feet sinking into sun-warmed sand as the clouds turn bright shades of orange sherbet and cotton candy. Macie is still caught up in her beading project, and Dad barely made an appearance long enough to sandwich a slice of Gramma's mystery meatloaf between two slices of purple taro bread before retreating upstairs to his bedroom-slash-office in what used to be Gramma's crafting room.

With Gramma otherwise occupied helping Macie with her beads and Dad buried under a pile of professor-ly emails, I'm on my own. I could call Jazz and see if she's around, but something in me is craving a few hours alone.

But right as I've found a comfortable walking stride and started down the beach, a familiar figure standing on a board bobbing offshore catches my eye.

"Hey!" The person waves, then uses a long paddle to push the board toward shore. "What're you doing here?"

"I live here." I jerk a thumb at Gramma's house as Malia paddles closer.

"You do?" She hops off her board into waist-deep water and squints at Gramma's house, then at me. "Where's Jazz? I thought you two were a pre-packaged pair. And Brander too—when he's around." Her eyes go a little glassy at the mention of Brander, and I lock my gaze on my bare footprint in the sand to keep from rolling my eyes.

"She's at her aunt's. And besides, I needed some alone time."

"I get you." Malia's gaze softens, and she offers a small smile. Her oversized surfboard scrapes along the sand as she pushes it onto the beach, and she steps closer, unfastening a long, black rope from her ankle.

"You tied yourself to your surfboard?"

Malia blinks at me like I'm in kindergarten. "For one, it's a paddleboard, not a surfboard. And for two, it's called a leash. So I don't lose my board if I fall off—which I never do."

Of course not.

"Dad taught me to SUP when I was little. I came in third in my class in the Lahaina Annual SUP Race last year. And the two girls ahead of me were both about to age out of the division. I should be in a good position to win this year." She practically preens as she says this, flipping her hair and adjusting her bikini straps like someone might want to take her picture for a magazine cover.

I open my mouth to ask what SUP stands for, then think better of it. No sense offering Malia another chance to remind me how much of a stranger I am to this unusual island lifestyle. "Good for you." I turn my head toward the last rays of light as the sun sinks toward the horizon.

"Jazz came in fourth."

"Huh?" I tear my gaze from the sunset and blink at Malia.

"In the paddleboard race. She was ticked off big time."

"Seriously?"

Malia snorts. "Yeah. She almost didn't congratulate me."

We both laugh. Though I've never watched Jazz compete before, something tells me she's as competitive as she is compassionate. In other words, *very*.

Malia rolls a hair tie off her wrist and throws her hair into a sloppy topknot. "Jazz kept teasing me about it, saying I'd better watch out because she was going to practice hard all year to come in first."

"That sounds like Jazz."

Malia nods and fiddles with her paddleboard leash. "Of course, that was before the amputation."

Malia's words are a punch to my gut—I guess I was assuming that Jazz still planned on beating Malia this year. Now that's impossible. "Does she know about the race yet?"

"It's an annual race." Malia takes a step back, her gaze icing over. "She couldn't *not* know. Not that it matters now that she's not competing."

I wince. "Why do you say that? She has a waterproof prosthesis."

"And you think she'd want to race out there in the open ocean? After she freaked out the last time she got in the pool?" Malia scoffs. "Whatever. As long as Jazz doesn't race, she's one less person for me to worry about. The grand prize this year is a thousand dollars *and* a gift card to the Hula Grill. I have to win."

I bite my lip. Things have been rough for Malia since her family lost their house a few months ago. The prize money *could* help them out. But since Jazz's last attempt at swimming got cut short thanks to a killer phantom pain, she's stayed as far away from the water as possible. Jazz should take this chance and race. She should *win*.

Of course, Malia would kill me if I said as much.

"Good luck then." The words sound hollow, as if my tongue knows they're meant for the wrong person. I should be wishing Jazz luck—not *Malia*. The thought pokes at my conscience as Malia and I chit-chat for a few more minutes.

And then, as Malia hoists her board and heads off into the evening twilight,

her words come running back to hit me.

She's one less person for me to worry about.

Malia didn't say she was sorry because Jazz *couldn't* compete. She said that she didn't think *Jazz* would want to race.

But what if Jazz *did* want to?

After all, why can't she race? Jazz is one of the strongest, most competitive people I know. She deserves a chance to race. To win—especially after everything she's told me about her mom—and I'm going to make sure she gets one.

Okay, Malia. Challenge accepted.

Chapter Nine

"WE NEED TO TALK." DAD POKES his head into the kitchen next Saturday morning, his words combining with the smell of scrambled eggs to make my stomach churn.

My eyes shoot up from my plate, but Macie is too busy shoving banana pancakes into her mouth to acknowledge Dad's presence. Even Gramma is too focused on tending her pan of bacon to pay much attention.

Not that it matters much what they're doing. Dad's gaze is fixed on me alone.

"What now?" The words escape before I can stop them, my tone of voice craggy.

Dad's eyebrows arch, presumably at my tone, and I drop my gaze. "Watch your attitude, young lady." He harrumphs under his breath. "Last I checked, it wasn't illegal for me to talk to you."

"Sorry." I scrape aside my eggs and spear a piece of pancake before looking at him. "What's up?"

Dad removes his glasses and rubs his eyes, as if questioning whether or not to keep talking.

Then, before he has the chance to decide, a knock sounds on the front door, accompanied by cheerful birdsong floating in through the open window in the living room.

"Who's that?" Macie asks around a mouthful of pancake, and I shrug.

Gramma moves to answer the door, and Dad leans awkwardly against the breakfast bar. His eye twitches behind his glasses, and he sticks his hands in his pockets. The change starts jangling a moment later. I open my mouth to call him out on it when the front door slams shut, and Gramma returns to the kitchen with Jazz in tow. "Look who stopped by for banana pancakes."

"Jazzie!" Macie shimmies in her seat, but even Jazz's sudden appearance isn't exciting enough to tear my little sister from a plate of pancakes for a hug. I guess nothing comes between my sister and a good meal—not even one of her favorite people in the world.

"Hey, Jazz." I pat the seat of the barstool next to me. "What's up?"

"Ruby's having a bunch of friends over for book club, but I got one look at the book cover and figured I'd be better off over here. You don't mind, do you?"

"Did you walk?" I squint at Jazz's prosthesis as she clambers onto a barstool. I haven't mentioned the race to her since I heard about it from Malia—I'm still waiting for that perfect opportunity—but she'd better not overdo it or pull something before I can tell her my plan.

"Ruby drove me. I think she was glad to get me out of her hair. Wanna go hang out on Front Street?"

"Sure!" I start to nod, but my chin suddenly freezes in place. My gaze drifts over to Dad, who is glowering at his pancakes. "But, um, I think Dad needs to talk to me first."

But Dad flaps his hand, as though waving me away. "Forget about it. You girls go have fun. We can talk later."

"Okay." My voice is small. Too small.

A chill creeps into the room, and I shiver before sneaking another peek at Dad. His eyes are glazed over, and he's staring at his pancakes again. Whatever he'd been about to say, it must not have been anything good.

"Let's go on a mission." As soon as Gramma's rattletrap station wagon pulls away from the curb in front of one of

Front Street's infamous ABC stores half an hour later, Jazz grabs my hand and flashes a grin.

I return the smile, though it feels a bit wooden—I'm still trying to figure out what Dad had on his mind earlier. "What kind of a mission?" The midmorning breeze plays with tendrils of my hair as a handful of frenzied shoppers push past us. "I don't know if I'm up for anything major." Between trying to appease Dad at every turn and coming up with a way to get Jazz interested in the paddleboard race, I have enough on my plate as it is.

"I thought we could do something cool for Brander—to welcome him home." Jazz links her arm around mine as my heart gives a strange kick at the mention of Brander, and I let Jazz drag me farther down Lahaina's tourist-trap-meets-Rodeo-drive shopping street.

"Something cool? Like what?"

Jazz shrugs. "A welcome-home present. Something silly, like a Hawaii survival kit. You know, since it feels like he's been gone for forever."

"Tell me about it." I speak the words to myself more than to Jazz, but she offers me a certain closed-mouth smile and waggles her eyebrows.

"Does that mean you're in?"

"For sure." I still can't get the way he sounded on the phone out of my head—tired, weary, and definitely in need of a surprise. "He's seemed so stressed lately—and busy."

"No kidding. I got a text from him last night, but it was super short."

"Yeah. I hear from his Instagram more than I do from *him.* He must be swamped." But hey, what kind of a career—even one straight out of someone's wildest dreams—keeps people too busy to talk to their friends?

Jazz bites her lip and shuffles her feet. "Then let's go whole hog on this thing. I'm thinking we buy him a Hawaiian shirt, tourist sunglasses—the works."

"Everything he needs to be an official island boy." I snicker. "Maybe we can drop it off at his house so it's waiting for him when he gets home. That way, even if he's swamped with newspaper interviews, there's no way he'll forget to come visit me—er, us."

Jazz laughs. "Somehow I doubt he'll *ever* forget about you."

I open my mouth to object when Jazz ducks into a store and motions for me to follow. "Let's divide and conquer. You find some snacks, and I'll get the other stuff."

Before I can ask what kind of snacks I'm supposed to get, Jazz is gone. The clunk of her prosthesis echoes as she disappears down an aisle filled with dashboard hula girls, plastic ukuleles, and—probably on the pricier side—bowls made from Koa wood.

Koa.

Despite my dislike for dogs, I can't help smiling at that name. Maybe, if Macie gets her way and we end up with a scrawny rat-dog in the house, it won't be the end of the world after all.

What am I thinking?

I stick my hands deep in my pockets before heading down one of several food aisles. What would Brander want with any of this? He's lived here longer than I have. He's probably had plenty of—I shudder—SPAM-flavored macadamia nuts in his lifetime.

Still, the idea of having something goofy waiting for him when he gets home is a good one. I take out my wallet and do a quick count before picking out a small assortment of items. Some look tasty, like the bag of oatmeal-macadamia-nut cookies, and others tacky, like a sample-size bag of those SPAM nuts. If nothing else, they'll give him a good laugh. Maybe I could even write little notes to go along with the dorky stuff.

Sorry to keep SPAMming you, but we're excited you're

home.

I roll my eyes at the corniness of that idea, but I can't ditch my goofy smile as I dive further into the store to find Jazz.

When I spot her pawing through a box of discounted dashboard hula-girls, however, that smile slides off my face in a hurry. Because Jazz is no longer alone.

"What about this one?" Malia holds up a hula girl wearing the world's ugliest purple grass skirt and holding a ukulele over her disproportionately small midsection. Jazz snorts with laughter and grabs for it.

"Perfect." She giggles and adds it to a half-filled shopping basket before turning to me.

"Hey, Olive. Look who we found." Jazz points to the hula girl. The hideous piece of junk stares up at me from the basket with a plasticky grin, but I'm more focused on Malia's smug smile.

"You okay?" Jazz squints at me and leans forward to wave a hand in front of my face. "If you don't like the hula girl, we don't have to get her. She's pretty funny though."

"Go ahead." I slap a smile on my face. "Aloha, Malia."

Malia opens her mouth as if to return the greeting, but her pocket dings before she can say anything. And just like that, she's got her phone pressed to her ear. I close my eyes for a millisecond to keep anyone from seeing them roll around in my head.

When it becomes clear that this *isn't* going to be a two-minute conversation, Malia shrugs and waves for us to keep shopping. "I'll catch you outside," she mouths before scooting out of the store.

"What was that all about?" Jazz squints at me.

"Huh?" I lift the SPAM nuts. "Check these out."

"Don't play dumb. Why did you glare at Malia like that? Are you two okay?"

"I didn't glare at her. We're fine." *As fine as a baby kitten and a pit bull.* "Don't you think Brander will like the nuts?"

Jazz narrows her gaze.

"What? Seriously, nothing's wrong."

Jazz's gaze softens a bit, though I doubt she believes me fully, and she finally turns her attention to the nuts. "Perfect. Let's buy this stuff and head out. Maybe Malia will have some more ideas."

I coax a smile onto my face and follow Jazz to the check stand, all the while something prodding my conscience. How can I be jealous of Malia when I know she needs Jazz's friendship as much as I do? It's not fair to her. Not fair to *me.*

But I can't shake the feeling that something about the newest member of our group isn't quite right.

Chapter Ten

"Sorry, guys, but I've gotta run. Thanks for letting me tag along. It was so cool to do something nice for the Hawaiian Heartthrob." Malia lifts her hand in a *shaka* after we've visited a few other shops, and my shoulders must drop about ten inches as we say goodbye.

"What's up with you two?" Jazz turns to me the second Malia is out of earshot and pulls me onto a bench overlooking the water.

"Nothing." I set the bags I've been carrying on the ground and cross my arms. "Why do you keep asking me that?"

"*Why?*" Jazz adopts a gaze suspiciously similar to the one Gramma uses when Macie is in trouble. "Maybe because you act like we're swimming with sharks whenever she's around?"

"I do?" I blink, feigning innocence, but the tilt of Jazz's chin tells me she's having none of it. "It's nothing. Really."

"*Right.*"

"Didn't we talk about this earlier? I don't like change. Isn't that okay?" The crashing of waves and chatter of shoppers washes over me as Jazz nibbles a hangnail. "You don't even like good change?" She cocks her head at me.

"Such as?" If Jazz considers trading Brander for Malia a *good* change, then...

"Since Malia started hanging around youth group, she's closer to God than I've ever seen her before. Brander is living his dream in Nashville, and he's changing lives while he's at it." Jazz hesitates, as if unsure of whether or not to go on.

"So?" A bird caws somewhere in the tree above us. "I'm glad that stuff is happening. But it doesn't make for an easy adjustment."

"I didn't say it would, but I also don't see what's so hard about reaching out to someone in need. I did the same for you last summer. Everyone needs a friend." Jazz brushes her lap before standing, then offers me a hand. "Wanna keep shopping?"

I let Jazz half-pull me to my feet, and I trail after her as she marches down the street toward one of those ABC stores.

She's right, a little voice in my head scoffs at me as I walk. *What's wrong with new friends, after all?*

The voice opens something in my heart that I thought had been covered over long ago, and I flinch. What's wrong with new friends?

Only the fact that, more often than not, new friends replace old friends.

A feathery memory of one of the many times I tried to find a place to sit in the school cafeteria back in Boston crops up. Should I tell Jazz? Admit that any "friends" I made on the mainland usually forgot about me as soon as someone cooler came along? Someone who liked to talk about guys and party on the weekends and read books that *weren't* on the school reading list?

I squeeze Jazz's hand and open my mouth as we slip into the ABC store. Surely she'd understand.

But, on the off chance that she wouldn't...

Maybe I'd better keep all of that to myself.

By noon, we've walked up and down Front Street half a dozen times, collecting enough bric-a-brac for what we've dubbed Brander's "Hawaii Survival Kit". And I'm starving.

"Want to grab something to eat?" Jazz gestures toward a burger joint on our right, and my stomach growls.

"Sounds, good, but I'm broke. Wanna head back to Gramma's?"

"For mayo-fish sandwiches?" Jazz wrinkles her nose. "No way. Ruby gave me lunch money before I left. I'll buy."

I open my mouth in protest, but one sharp look from Jazz has me snapping it shut. We climb the steps to an open-air dining room and get settled at a table positioned directly overlooking the walkway below.

"Hey." Jazz nudges my foot and gives the restaurant a quick scan after a waitress brings us waters, as though checking to make sure no one is listening. "I'm sorry."

I take a sip of my water and duck my head, staring at the menu without actually reading it. "Sorry?"

"Yeah. I know the Malia thing was a surprise. But I couldn't make myself turn her away. Not after she got so excited when I told her about Brander's survival kit."

"Because it was for the 'Hawaiian Heartthrob'?" I make air quotes and pretend to gag.

"Be nice." Jazz waves a finger in my face.

"*Sorry*. But you have to admit she's kind of starstruck."

"Who wouldn't be? Besides, what better person to have a celebrity crush on? Malia needs a good influence in her life." Jazz twirls her paper straw around in her glass. "Besides, I kind of like hanging out with her. It reminds me of swim team, which isn't a bad thing."

"You know, if you're missing swim team that much, I think you should try—"

"Try what?" Jazz's eyes grow dim, almost as if someone threw the shutters closed across her gaze. "Don't you remember what happened the last time I got in the water? It's like Mom says—sink or swim, unless you're a Whitaker. Then you might as well be a lead weight."

I flinch. "She doesn't really say that. Does she?"

Jazz shrugs. "Not in so many words, I guess, but yeah. Pretty much."

Ugh. "Don't listen to her then." What I wouldn't give for the opportunity to give Jazz's mom a good and proper chewing-out. "Let me say one more thing, then I'll shut up—I promise."

"Why bother? Even if I magically did make the team, it wouldn't be enough to make Mom happy. Besides, there's no way I'm getting in the water, let alone on the swim team."

"What if you didn't have to get in the water?"

One corner of Jazz's mouth twists up. "Um, I have to get in the water if I want to swim."

"But what if you weren't swimming?"

Jazz stares at me like I'm nuts. A waitress seizes the opportunity to swoop in to take our orders, but I'm quick to continue as soon as she's out of earshot. "I'm talking about paddleboarding, Jazz. Don't you still want to beat Malia this year?"

Jazz keeps staring.

"You know what I'm talking about. Malia told me about the race—how you almost placed last time, and how you're planning on beating her this year. But I haven't seen you training."

Jazz lets out a noise that's half-scoff, half-laugh. "Is this some kind of sick joke? I can't paddleboard."

"You said your balance was getting better."

"So?"

"I see you standing up all the time. Isn't that what paddleboarding is? Just—you know—on a board?"

Jazz nods for a millisecond before her chin changes directions and jerks from side to side. "You don't get it."

"What don't I get?" My voice is a little louder than I'd intended, and Jazz jabs a finger to her lips.

"Keep it down."

I cross my arms and huff. Was I ever this crabby when Jazz talked *me* into doing something I was afraid of? On second thought...I don't want to answer that.

I clear my throat to try again, but the words leave my mouth when the waitress reappears with our lunch. She deposits two plates loaded with burgers and onion rings at our table, and for a few moments the only thing in my mouth is one heavenly bite of my *kalua*-pork-and-pineapple-topped burger.

But I can't let Jazz go down without a fight. She never let me take the easy way out. Now's my time to push her—only a little. But enough.

"So." I set down my burger and lean across the table. "When did you turn into a quitter?"

Jazz's eyes bug out. "Huh?" Good thing she hadn't taken a bite of her burger yet, or she would've choked.

"Are you seriously going to let Malia beat you this year too?" I do my best to pin her under my gaze, but it's harder than I'd expected. How long did it take Jazz to perfect her own power-stare technique?

"Why do you say it like I have a choice?" Jazz shifts in her chair. "It's hard enough thinking about everyone who gets out of bed in the morning without having to strap a fake leg onto Clyde—er, their stump. I don't need you reminding me about all the other things normal people do." *That I can't.* Jazz doesn't say those last three words out loud, but I read them in her eyes.

"That's exactly it." I plant my hands on the table. "You've given up before you've even thought about it."

"I have too thought about it."

"How could you have? I told you, like two minutes ago. Come on—how hard is paddleboarding? Seriously?"

"It's easy. For people with two legs." Jazz picks up her burger and stares at it, but she doesn't take a bite.

"Last time I checked, you were wearing both *slippas*."

Jazz scrunches up her nose and stares at me over her behemoth of a burger. "This is mean, Olive. Don't you know how much time I spend staring at the water, wishing I could get out there? Wishing I could prove to my mom—to *myself*—that I can still swim? Still do something with myself—and my life?"

No, because you'd never admit it to me. But that's a conversation for another time. I, more than anyone, know how hard it is to be vulnerable. "All I know is that you want to get in the water, and I think you should. You *could.*"

Jazz snorts. "You sound exactly like Doctor Freeh."

"What do you mean?"

Jazz picks up an onion ring and eats all the breading off it. "He keeps saying that I should try swimming. That my prosthesis is made to transition from land to water. He doesn't get it."

"Actually, I think you're the one who's not getting it."

"Nuh-uh. You and Doc Freeh haven't ever dealt with phantom pain. You can't understand what it's like. How scary it is."

"But if you get a pain, you can sit down on your board. It's not like you have to swim across the channel or anything. You could do this, Jazz. For real."

"Why're you trying to give me false hope? I don't need it." Jazz takes a huge bite of her burger and swallows it in one gulp. "Listen. It's nice that you want to help me, but you don't *get it.*"

"But—"

"These are good burgers, aren't they?" Jazz nods so pointedly at my nearly untouched plate that I can't help but pick up my burger and drop the subject.

For now.

Chapter Eleven

"WHAT'S THE PROBLEM?" GRAMMA CORNERS ME after dinner and hands me a box of—I peer inside—jeweler's twine. Tangled.

"What problem?"

"You look like you're preparing for battle. Help me untangle this mess and we'll talk about it."

I follow Gramma, the scent of plumerias greeting me as I step onto the front porch and sit on the swing next to her. Reaching into Gramma's box, I pull out a mass of woven-together twine. The evening breeze plays with my hair as I begin the work of untangling, my fingers worrying the twine, my brain worrying about everything *else*.

For a while, the ebb and flow of the ocean waves moves in rhythm with the gentle rise and fall of Gramma's chest, and the only sound is the gentle symphony of a Hawaiian evening. Somewhere down the street, laughter erupts from a group of kids—Macie included. Last I heard, they're obsessed with some sort of game involving pretend molten lava from Maui's all-too-real resident volcano, Haleakala.

"Ready to talk yet?" Gramma's voice splits through the calmness in the air when we're about halfway through the box.

I push back my hair and lean my elbows on my knees. "Jazz is giving up."

"Giving up on what?"

"Her mom. Her leg. Herself." I drop an untangled piece of twine into the box. "I'm worried about her."

"Hmm." Gramma plucks at a strand of twine with her

knobby fingers, then hands it to me. "Can you get this one? My hands don't work like they used to."

I take the piece and get to work as I tell Grams all about my conversation with Jazz over lunch. "It sounds like her mom's being a mega jerk about it all. Like it's Jazz's fault that she can't swim anymore." I hiss under my breath as I encounter a particularly gnarly knot in the twine. "I think she needs to get in the water somehow—even if she doesn't swim. There's this paddleboard race coming up that she should enter. She could show herself—and everyone else— that she's still a star, but she doesn't want to do it."

Gramma hums again, then tucks a strand of salt-and-pepper hair into her messy chopstick bun. "Why do you think she's so hesitant?"

"Beats me." I hand Gramma the length of twine—now tangle-free—and she twists it into a circle before laying it aside. "Jazz has always been so fearless. I don't know why she's holding back now."

"Well, why are *you* holding back?"

"Me?" I blink at Grams.

Gramma squeezes my shoulder. "You and Brander raised thousands of dollars to buy Jazz a leg, even when you didn't know if she would live to use it. You let a dog come into your house—learned to love it, even—to help Jazz out of a tough spot. You bared your heart to the kids at the support group, even when opening up was hard."

"How—"

Gramma holds up a finger. "Jonah told me that one."

"So much for confidentiality."

Gramma shoots me a look.

"Okay, so maybe I'm not the scaredy-cat I think I am. What does that have to do with anything?"

"I was thinking...you can't understand why Jazz, who's gone through so much and come out on top, would back down now. Aren't you doing the same thing?"

"How?"

Gramma raises a brow. "I think we both know."

"You mean with Malia?" To say it out loud like that makes me sound like I'm in middle school. "I'm not scared of her."

Oh, come on. That voice in my head has returned. *Admit it. You are scared. Scared she'll steal your place. Scared that Jazz'll end up dumping you for her.*

No. Jazz is a true friend. She wouldn't do that.

Would she?

"I don't know what's going on between you and Malia, but that's not what I meant." Gramma's words bring a breath of fresh air to my heart, and I sag onto the swing. Disaster averted. "I'm talking about Macie—about that puppy she wants."

"Oh." The words, while they dig a cold, dark pit in my stomach, don't make me cower like they would've a few months ago. After all, I hate the thought of living with a scruffy rat-dog in Gramma's house, but I hate the thought of living anywhere else even more. "You're going to get it for her, aren't you?"

"Her birthday *is* coming up soon."

Every bit of uncommon sense in me begs to lay into Grams right then and there and ask her what she's thinking, letting Macie adopt one of my worst nightmares. But a picture of Koa comes to mind, the gentleness of his puppy-bark echoes in my ears, and I don't have the heart to put up a fuss. "What kind of dog is it exactly?"

Gramma's eyebrows arch—I'm sure she's surprised I didn't put up more of a fuss—and she takes a moment before answering. "They're Shih Tzus."

"Boy or a girl?"

"There are a few of each to choose from. If all goes as planned, maybe you can help me decide."

My heart hiccups. "What do you mean—if all goes as

planned?"

"Your dad's still a little wary."

I breathe in a deep, relief-tinged breath, then mentally kick myself. Don't I want my little sister to have a happy birthday?

Besides—if I want to convince Jazz to work up the courage to give this paddleboarding thing a try, maybe I have to be the one to show some of that bravery first.

The next weekend, Jazz is headed back to visit her mom, and Dad makes it clear that he needs peace, quiet, and *absolute privacy*—his words, not mine—until he alerts us otherwise.

Since Grams left to work a shift at the gallery right after she pulled a loaf of streusel-topped banana bread out of the oven, that means it's down to me and Macie.

"Let's go to the beach and play sharks and mermaids." Macie hunts me down right as I finish drying the stack of breakfast dishes and nearly dislocates my arm as she drags me toward the front door. "You be the shark, I'll be the mermaid."

I roll my eyes over Macie's head and bite back a groan. Sharks and mermaids is another island-kid game. A very intense, very weird game. But at least playing outside will keep Macie out of Dad's hair. "Let me put my suit on first." I disentangle myself and run upstairs to change.

As I fold my shirt and put it in a drawer, I peek outside. A knot of swirling gray clouds covers Lanai, one of the neighboring islands. Hopefully it'll stay over there until I've chased Macie around the beach long enough to tire her out.

As we trot across the street, though, the clouds seem to grow even darker.

Macie doesn't even have time to finish explaining the

rules of the game—which happen to be more complex than I'd given her and her friends credit for—when the first raindrops splash on her nose.

"It's raining." Macie sticks out her lip in a pout.

"Does it matter? We were already planning on getting wet."

Macie doesn't have time to answer before the heavens open and a sheet of rain sweeps across the shoreline. A collective squeal goes up from the other beachgoers, and Macie tugs on my arm. "Run for cover!" She points across the street toward Gramma's house, and we break into a sprint.

By the time we reach the porch, we're both completely drenched, and the rain is pounding on Gramma's roof like a pro drummer. So much for keeping Macie occupied outside.

"Come on, squirt. Let's get dried off."

Too bad the walls in Dad's room aren't soundproof.

By the time Macie and I are wrapped snuggly in warm clothes and I've checked the weather—it's supposed to rain all morning, maybe into the afternoon—barely an hour has passed, and Dad is still shut away in his room.

"What do you want to do now?" I follow Macie into the living room, crossing my fingers that she'll be happy to watch a cartoon.

"Let's make Valentines." She balances on her tiptoes and twirls a corkscrew curl around her pinky finger. "It's almost February."

"Valentines?" Seems quiet enough. "With what?"

"Gramma has lots of scraps, doesn't she?"

"Well..."

"That's a yes, isn't it?" Macie jumps and claps her hands.

I nod, pressing a finger to my lips. "Dad's trying to work, remember? Stay here—and *stay quiet*—and I'll see what I can find."

Macie mimes zipping her lips, and I take off upstairs.

"I'm going to make a card for every single person in my class." Macie waves a crayon at me over the coffee table, which is barely recognizable under stacks of cardstock, ribbon, and other crafty odds and ends.

"Every single person, huh?" I fold a sheet of purple paper in half, then hand it to Macie, who immediately goes to work with a hot pink crayon. "Even the guys?"

"Why not?" Macie draws a lopsided heart on her paper.

I smile, though a tinge of envy flutters in my chest. If only my life was as simple as Macie's. As it is, I haven't made a Valentine for anyone other than a family member in years. Pulling out my phone, I scroll around online for ideas before settling down to make Jazz a cheesy card, complete with a doodle of a sea turtle and the message "you're turtle-y awesome." It makes me cringe a little, but Jazz'll think it's hilarious.

By the time I finish—who knew drawing a turtle could be so complicated?—Macie has accumulated a teetering pile of hastily-scrawled cards. I lay my Valentine aside, and Macie stares at it. "You're only making one?" She lifts a glue stick to her mouth, but I yank it out of her hand before she can take a lick of paste.

"No eating glue."

"But I'm *hungry*."

"You ate three pieces of banana bread this morning. Surely you can wait until lunch." I wrestle the stick out of her hand, and she scowls.

"Where are your cards for Daddy and Gramma and

Brander?" Macie tears her eyes from the glue stick and fixes her gaze on my one lone card.

"You think I should make a card for Brander?"

"Of course. Don't you love him?"

I squeak and drop the glue stick, ducking to grab it before Macie can see the fiery inferno that must be spreading across my face. By the time I raise my head, I've garnered barely enough composure to choke out a response. "Sure, I love Brander. Jesus wants us to love everyone. But I don't know—I mean, I don't *love* love him. I do like him a lot though."

"Huh?" Macie doesn't look up from her latest masterpiece, but her gaze narrows anyway. "If you love him, then make him a card."

"If only it was that simple."

"You mean it isn't?"

"Not a chance, squirt."

The pounding of rain overhead fills in the silence that follows, but it doesn't do anything to help quiet my thoughts.

What exactly *are* Brander and I? We're friends—I know I can be sure of that much—but then where do those kisses fit in? We're certainly nowhere near the happy-sappy-honeymoon-eyes stage that seems to signify more-than-friends.

But, like I told Macie, I definitely care about him.

A lot.

"It's not like I'd be singling him out by giving him a card." I lay a finger alongside my chin and watch as Macie draws another lopsided heart. "You're sure this is a good idea, Mace?"

"Yep." She squirts half a tube of glitter glue onto her paper and smears it around with her thumb.

"Okay then." I reach for another piece of paper and fold it right down the middle. I can at least make one. If things get awkward between now and February fourteenth, I don't have to give it to him. But just in case...why not give it a try?

I start with the inside.

Dear Brander...

I drop the pen like it's suddenly as hot as boiling magma and crumple the piece of paper. *Dear?* For real? No way.

Try again.

I know we're not together or anything, and Valentine's Day is supposed to be all couple-y and stuff, but the truth is I care about you. A lot. And I felt like I should tell you that.

Ack. Even when I'm just writing this stuff I get all rambly and...well, I hope it's not mushy. I should crumple the whole thing up right now and be done with it. But I can't. One way or another, I have to finish this thing. Because, when it gets down to it, I *would* like Brander to know that I care.

Anyway, what I want to say is happy Valentine's Day. Not romantically or anything—but from one friend to another. I mean, this card doesn't even have a heart on it. So basically, it's a card saying hi. And yeah, I really care about you too.

Chapter Twelve

"WHO'S THAT FOR?" THE VOICE COMES out of nowhere. My pen jerks in a slash across the front of my almost-finished, sort-of Valentine for Brander. *Rats.*

"A friend." I cap my pen and flip the card over before turning toward Dad, who is peering over my shoulder with a bit too much interest for my own personal liking. "It's a Valentine."

Dad knits his brow together and peers at the card, as if hoping to develop x-ray vision. "It appears you two have made quite a mess in here."

I get to my feet and survey the table, which is covered in paper scraps, stray sequins, and smears of glue—not to mention Macie's mountain of cards. "I'll clean it up."

Dad pins me under his gaze, then spins on his heel and marches out of the room. "You do that. Then we need to talk."

My stomach pinches at his tone, and I clean up Macie's mess as slowly as I can. Could he have seen Brander's name on the card? Not that there's anything lovey-dovey or remotely romantic in it, but it *is* a Valentine. For a guy.

Dad reappears as I toss the last bit of paper in the trash can. "Hey." My eyes flick to Macie, who is now curled up in front of the TV with a bag of Maui onion chips, and I lower my voice. "Is this kid-friendly?"

Dad shrugs.

"Let's go out front." I lead the way, pushing through the front door into a humid, slightly chilly afternoon. The rain's still coming down, and the street is half-flooded.

"What's wrong?" The words pop out of my mouth as soon as we're settled on the swing, a damp breeze washing over the bridge of my nose.

"Why do you assume something's wrong?" Dad removes his glasses and wipes them on his rumpled gray shirt.

"You look serious."

"That's because I am."

"Is this about that Valentine?"

"No." Dad squints at me, and I mentally kick myself for bringing it up. "Unless there's something you're not telling me about it."

"Nope. Not a thing." I shake my head fast. Too fast?

"All right, then. How to start?"

"Words work best."

Dad narrows his gaze slightly, and I laugh. "I'm kidding, Dad."

"Oh." His shoulders drop, and he presses his fingers to his lips before beginning. "I saw on the parent portal—"

Not this again. "Dad, relax. Ask Jazz, ask Gramma, ask my teachers online—I'm not slacking."

"I didn't say that you were." Dad knits his fingers and rests his hands behind his head. "Listen to me for a few minutes, okay?"

I swallow every smart response that I have in me and nod. "Shoot."

"You realize you're on track to graduate this year, right?"

"Huh?" Now it's my turn to squint at Dad. "I'm a junior."

"But you've accumulated enough credits to get your diploma a year early. You should seize this opportunity and get a head start on college. Speaking of which..." Dad pulls out his phone, taps the screen a few times, then hands it to me. "Read this."

Harvard University Announces the Sophia Galloway Scholarship Program.

The board of trustees has put out a statement regarding a new scholarship program specifically targeted at children of alumni who are particularly gifted in English and the literary arts...

My heart gives a kick, and I scroll down a bit.

...accepted students will receive full-ride scholarships, with the option of majoring in careers focused on liberal arts studies. Dr. Alexander Galloway, who played an integral part in the foundation of this fund, has named the scholarship after his late wife, a cum laude graduate of Harvard's Faculty of Arts and Sciences. The Sophia M. Galloway Scholarship will be open for applications on February 1st. Interested and eligible high school seniors may apply...

I don't finish reading.

Don't say a word.

Just hand the phone to Dad and gape.

"Well?" Dad pockets his phone, his voice soft and velvety—like it used to be Before. "What do you think?"

"I—I'd never...I mean, isn't it kind of a pipe dream?"

"What?" Dad bursts out laughing. "With your grades, you're sure to win."

"But it's named after Mom. Doesn't that mean I wouldn't be eligible?"

"It's named after Sophia, but the fine print clearly states that any alumni's offspring would be eligible. I'm not judging the submissions. There's no reason why you can't enter. Have you taken the SAT?"

"Over Christmas break." The answer comes without me bidding it, my tongue moving on autopilot. *Go to Harvard? Me?* It's been my dream practically since I was born, but now? A whole year early?

"When do you get your results?"

"Dunno. So this means I'd start school in the fall?"

"Isn't that what you've always wanted?" Dad's vision clouds. Is that a tear winking in the corner of his eye? "I did this for you. And your mother, of course. I thought..."

The wetness in Dad's eyes spills over into my own. Suddenly my heart is brimming, I'm beaming, and the tears are falling. "You did this. For real?" The words squeak in my throat like I'm in one of those sappy tearjerker movies Mom used to love. All these months, I sat here thinking that Dad hated my guts and wished I'd fall off the face of the earth...

All these months, he was working on this. For Mom. For *me*.

Before I know what I'm doing, I'm wrapping my arms around Dad in a hug that's long overdue.

Dad clasps his hands behind my back. His English Suede cologne ushers in memories from another lifetime, only increasing the flow of my tears.

"I read one of your essays—the *Pride and Prejudice* analysis. Your mother would be so proud." Dad pulls away and swipes at his eyes. "Harvard is waiting for you, Olive."

"You think I have a chance?"

"Take it from someone who's on the board. I know the people who will be reviewing applications, and I know you." Dad leans in close. "You send in an application, you're in."

Gramma gasps when I tell her late that afternoon.

"Sweetie, that's wonderful." She wraps me in a hug and pecks the top of my head. "Your mother would be thrilled."

"You think so?" I ask, and Gramma nods, her face plumping in a smile as I swallow more tears. "I can't believe it. I've been wanting to go to Harvard for forever."

"And Sophie always hoped one of you girls would go to her alma matter." Gramma squeezes me again, and I squeeze her right back.

"I hope I can do her proud."

"Of course you will. To think—I'll have another Harvard graduate come out of my house. There must be knowledge in these walls." Gramma knocks on the kitchen wall, then winks at me. "More likely you got your grandpa's genes. He was a correspondent for the *New York Times* here during World War Two, you know."

I nod. Grandpa died when Mom was in college, but I've heard a few stories about his journalistic greatness over the years.

Before I can say anything else, Gramma claps her hands and cheers. "We should go out to dinner to celebrate. It's not every day one of my granddaughters gets into Harvard."

I laugh. "It's not like anything is official. If I even apply for the scholarship, who's to say I'll be accepted?"

"*If?*" Dad's voice bounces off the walls as he steps into the kitchen. "Surely you'll apply—and mark my words. You'll get in. Have you read most student papers these days? The grammar and sentence structure are atrocious."

That's enough for Grams and Dad to get into a conversation about the decline of the public-school system, which couldn't interest me less, so I inch away and pull out my phone.

Jazz should be home from visiting her mom by now—I have to cross my fingers and pray she hasn't already eaten dinner.

"Harvard?" Jazz's eyes balloon to the size of sea urchins when I tell her before we leave for dinner that night. "Like, in Boston? Why not go to college here?"

"Here? I didn't even know Maui had a college." Of course, that was before I came *here.*

"Sure they do. The University of Hawaii has a satellite campus in Kahululi." Jazz sprawls across the pillows on my bed as I dig through my closet—Gramma's taking us to a white-tablecloth restaurant and everything, and she said to dress fancy. I thought my short, swingy halter dress was fine, but then Jazz showed up in a floor-length white maxi skirt I haven't seen her wear anywhere but church.

"Oh. Okay. But that's not the point. Harvard's been my dream school since I was six."

"I didn't even know what college *was* when I was six."

"Oh. What about this?" I pull out a white eyelet dress that's longer in the back than it is in front. Kind of plain on its own, but it would make my shell necklace stand out.

"It's fine." Jazz rolls over onto her stomach. "So you're getting a full-ride? To do what?"

"Literature. Journalism. That thing." My voice is muffled as I pull the dress over my head.

"They have classes like that at the University of Hawaii."

Before I can explain that there's a *big* difference between Harvard and the University of Hawaii, Macie hollers up the stairs that it's time for us to go.

"Yeah, like it'll be time for you to go in a few months." Jazz's hands clench into fists as she clambers off my bed. "Didn't you decide you don't like living in Boston?"

"That was an apartment. This is Harvard." I cross my arms, as if to hold in my impatience, but something in my chest stirs, like my heart agrees more with Jazz's words than my own.

"Harvard schmarvard. You'd be way better off staying right where you belong. And right now, that's here with us. So let's go before I starve to death, okay?"

I open my mouth to argue, then close it as Jazz takes my hand and pulls me downstairs. This is supposed to be a nice night—a celebration of my dream-come-true. Why ruin it by arguing?

And besides. Some strange, foreign part of me is far too tempted to agree with Jazz.

Though my own face is wavering between a goofy grin and a confused grimace, a full-on smile has replaced Jazz's earlier look of dismay by the time we reach our destination—a fancy French restaurant tucked away on a side street right off of Front Street—and get seated. Just like Gramma said, it's a cloth-napkin kind of place, with tables spilling out from the dining room right onto the porch of an old-fashioned house that could've come straight from an old movie. *Gone With the Wind,* maybe.

Something tells me the bill for this meal will be almost as much as the scholarship we're celebrating.

The scholarship to *Harvard.*

My dream school.

The same one that happens to be over five thousand miles away.

"To Olive, and all the other smart people gathered here tonight." Jazz lifts her water glass in a mock salute after we've gotten settled. Everyone clinks glasses, and my cheeks heat—which was probably the whole point of Jazz's impromptu toast. Thankfully Macie is quick to take the attention off of me.

"Why are we only celebrating Olive's brain?" She grabs a piece of bread from the basket and coats it with butter—both sides. "Isn't my brain important too?"

"Of course your brain is important. Jesus made *all* of our brains different and beautiful—including yours." Gramma tweaks Macie's chubby cheek as the waiter appears, but my sister doesn't look much happier.

After we place our orders, Gramma fishes a piece of paper out of her overflowing handbag for Macie to doodle on while the rest of us make small talk. We keep up a fairly good conversation until the waiter returns with our appetizers, at which point I guess Dad decides it's time to get serious. "Jazz, have you ever thought of studying at Harvard? I have connections in the financial aid office." He nibbles on a taro chip and blinks at Jazz through his wire-rimmed glasses.

Jazz's face grows as red as the seared ahi tuna on her plate, and I stretch my legs—to see if I'm close enough to kick Dad under the table. I'm not. *Darn it.* For someone so smart, he sure doesn't have much tact.

"Sorry, Mr. Galloway, but even if I was smart enough to win a scholarship, I don't think Harvard and I are cut out for each other."

Dad's eyebrows jump at her response, but he simply shrugs and fidgets with his glasses. "Where do you plan to go then?" he asks. Like Harvard's the only college in the country.

"Dunno." Jazz shrugs. "Guess I'll figure it out next year."

The conversation continues around me, and I find myself joining in, but everything feels off-kilter. Like all of a sudden, the only thing my brain can focus on is the fact that Harvard is so far *away*. And that, when I start classes at Harvard in the fall, Jazz won't be going with me.

She'll stay here in Hawaii while I go off.

Alone.

I open my mouth to voice my concern, but our dinners arrive before I can say anything. Grams splurged and ordered us all the catch of the day—panko-crusted and basted with butter sauce—and the sight of it sends my stomach grumbling despite the tangle of nerves growing inside.

Gramma bows her head and offers a quick blessing before we dig in. "I can't believe you'll be going home to Boston. To Harvard." Gramma smiles at me from across the table, and I resist the urge to wince.

I can't believe it either.

Do I *want* to believe it?

I open my mouth to ask exactly that, but the food is so good, the mood so jovial, that I don't dare ruin the moment. Instead, I field questions from Dad about how I'll adjust to college life—like I've started thinking about that in the five hours since I've known about the scholarship—until we push away from the table after dessert.

Jazz stayed fairly quiet during most of the meal, but Macie is the one who surprised me the most. She kept her chatterbox latched shut the whole time—unless she was shoving in bites of her dinner. Even then, she didn't look too happy.

Then finally, on the walk back to Gramma's station wagon, Macie's stoic frown cracks.

"Why did we have to eat on their porch?" She scuffs her sparkly Velcro sandal alongside the sidewalk. "We could've had something better on our porch."

"Hey, I thought the food was good," Jazz cuts in. "It's not every day you get to go to a real-deal French restaurant."

"What if I don't *like* French food?" Macie sniffs, and she lets a tear slips out, then another, followed by a wail that causes several passers-by to crane their necks in our direction. Seemingly oblivious, Dad kneels in front of Macie and pats her back. "What's wrong, princess?"

"You don't think I'm special." Her voice is watery—either she's milking this opportunity for all it's worth, or her feelings are *really* hurt. "You went out to dinner to celebrate Olive, and you didn't even try to give me any toast like you did her. All I got was bread and stinky fish."

Jazz catches my eye and scrunches her nose. I hide a giggle behind my hand as Dad turns to Gramma for help.

"Macie, sweetheart. Let's sit down." Grams motions to a nearby bench, and she and Macie settle onto the weathered wooden slats. "We celebrate different people at different times—and for different reasons. Today was Olive's big day, but isn't your birthday coming up soon?"

Macie nods. "So?"

"We'll celebrate you then, Mace." I walk over and ruffle my sister's curls, but I keep an eye on Grams and Dad as they exchange a huge grin. Has Gramma managed to get Dad on board with that puppy?

Dad takes a step closer to Macie and reaches for her hand. "Think you can hold out until your birthday?"

Macie squints up at him in the evening light. "Maybe. If waiting means I get a puppy."

"Ah, sounds like I'm raising a shrewd negotiator. A future graduate of Harvard's law program, perhaps." Dad chuckles, and he trades another sneaky smile with Gramma. "Why don't you wait a few weeks and see what kind of birthday magic happens before you keep pouting, all right?"

With that, Macie hops off the bench, and we continue on our way. Jazz hangs back to walk alongside me, her prosthesis clunking in a comforting rhythm, but my heart is pounding in a way that's anything but comforting.

Go off on my own to Boston?

Stay here with a new, canine-toothed family member?

I might be trying to be brave and all that, but still...

God, what do You want me to do?

Chapter Thirteen

"JAZZ, YOU'VE GOTTA HELP ME." I grab her arm after church the next day, before Malia or anyone else can snatch her away from me. "Can you come over?"

"What's up?" Jazz tugs on her braid. "Trying to figure out what to pack for Harvard?"

Her joke needles my heart. *Harvard.* Going to school there sounds so intimidating now that it's no longer a dream.

Now it's reality. Or maybe even a nightmare.

My chest twinges, but I take a deep breath and answer Jazz. "No. This is a lot more important."

"More important than *Harvard*?" Jazz says it with a smile, but I get the niggling feeling that she's being sarcastic. Before I can do any digging to be sure, Ruby appears, a new hoop embedded in her right eyebrow. How many does that make now? I lose count after five, when Ruby clears her throat and snaps her fingers at Jazz.

"Come on, kiddo. Time to go. I've gotta leave for work soon."

"I'm hanging out with Olive." Jazz jerks a thumb at me, and Ruby shrugs.

"Whatever." Ruby runs one hand over her half-shaved head of hair and turns to leave. "See ya."

"What's the problem?" Jazz turns to me the second Ruby is out of earshot.

"You are." I blurt it out before I can stop myself, then slap a hand over my mouth. I've run through a million different versions of this conversation since we dropped Jazz off after dinner last night, and none of them started like *that.*

"I'm the problem?" Jazz's brow crumples, and I clamp my eyes shut. *Nice going, queen of social skills.* At least Malia knows how to speak properly—even though the words she speaks aren't always the nicest.

Opening my eyes, I find Jazz goggling at me like I grew a coconut between my two eyeballs. I've got to fix this before Jazz decides to ditch me and chase Ruby down to take her home.

"That came out wrong. Honest." I clear my throat to say what I've wanted to all along—that Jazz seriously needs to reconsider the paddleboard race—when Gramma waves us over.

"Come on." I give Jazz's arm a tug, and we follow Gramma, Dad, and Macie out of the church pavilion. "I'll tell you later."

"Are you going to tell me what's up?" Jazz follows me out front after lunch, her gaze one frown line short of testy. She'd probably feel a whole lot better if she would get in the water.

"I want to learn how to paddleboard." I point at the small beach across the street from Gramma's house. "You're the only person I know who can teach me."

"Paddleboard, huh?" A flicker of what I can only hope is interest gleams behind Jazz's eyes, but her expression stays grim. "What about Malia?"

"Malia?" I hadn't been expecting that. "Something tells me she isn't the gentle, encouraging type. Besides, she'd probably want to spend the whole lesson telling me how great she is. Or grilling me about Brander's life of fame and glory."

"I was kidding." Jazz cracks a smile. "But seriously, why would you want me to teach you when I can't even get in the water? Wait for Brander to get home. He's pretty good at it."

My heart nearly dances at the mention of Brander's return, but I can't let anything distract me—not even the thought of seeing him again. "You don't get it. I want *you*."

"You want a peg-legged pirate to teach you how to paddleboard?" Jazz dips her head, and her blonde bangs shade her gaze from view.

"Wouldn't a peg-legged pirate make a cooler coach than a rising pop star?" I lean over to knock my shoulder against Jazz's. "Besides. It'd be fun."

"If you think hanging out with a pirate's fun." Jazz doesn't lift her head, but I catch a spark in her words.

"I've always thought pirate ships were pretty neat." I reach over and give Jazz's braid a tug. "Isn't there a paddleboard rental place on the south end of Ka'anapali Beach?"

"*Maybe*." Jazz draws the word out for what feels like forever, but she finally raises her chin enough for me to catch the tail end of a smile.

"Is that a yes then?"

"Aye, matey. Them's be a yes." Jazz finishes with a pirate-like growl that sends laughter bubbling up in my throat.

Maybe this won't be as hard as I thought.

This is so much harder than I thought.

Not getting Jazz out on the water—the surfer dude working the counter at the board rental place did that part for me. With a few encouraging words and a killer smile from him, Jazz was standing on her board and paddling through the surf like an old pro in minutes.

I, on the other hand, can barely balance in a kneeling position, let alone think about standing and using my long, oar-like paddle to steer.

"Isn't this fun?" Jazz pulls alongside me as the ocean swells beneath us. "It's way easier than I thought it would be."

I glance up to smile at Jazz, but the bright sunshine hits my eyes, and I grimace instead. "See? I knew you could do it."

"You'll get the hang of it too. Just make sure you're working *with* the ocean and not against it." Jazz laughs and paddles away, spraying me with water as she goes. "Come on, slowpoke," she yells over her shoulder.

I plant a hand on the board and try to push myself onto my feet, but a wave crops up before I can stand. I groan, holding tight to the board as it pitches in the surf. I've never been one to get motion sick, but if I keep sitting here, bobbing like a ship lost at sea...

"Wow. Guess you talked her into it, huh?" The voice comes out of nowhere.

Turning to look behind me, I send my board rocking even more than it already was. Malia towers above me on a pink-striped board. She looks so at ease that I wouldn't be surprised if she told me she was born with a paddleboard leash around her ankle.

"Fancy meeting you here." Embarrassment sparks in my chest. I must look like a baby, crouched on this board, holding onto my paddle for dear life. "This is my first time," I add—like *that* needed any explanation.

"You don't say." Malia snorts. "So Jazz is going to do the race? For real?"

"Yeah." The ocean shifts beneath me, and I let go of my paddle to grip one edge of my board. I hope the rental shack won't mind if I return their paddleboard with a few fingernail marks on it—maybe more than a few. "She just doesn't know it yet. All I did was ask her to take me out today and show me the basics."

"Wow. Guess you're a natural."

Ouch. I wince, though Malia's sarcasm is right on target. "Hey, I never said I was coordinated."

Malia heaves a mighty sigh, her eyes rolling up toward the sky. "Turn around and face the right direction. I'll help you."

"You...will?" The offer seems strangely selfless, coming from Malia.

"Yeah. But I don't have all day."

Malia paddles alongside me, and we wait in silence for the ocean to calm before Malia coaches me into a standing position. "That's it. Keep your feet even, otherwise you'll fall overboard before I can say SUP. Now paddle."

I fumble with the paddle a few times before settling into a rhythm, and Malia joins me as I work my way down the coastline toward Jazz.

"Not bad." Malia's eyes soar over me like a hawk scouting for prey. "Not good enough to race or anything, but at least you don't look like an idiot anymore."

High praise. I dip my paddle into the frothy surf, smiling when the water splashes up against my legs. Maybe I should ask if Malia would like to join me and Jazz—now that I've gotten the hang of this and she won't be able to make fun of me. I open my mouth to invite her, but something knots up my tongue, and I change tactics. "I guess this *is* kind of fun."

"Of course it is. Now get out of my way. I need to get in shape for that race." Malia makes a sharp turn, heading farther out to sea, and I continue on my way toward Jazz.

"Hey, you finally made it." Jazz's eyes are wide, and she's wearing a brilliant smile when I catch up with her. "Isn't this a blast? Thanks for getting me out here."

"No problem." A wave swells beneath me, and I nearly

lose my balance. "It's harder than it looks, though."

"Yeah, but you're doing great."

"I guess." *Thanks to Malia.* I open my mouth to say that, but a strange part of me isn't willing to acknowledge Malia's role in my improvement. Like mentioning her name will throw an otherwise perfect afternoon off-kilter.

Instead, I pour my focus into keeping pace with Jazz. My breath comes out in little puffs, and a deep ache seeps into my arms as I strain to keep from being left behind. Even on land, Jazz is a fast mover—but when her prosthesis isn't part of the equation?

It's exactly like I've suspected all along—Jazz is unstoppable.

"Let's race to shore."

I nearly topple off my board when Jazz's suggestion cuts through the balmy air a while later. "Race? I thought you weren't into competitive water sports anymore."

"Don't be silly. This is just for fun—come on."

I shake my head, that simple movement throwing off my newly developed center of balance. I sway on my feet, and my heart launches into my throat as I prepare for impact with the water. Jazz squeals and closes her eyes, as though afraid to watch, but I manage to steady myself before I wipe out completely. "I don't think I'm good enough to race."

"So? An hour ago, I didn't even think I could paddleboard." Jazz's gaze slides over to meet mine. "We do this a few more weekends in a row, I might even have to think about going out for that race."

Score. "The race, huh?"

"Yeah. But first, I want to see how fast I can go."

"Fine." Though my arms feel like overstretched rubber bands, I grip the paddle tightly in both fists and prepare for blastoff as Jazz counts us down.

"Ready...go!" Her shout rings out over the rippling sheet of blue water, and she takes off like a supersonic jet. Every muscle in my upper body protests as I dig my paddle into the water, but I have to at least try to give Jazz a run for her money.

As we race, a breeze coming off the shore finds me, blowing in my face and wrapping itself in my hair. The only sound that fills my ears is that of the gentle ebb and flow of the water beneath me.

I guess I can see why someone would want to spend their free time doing this...

"Look at you two." A voice comes from my left, and Jazz and I slow as Malia paddles closer. "Nice form, Olive. Exactly like I showed you."

"Malia helped you?" Jazz quirks an eyebrow.

"You didn't tell her?" Malia makes a tiny growling noise that's barely loud enough for me to hear over the cawing of a seabird.

"That's cool." Jazz's eyes dart from me to Malia, then back. "You should've joined us, Malia."

"Didn't want to. I have a race to train for." Malia rolls her neck, caramel-colored skin glistening with a sheen of moisture. How does she manage to make sweating look like the next big fashion statement? "I've gotta beat my time from last year." Malia's words are breezy, but she fixes her eyes on Jazz, like she's already trying to psyche her out.

If it works, Jazz sure isn't about to let it show. "I bet you will. When's the race?"

"In a couple of months. You should come watch me." Malia's voice leans heavily on those words—*watch me*—and she juts her chin toward the shore. "I'm beat. Wanna head in?"

Jazz nods. As we paddle the rest of the way in silence, Jazz's words roll around in my mind.

Malia should've joined us.

But when I had the opportunity to invite Malia to do exactly that, I choked.

Why?

When did I become so afraid of change that I'd be willing to make someone *else* feel excluded in order to keep things safely within my own comfort zone?

When Mom left.

Forever.

Mom's face blooms in my memory, the mere image of her threatening to overpower everything in the here and now. I blink a few times and wait for the image of Mom, plus the few tears it brought out, to fade away.

As we near the shoreline, a shiver starts at the very base of my spine and runs all the way up my back. I should be ready. Ready to heal—to make it through life without Mom.

This is supposed to be my year of surviving and *thriving.* Instead, I'm a mess. Afraid to share Jazz with anyone else. Afraid to give Brander a Valentine—or not.

Afraid...

Afraid I'll never know what it means to be truly brave.

Chapter Fourteen

"WE NEED TO DO THAT AGAIN." Jazz practically skips down the path to Gramma's as we head home after turning in our boards. In fact, though her prosthetic makes it a little uneven, she *is* skipping. "Wasn't it fun?"

"Fun." I bob my head in a weak attempt at a nod. There are still too many questions flitting around in my brain for me to make conversation.

"Except next time, we should make it a party and invite the kids from youth group—especially the swim team ones. It'd be a blast. And it'd be good for Malia too."

"Yeah." I picture myself trailing behind Jazz's group of swim team friends, paddling across the water like a pathetic slug. "A blast."

"Aargh, matey, you be turnin' into a parrot right befer' me eyes." Jazz jabs me with an elbow, then drops the goofy voice. "Seriously though. What's up?"

"It's nothing."

One glance at Jazz's eyes lets me know she's not buying it. "It's *something*."

"I'm just..." *Jealous.* That little voice is such a liar. I'm not jealous. Okay, maybe I am a little bit. "Malia keeps showing up everywhere. It's a little strange, isn't it?"

"Maybe. But sometimes God has to do strange things before we understand what He's trying to tell us."

A cool breeze wafts through the air, bringing with it a light drizzle. I shiver and shove my hands in the pockets of my sweatshirt cover-up. "You think God wants to tell us something about Malia?"

"Yeah. She needs a friend." Jazz's eyes grow warm. "And so do I."

Her words punch a certain soft spot in my gut that hasn't been hit since before I left Boston. "What does that mean—that I'm not good enough for you anymore?" The words come out in one breath—like the swing of a freshly sharpened machete. And they're not at all light and teasing like they'd sounded in my head.

"Whoa, back up." Jazz opens her mouth, the sun dancing over a few stray freckles on her nose. "I didn't mean it like that. But if you're going to go back to Boston, and if Brander decides to stay in Nashville..." Jazz swallows. "I'll get pretty lonely."

My throat constricts at the idea of Jazz—sweet, sunny Jazz—being lonely. But at the same time, the thought of her filling my place with Malia makes my chest ache. "Maybe I won't go."

"Not go to Harvard?" She adopts a superior tone of voice as we turn onto Gramma's street. "But it's *Harvard*. Your *dream school*."

Is that what I sound like when I talk about Harvard? I hope not. "Sure, Harvard used to be my dream school. It's, like, five minutes from my old house." I lower my voice as we reach Gramma's and start up the front walk. "But now that I'm here, Harvard seems awfully far away."

"You're having second thoughts?"

"Maybe. All I know is, *if* I go, I'll miss this place. A lot." I also know Dad will kill me if I decide not to apply, but that's beside the point. "Maybe I should pray about it first—before I make any for-sure decisions."

Jazz relaxes at my words, and something in my chest eases too—like the simple admission that I can choose where and when to go to school released me from a trap I didn't even know I was stuck in.

"Hey, Olive." Brander's voice—deep and rich, like a bar of gourmet dark chocolate—rumbles in my ear when I answer the phone late the next evening. "Are you free to talk?"

"Of course." I scramble from the couch and wave to Grams, Macie, and Dad, who are bent over a Candy Land board, before heading outside. Anything to avoid one of Dad's I'm-not-eavesdropping-but-totally-am charades—the kind he likes to pull any time he's around when I talk on the phone with Brander.

Outside, I press the phone closer to my ear and lean on the porch railing. The sun hovers over the horizon, beginning to melt into a sheet of rippling water—the days sure are getting longer. "What's up? Shouldn't you be packing?" I settle onto the swing.

"No—I..." Brander groans. "I don't even know where to start. Can you pray for me?"

"I pray for you every day." The words slip out before I can stop myself, and even though it's the truth, I can't help but flinch. That didn't make me sound like a creeper, did it? "I mean, you know. We all pray for you. Me and Grams and Macie and—"

"I appreciate that." Brander doesn't seem creeped out. If anything, his nubby flannel tone has grown even warmer. "Honest—it means a lot. But I was wondering if you could pray for me, like, right now."

Despite the genuine warmth in Brander's tone and the kindness of his words, something stirs in my stomach, like a riptide tearing through a placid coral reef. "Is something wrong?"

"Yeah. No. Kinda. It's—oh, man." Brander groans, and another wave of uncertainty sweeps through my stomach. "I wish we could talk about this in person."

"Then let's wait. Aren't you flying out tomorrow?" I tighten my grip on the phone with one hand, crossing my fingers on the other, even though I have a sinking suspicion I already know the answer.

"That's part of the problem. I won't be able to make it out until next weekend, at the very earliest."

"For real?" The small flame of excitement in my chest that sparked when I answered the phone gets doused in a wave of disappointment. Another weekend adventure with Jazz and Brander down the tubes. "What happened?"

Brander mutters something about the label needing to do some damage control, and my gut twists. "What's going on out there?"

"It's not that big a deal. Honest." But Brander's voice wavers all the same.

"What is *it*?"

"Nothing. But Mike and the higher-ups at the label are all up in arms over it. They want me to stay for a few more days. To talk about my *image*."

"Your image is so spotless you could replace Mr. Clean, and no one would notice. What aren't you telling me?"

"Not that much."

Like he thinks I'll buy that? "Come on. Spill."

"I don't know if I should."

"Why? Is it confidential or something? I'm good at keeping things under wraps."

"No. But I'd rather talk in person. Where there aren't so many people around. But can you still—would you mind still praying for me?"

This time, as soon as the request meets my ears, I bow my head and offer up a prayer for peace and wisdom for Brander—and patience for the rest of us as we wait for him to come home.

"I guess this means we won't be driving the road to Hana this weekend?" I ask after finishing my prayer.

"I'll try and make it up to you." Brander's voice is thick. "I promise."

"That's not what I meant." Rats. I probably made him feel even worse. "Don't feel bad. Just keep me posted on when you're coming back, 'kay?"

"I'll let you know as soon as I hear anything." Brander sniffs—he isn't crying, is he?

"You sure you don't want to talk?"

"Nah. It's too—I mean, we can do it later. I...*aloha*, Olive."

Before I can say goodbye, the line goes dead, and I'm left standing on the porch, the phone a sudden weight in my hand. Did Brander hang up on me?

The thought makes my heart pound against my ribcage. First Jazz started getting ideas about finding a replacement for me, and now Brander's falling apart. What will he think when I tell him I might be going to Harvard next year? He'll probably dump me like I'm last week's leftovers.

Not that we're together or anything.

"Olive?" Dad nudges the front door open and steps outside. "Who was on the phone?"

"Brander." *Like you didn't already know that.*

"Ah. Yes." Dad takes off his glasses and pinches the bridge of his nose. He opens his mouth to speak, and I cast about for something to say to cut him off. Knowing Dad, he's trying to think of some way to bring up The Talk. The one Mom had with me in the hospital before she died. About guys and love and a bunch of other stuff I have no business hearing about from my dad—or anyone else, for that matter. Especially when Brander's never done more than kiss me.

On the *forehead.*

"You know Brander and I are only friends, right?"

Dad blinks at me, as though questioning why I would assume he was thinking about Brander. *Maybe because it's written all over your face?*

"Brander isn't even going to date until he finds the person God wants him to marry." And there's no way that's going to be me. Especially now that he's surrounded by Nashville's finest—a bunch of girls prettier and more godly than I could ever be.

Dad purses his lips, almost like he doesn't believe what I'm saying. If only he could meet Brander—then he'd have an easier time getting it through his head that we're *only friends*.

"Scholarship applications open soon." His words send my shoulders shooting up to brush my ears, and all thoughts of Brander fly from my head.

After all, I haven't found the right time—probably because there isn't one—to tell Dad about my case of cold feet. "How long do I have to turn it in?"

"You have a while after applications open, but I highly suggest you get yours filled out and submitted as soon as possible. Punctuality is important."

"What if..." The words teeter on my tongue, one on top of the other, until they tip over and spill out into the quiet evening. "What if I'm not sure yet? About going to Harvard? Because it's far away and a year early and—I mean, can't I wait a year? Go off to school with the rest of my friends?"

Dad's face pales, like I suggested I'd be better off joining the circus than going to college. "You're second-guessing your entire life goal?"

But what if Harvard isn't my life goal anymore? "Going to Harvard this fall hasn't been an option for more than a couple of days. You've got to give me some time to think about it. And pray." Despite my irritation, a smile slips onto my face. I haven't always been the pray-about-it-then-decide kind of person, but I like the sound of the words as they leave my mouth. After all, I'm sure God knows something about this mess that I don't.

"How long?"

"Huh?" I blink at Dad.

"How long to pray?"

"I'm not exactly sure." Maybe I should ask Gramma about that part.

Dad huffs.

This obviously isn't how he imagined our conversation would go, but at least I managed to get him off Brander's case. The bad thing is, now he's on mine. And I have a feeling he won't let up until he gets the answer he wants.

An answer that, right now, I'm not sure I'll ever be able to give.

Chapter Fifteen

GRAMMA MUST'VE KNOWN SOMETHING WAS WRONG the second Dad and I walked inside after our talk last night, because she pulled me aside before bed and asked if I'd be willing to help her scrounge for "ocean treasures" on the beach before school the next morning.

Which is why I'm now up to my knees in chilly saltwater before the wild roosters have even begun to crow—and the chickens in Hawaii are serious early birds.

Oops, bad pun.

"Would you like to talk, or are we pretending that everything's fine this morning?" Gramma peers at me from beneath her wide-brimmed sunhat as I wade out of the bay and drop a smooth sphere of white glass into her mesh collecting bag.

"Why would you think something's wrong?" I watch Gramma's face, the early-morning light reflecting off the water and playing hopscotch over her collection of smile lines.

"Because you didn't think to check that the window was closed before you made your escape from the living room last night."

I drop to my knees and pretend to examine a broken shell to hide the guilt that must be spreading across my face. "You mean you guys heard the whole phone call?" My brain whirls as I scour my mind for a transcript of all that I said to Brander during our talk, but Gramma cuts in before I can figure out how much Dad overheard.

"I got an email from Brander last night. He sounded

thankful for your prayers."

"Did he say anything else? Like about what's bugging him?" I stand and toss the broken shell into Gramma's bag—the colors are pretty enough that maybe its jagged edges won't matter.

Gramma bites her lip. "He mentioned he's been having some trouble with the paparazzi. It sounds like his label wants to keep an eye on him until things blow over."

"The paparazzi are hung up on a teenage Christian singer?" I wrinkle my nose. "They must be running out of hot news." Not that I don't think Brander is newsworthy, of course. But he isn't the sleazy type those camera hounds usually gravitate toward.

"That's the problem. They're trying to turn something into news that…isn't."

"Huh?"

"You know how the pharisees tried to make people believe Jesus wasn't the perfect, faultless Son of God?"

I nod.

"People try to do the same thing with Christians today. They see someone—Brander—who's living a pure life and trying to serve Jesus in all that he does, and they start digging."

"Digging?"

"Looking for fault where there isn't any." Gramma picks up a handful of sand and lets it run through her knobby fingers. "I suppose they found—or *think* they found—something."

"Grams, what happened?" I stoop to pick up a shell, but I barely even look at it before pitching it in the bag. "What could be so bad that Brander is afraid to tell me about it?" Honesty and openness have always been two of Brander's favorite principles. What could've happened in Nashville to change that?

Gramma presses her lips together and gazes at me,

almost as if gauging my level of trustworthiness. I keep my expression cool and solid—dependable—as I meet her gaze. *You can tell me.*

"I shouldn't say."

Rats. I should've known better than to hope she'd spill. "I promise I won't say a word. Not even to Jazz. Brander'll never know that I know."

Gramma opens her mouth, and I allow hope to bloom in my chest once more. But then her eyes grow dark, and all of my optimism withers.

"You know I'm not keeping this from you to be mean." Gramma reaches out as if to pat my arm, but I duck away and reach for another shell. "It's not even that Brander asked me to keep this from you. But relationships are complicated things. I'd hate to do or say anything that might get between you and Brander."

I open my mouth to argue. After all, Brander and I don't *have* a relationship—other than a friendship that's more precious to me than gold. But Gramma keeps talking. "I don't know about everything that's going on in Nashville, but I know that Brander's ready for a break. But you should be prepared. When Brander does come home, he might not be the same person he was when he left."

"Of course. I'm not the same person either." But something tells me that Brander's changed a lot more than I'd care to know. "He's not mixed up in drugs or anything like that, is he?"

Gramma's eyes bug out. She covers her mouth and coughs, though it sounds more like she's trying to disguise a laugh. "No drugs. Or alcohol. Or anything remotely scandalous like the press would have you think." Her eyes widen even more, and she keeps her hand over her mouth— almost like she's said too much. "Remember, in case you see something you shouldn't—not everything you read on the Internet is real."

We walk in silence after that, the noise and confusion in my brain roaring louder than the ocean waves. What on earth is Grams talking about? Brander and the paparazzi aren't a good fit. They don't even sound good in the same sentence, for crying out loud.

And what would I find if I tapped Brander's name into a search engine? Obviously, nothing good.

The thought of a bunch of scummy shutterbugs throwing Brander into their fake news reports curdles my blood, and I kick at the sand as I walk. Brander had better get home where he belongs.

"You don't want to go to Harvard, do you?" Gramma says after a while. Her words, instead of making me panicky, warm my heart—almost like I've been waiting for someone to know the truth ever since Dad told me about the scholarship. And maybe I have.

"When did I say that?" I bend to pick up a broken piece of sand dollar.

"Grandmas have a way of hearing the things you don't say better than the ones you do." The sun ducks behind a cloud, and Gramma pushes off her hat, letting it dangle behind her as we walk.

"Then tell me something else about myself I don't know." I kick off my shoes as we continue to scuff through the sand. "Harvard's been my dream since I was a little kid. Why wouldn't I want to go?"

"Sometimes God has a funny way of giving us new dreams to replace the old."

"Huh." I pick up a shell, so smooth it feels like glazed porcelain, and throw it in the bag. "But if what you're saying is true, then why hasn't God given me a new dream yet?"

"Maybe He already has." Gramma kneels to scoop up a handful of perfect, tiny shells, some so small they'd fit on the tip of my pinky finger. "Have you been listening for His voice?"

"Not much. I've been trying to pray about it, but it's all so complicated. I don't even know where to start."

Gramma clambers to her feet, brushes sand from her knees, and lays her hand over her heart. "Start here. Tell God what's wrapped up inside—those secrets, the ones you're afraid to admit even to yourself. Give them to Him. Then wait and watch Him work."

"What if there's no time to wait?" I stop mid-stride to grab a chip of frosted blue sea glass. "Dad wants me to get my application in, like, yesterday."

Gramma hums under her breath, her brow knotted, mouth twisted. "Your father is a brilliant, kindhearted, and passionate man. But since your mother died, I've come to learn that he acts more on his emotions than on what the Lord tells him to do. That's not to say that he makes bad decisions, only that it's sometimes best to ask your *Heavenly* Father for counsel first."

"You mean Dad might be wrong about all of this?" A knot in my chest goes slack, and I take a breath of relief.

Grandma raises her palms in the air, as though hesitant to agree with me. "I can't tell you where and when you should go to school, and neither can your father. That's a matter that should be between you and God."

As Gramma speaks, the knot in my heart eases even further, until I can practically feel the tension leaving me, rolling out to sea in loose, loopy waves. Maybe Grams is right—maybe I don't have to make a decision now, tomorrow, or even next week. Maybe I don't have to make a decision at all—maybe I should leave that up to God.

Chapter Sixteen

"WE NEED TO GOOGLE BRANDER." I plop next to Jazz, laptop in hand, after we've finished our history assignment late Wednesday afternoon.

"Huh?" Jazz peers at my laptop screen as I pull up my web browser. "Wouldn't it be easier to text him?"

"Very funny." I cross my eyes at Jazz before typing in Brander's name. I move to hit enter, but my pinky hovers over the key, quivering a little. Am I sure I want to do this?

Jazz gives me a poke. "Seriously though. Why are we Googling Brander?"

"Grams said something yesterday." I bite my lip, then launch into an explanation of Gramma's cryptic references to Brander and the paparazzi. "She wouldn't say much, but I think he's in trouble."

Jazz frowns. "Are you sure we should start digging around online? Wouldn't it be better to talk to Brander in person?"

"Maybe."

"For sure." Jazz nods, but as soon as she does, something flashes in her eyes, and she doubles over.

"Jazz?"

"Just a phantom pain. Maybe Andy doesn't like paddleboarding as much as I do." The words are muffled, as though they come from between clenched teeth, and Jazz grips her stump—er, Andy. Guess she still hasn't picked out a name for it. "Don't worry. It shouldn't last much longer."

And she's right—only a few moments later she raises her head and shoots me a wavering smile. "I haven't had one that bad in a while." She squeezes her leg one last time, then adjusts her position on the couch, her elbow knocking mine.

Reflexes kick in, and my arm jerks. Before I can stop myself, my pinky taps the search button, sending the computer's hard drive whirring.

Almost instantly, a page of results pops up. At the top of it are three different article excerpts—each of them headed by the same picture. A picture of...

Whoa.

My stomach grows cold, iced over by the image coming at me in a triple threat.

The shot is in silhouette, but Brander's jaunty cowlick gives him away. I can't tell who the other person is, but from their soft, curvy figure it's obvious that whoever-it-is happens to be of the female variety. And Brander is holding her hand.

Jazz makes a funny squeaking noise, but it barely registers as I stare at the picture. Maybe it wouldn't be so bad if he was just holding this gal's hand, but he's not. Brander's head—the one with that cowlick that I know so well—is lowered, his mouth parted slightly. As if he's about to...

No way.

Everything I've told myself and everyone else about me and Brander—that we're not a couple, that we're not in a relationship, that we're nothing more than friends—crumbles away as the picture slowly burns itself into my brain.

Brander—*my* Brander—is about to kiss another girl.

Not that he was ever *mine* to begin with, of course. But still.

"I can't believe it." My words catch in my throat. "He said he wasn't going to date until he found the person he wanted to marry." Maybe I'd been hoping I was that person a little more than I'd been willing to admit to myself. "Why didn't he tell us when he found The One?"

My eyes slide over to see what Jazz makes of this whole mess, but her face is blank. "Jazz?"

She reaches over to tap one of the links, then turns to face me, a kind of sparkle in her eyes that makes my chest burn. "This is so bizarre."

"That he'd fall in love in *Nashville*? No kidding." I cross my arms and lean back on the couch as Jazz pulls the laptop onto her lap. "I can't believe it."

"And *I* can't believe the paparazzi think anyone will buy this." Jazz snickers, then falls silent as she scrolls through an article from one of those teen-queen online zines. "Hot new pop star Brander Delacroix has found his future love?" She snorts.

"I can't believe it."

"Stop saying that. It's obviously fake." She clicks over to the search results, then selects another article. "Are you reading this garbage? It's ridiculous."

"What do you mean?" That same picture flashes by on the screen, and I close my eyes to block out the image—not that it does a lot of good, seeing as it's already seared into my memory.

"You think this is for real?" Jazz rolls her eyes at me. "Didn't you say *Tutu* told you not to believe everything you read about him? Somehow I doubt you'll be the last to know when Brander finds his forever love."

"Whatever." I slam the lid of my laptop shut before Jazz can find another article, then turn to face her. "If this is a hoax, then how do you explain that picture?"

"I can't." Jazz shrugs. "But something tells me Brander will be able to."

Good grief. *God, help him get home soon.*

Even hours later, my shock at seeing Brander on the Internet with another girl must show, because Gramma takes one look at me when she comes home from a late shift at the gallery and envelops me in a warm embrace.

She doesn't say a word, just holds me, long and tight. I breathe in her sweet plumeria-and-sugar essence—the same perfume Mom used to wear—and I open my mouth to speak when someone beats me to it.

"Grammy!" Footsteps pitter-patter across the floor as Macie's voice comes nearer. "Alani said her puppies are almost ready to go to their new houses."

I swallow a groan as Gramma pulls away, but she doesn't get too far before stopping to squeeze my arm and whisper in my ear. "Remember—not everything the Internet says about Brander is true."

I nod and swallow hard, then stand to the side as Macie barrels forward and wraps herself around Gramma's generous waist. "Can I get one of the puppies? Please?"

I give Macie's hair a ruffle and slip out the front door before I can get dragged into any puppy drama.

Instead of getting myself mired in a conversation that will only end in Macie begging and pouting—unless Gramma decides to cave right here and now—I jog across the street, kick off my shoes, and scuff barefoot through the sand.

My fingertips itch to pull out my phone and dial Brander's number—to ask him what on earth is going on— but Gramma's gentle reminder keeps me from giving in. There's no point in bugging Brander about something that could be nothing more than the repercussions of a lazy paparazzo's project on a slow news day.

Then again...

Before I can second-guess myself, I grab the phone and

dial, then hold it to my ear as the ocean waves wash over my gritty feet. There's no answer on Brander's end—maybe that's for the best.

I leave him as cheerful a message as I can, assuring him that I'm only checking in and hoping he has a new date set to fly home, before I hang up.

And then, before I even pocket my phone, it buzzes.

"Hey." Brander's voice floods my ear when I answer. "Sorry I didn't answer. Mike was on the other line."

"Oops, sorry. You didn't have to hang up because of me, you know." *Especially now that you may well have met the love of your life.* Because even if that article is fake news like Gramma and Jazz seem to think, I'm no idiot. Nashville must be crawling with girls. Girls a whole lot nicer, prettier, and more godly than yours truly.

"I know I didn't *have* to. But I wanted to." A smile that I can practically see through the phone warms Brander's words. "What's up?"

"Nothing much." The fib catches in my throat, but I think it's for the best. Brander will tell me about his new love—or lack thereof—when he's ready. "I was wondering if you have a new date to fly out yet."

"I do, actually. My flight gets in on Sunday."

"That's not so bad." I pause for a breath and then, crossing my fingers that I'm not being too forward, open my mouth. "What time do you land? I bet Grams could take Jazz and Macie and me to the airport to pick you up. If that's okay with your parents, I mean."

"I'd like that."

"Are you flying in by yourself?" The words pop out of my mouth before I can stop them, and I wince. Hopefully that wasn't too obvious.

"Me and my guitar."

Thankfully, before I can say anything else that makes it sound like I'm prying—which I totally am, by the way—a voice on Brander's end of the call cuts in. "Yo, dude! We need you for a mic check in five."

"Rats." Brander's groan rumbles in my ear. "I haven't even warmed up yet. Can we talk later?"

"Of course."

We say our goodbyes, and I slip my phone into my pocket before retrieving my shoes and heading across the street to Gramma's.

Whether or not Brander has found his future love, at least he'll be coming home soon. And then—even if it's only for a few weeks—everything will be okay.

Chapter Seventeen

"I'M GONNA DO THE PADDLEBOARD THING." Jazz flashes a cheeky grin and pops a piece of pineapple into her mouth the night before Brander's due to fly in. "Malia talked me into it."

"Malia?" My mouth buckles under the sudden weight of a frown, and I push away the bag of barbecue potato chips sitting between me and Jazz on the porch swing. "When did you talk to her?"

And why are *we* talking about her now?

Between trying to forget about the fact that Brander may or may not have fallen in love, keep Dad off my case about Harvard, and convince Macie that there's *no way* she's getting a puppy—when I know full well Grams is in serious negotiations with Alani's mom—the last week has been a zoo. And I've been locked in the tiger's cage.

Having Jazz over to spend the night before we meet Brander at the airport tomorrow morning is supposed to be fun. I thought the plan was to camp out on the porch, eat as many snacks as humanly possible, and talk—about anything *but* Malia.

"We got talking after youth group." Jazz shoves more fruit into her mouth, and I internally kick myself for missing the Wednesday night service this week. If only Dad hadn't decided to keep me busy working on that application. "I don't think she was trying to help, but she kept reminding me how fast I used to be. Then she started bragging about how she's got this year's trophy in the bag. And peg-legged pirate or not, I'm still competitive."

"Good for you. I'm glad you're doing it." And I am. But why was Malia able to talk Jazz into competing when I couldn't? Does my opinion not matter anymore? "Do you want me to help you train?"

"No thanks." Jazz half-sneezes into her napkin.

"You sure? I know I'm not as good as you are, but I bet I could still help somehow. Even if I paddle behind with a bag of snacks or something."

Jazz sneezes again, except this time it sounds more like a laugh. That's it—she's laughing. *At me?* "Thanks, Olive. I appreciate it. But I think I'm better off with Malia. Since she actually knows what she's doing."

"Huh?" I nearly fall off my seat on the swing. "You asked Malia to help you?"

"Not yet."

I breathe in a breath tinged with sweet relief.

"But I'm going to."

Oh. "Does Malia usually make it a habit to train her competition?"

"No." Jazz waggles her eyebrows. "But I have my ways."

Before I can ask what those *ways* are, something else jumps out of my mouth. "Glad you're not waiting to find a stand-in for me. Next time you decide to replace your best friend, maybe you could wait until they're actually sure they're going to need replacement." *Where did that come from?* My cheeks heat, and I have no doubt they're turning lobster-red.

Jazz gapes at me and lowers a handful of macadamia nuts. "Who said I'm trying to replace you?"

I shrug. "It sure seems like it. You're getting all caught up in this paddleboard thing—"

"Which was *your* idea."

"Yeah, but I thought it would be something fun for the both of us to do. Now it's all about Malia. You're pulling away from me. Why?"

"Because." Jazz nibbles her bottom lip. "People always leave. My dad, my mom. My friends."

"So now *you're* leaving *me?* I don't even know if I'm going to Harvard yet." I pick up a piece of Gramma's shortbread but don't take a bite. "Even so, I wouldn't be *leaving* leaving. You'd still be my best friend."

"For real? With five thousand miles between us?"

"Of course. And it would totally kill me to leave you, but it's...it's Harvard, Jazz."

"That's what you keep saying." Jazz raises her fingers to make air quotes. "'It's Harvard.' But what about 'It's Jazz' or 'It's Maui'?"

I open my mouth in protest, but Jazz keeps going. "This was your dream since you were in diapers. I get it. But there are other things in the world besides Harvard. Like *me.*"

"I know! That's why—"

Jazz holds up a hand. "Sorry, but that's how I feel. It's like your dad is making you choose—Harvard or me. And I think I know which side is winning."

"So that makes it okay for you to go and replace me with Malia?"

"Leave Malia out of this. I've known her my entire life, and she needs a friend. Besides, I don't want to be left on my own when you and Brander both end up on the mainland, chasing your dreams. Especially since I won't be making the Olympic swim team anytime soon." Jazz grimaces and raps on her prosthesis, and something within me crumples.

"Jazz, I—"

"You're not the only person in the world who gets jealous, you know."

Oh.

Jazz's words shut me up fast.

All this time that I've been jealous of Jazz and Malia—of the new friendship they're forging—I hadn't thought that

Jazz could get jealous too. Of me. Of Harvard. Of the fact that I'm still able to reach for the dreams I've had my entire life.

Jazz—the girl I once found invincible—is jealous. And why shouldn't she be? Somewhere along the line, when her dream died…a part of her must have died too.

And here I thought she was actually happy.

The wind whips across the porch and twists around me as I sit, wrapping my necklace around my hand until I can no longer feel my fingers.

"Jazz, I am so, so sorry." The words feel flimsy and pathetic as they leave my mouth. If the look on Jazz's face is anything to go by, she thinks so too. "I've been so wrapped up in myself. I guess I haven't taken the time to think about how you've been feeling. About the swim team, your mom…about how this college thing might affect you too."

Jazz nods. "Exactly. You haven't." A gray cloud blows across her usual sunny expression, and even in the dim evening light I catch something wet shining in the corner of her eye. "You've been so caught up in *you* that I'm starting to wonder how much you care—about your sister, about *Tutu*…about all of us."

Jazz's words needle my pride, but even more than that, they jab at my heart.

"Can I make it up to you?"

"I don't know how you could. It isn't your fault—I mean, it kinda is. But it's more…I dunno. Stress, I guess."

"What about?""My mom's going to be coming home soon, and I don't—I can't." She hiccups. "It's like, you might be leaving so I get my mom for company instead of you? Not a fair trade."

So that's why you're trying to exchange me for Malia instead? I almost kick myself for that thought. "Don't get too hard on your mom, Jazz. I'd do anything to get my mom back. Even if it was only for a few minutes. Maybe things will be better with her once she gets out of treatment."

"You don't know *my* mom. Throw in the right guy—or the right bottle—and she could be out the door in the first week. It's not like she'll stick around, and even if she does, I don't know if I want her." Jazz slowly stands before stepping toward the screen door. "It's getting late. I'm gonna get ready for bed."

"Jazz?" I whisper the word once we're both tucked in for the night—me in a sleeping bag on the swing, Jazz settled on an air mattress beneath me—but my voice is buried by the sound of the waves.

"Jazz?" I try again. Louder.

"What?"

"I'm sorry. Really sorry. I haven't been a good friend lately."

"Don't worry about it." Jazz's words are muffled, and I hang my head off the swing to hear better. "I forgive you."

"But?"

"There are no *buts*." Jazz snorts. "You know that."

"Come on." I slip out of my sleeping bag and slide off the swing before perching on the edge of Jazz's air mattress. "I've been a jerk and we both know it. So lay it on me. How can I be a better friend?"

Jazz breathes in, then out, then in once more before she clears her throat. "You're the best friend I could ever ask for." Her words, though sweet, are surprisingly thick. "That's the problem. I'm afraid that you'll get so busy trying to figure out your own life that you'll..."

"Forget about you?"

"Yeah." Jazz's voice is small.

I open my mouth to object—tell Jazz that she's far from an afterthought—but a load of guilt chokes me. When *have* I been there for Jazz lately?

You haven't. The voice in my head—one that, right now, sounds suspiciously like Mom when she used to give me one of her famous talking-tos—sighs. *You've been so caught up in yourself that you haven't been standing strong for Jazz when she needs it.*

I rub my temples, as though the realization snuck up and clobbered me on the head. Why do I have to figure this stuff out *after* the fact? Can't my conscience at least be nice enough to give me a warning before I botch things?

"Jazz..." The word is swept away in the evening breeze, and maybe it's better that way. In a few minutes, a new sound joins the crashing of ocean waves—soft, rumbly snores coming from Jazz's direction.

Holding my breath so as not to wake her, I stand and climb into my sleeping bag.

Maybe things'll be better in the morning.

But even though I tell myself that, I lie awake for hours, staring at the stars beyond the porch, wishing hard on each and every one of them.

I wish I was a better friend.

I wish Mom was still here.

I wish Brander had never gone to Nashville.

But wishing doesn't get me anywhere, so eventually I find myself praying—asking God to take the broken, messed-up pieces of my life and turn them into something better. To turn *me* into something better.

I don't know how He'll ever manage it, but He is the God of miracles, so I guess I have to cross my fingers and hope that's true.

Deep down inside, I *know* it is.

Now I have to believe that for myself.

"Olive?" Macie's face appears through the window screen separating the porch from the living room early the next morning, and I press a finger to my lips.

"Quiet. Jazz is still asleep." I slip off the swing, careful not to step on Jazz's air mattress, and tiptoe inside.

"Why aren't you still in bed?" Once I'm in the living room, I motion for Macie to come away from the window. She tugs at one of her many tangled curls and joins me on the loveseat as a ray of light spreads across the floor.

"I need to say I'm sorry." Macie dips her head and pooches out her lip. "I'm being self-y."

"Do you mean selfish?" Someone should tell Dad he needs to work on his youngest daughter's vocabulary. Maybe it would even get him off my case for more than five seconds.

"That too." Macie itches her nose.

"How are you being selfish?"

"Because I've been asking Grammy for a puppy, even though I know you hate—I mean, you really, really don't like doggies."

My heart twists at Macie's wide-eyed sincerity. Before I know what I'm doing, I'm wrapping my arms around her and squeezing. Tight. "It's okay, Mace."

"No, it's not!" Her words creep up to an outdoor-appropriate volume, and I shush her again. "I mean," she says in a softer voice, "being selfish isn't okay. It makes other people feel bad."

"Who told you that?"

"Grammy. We were talking before bed last night."

"Huh." Wish I could've been in on that conversation. I bet it could have helped me figure out things with Jazz. "What got you talking about something like that?"

Macie bites her lip. "I heard you and Jazzie talking."

My stomach drops. "Oh."

"Jazzie wasn't very nice."

"That's not true. It was my fault. I messed up. Big time."

Macie scrunches up her nose. "So did Jazzie."

"I don't know about that." I sigh. "Do me a favor Mace—don't end up making mistakes like I do when you're a teenager."

She yanks at another curl. "But I'm already making mistakes. I still want one of Alani's puppies for my birthday. Even when I know you don't."

"It's okay, Macie. I'm cool with it." And, as I say the words, I realize something.

I believe them.

Somewhere down the line, the thought of having a dog in the house has become a lot less frightening than other, more pressing issues. Like what's going on with Jazz and Brander—and, okay, me too. "Seriously. If having a mutt of your own will make you *that* happy, then I'm all for it."

Macie's eyes grow wide. "For real?" She doesn't wait for an answer before throwing her arms around my waist and squeezing. Tight. As she holds on for dear life, something takes hold of my heart, and my chest grows warm and fuzzy.

If giving up my own hang-ups feels this freeing, why haven't I done it before? Why don't I start doing it more often—with Jazz, with Brander…even with Dad?

Maybe I will.

Thank you, God, for little sisters.

Chapter Eighteen

"YOU TWO HAVE BEEN AWFULLY QUIET." Gramma meets my eyes in the rearview mirror as she steers off the highway, following the signs for the Kahului Airport.

Alani's mom picked up Macie to take her to church before the rest of us left this morning, so the faint aura of awkwardness in the air between me and Jazz has been painfully apparent the entire car ride. I never thought I'd wish for my little chatterbox sister to tag along—especially when I'm about to see Brander for the first time in months, but...

"We're just excited, I guess." Jazz words lack their usual spark when she answers Gramma. The station wagon veers onto Kahululi Airport Road, but Jazz stares out at the road like she's looking at a barren wasteland, not an airport that will soon be welcoming back one of our best friends.

"You sure *sound* excited." I reach across the bench seat to poke Jazz's shoulder, but she doesn't laugh or smile in return. Instead, she shifts awkwardly and scoots closer toward the window.

Maybe things between us aren't okay after all.

Gramma's eyes meet mine in the mirror once more before she turns to enter the airport's short-term parking lot. Once we've gotten out, I lag behind to talk with Jazz as Gramma leads the way to the baggage claim.

"You know I'm really, *really* sorry. Right? I wasn't trying to hurt you. But I knew if—" I bite down on my tongue. "Never mind. I'm done making excuses. I haven't been the friend you need, and I'm sorry. Really, really—"

"You already said that. And I forgave you—last night, as a matter of fact." Jazz's mouth twitches in what could almost be called a smile. "It's fine."

"Then why don't I believe you?"

"Beats me. I thought I'd proven myself to be pretty trustworthy." Jazz's words are soft, but there's a spark in her eye that wasn't there before. "I didn't steer you wrong when I got you to try shave ice or hang out with me at youth group the first time. I'm not pulling your leg now." The half-smile returns to flit over Jazz's face, lasting a second longer this time.

"You're sure?"

She nods. "Sure, I'm sure. And sorry for being all weird. It's not you. It's my mom."

"Your mom?" The words come out in an almost-growl. "What'd she do this time?"

"I'll tell you later, but it's not important now." Jazz links her arm through mine, and we pick up our pace so we don't lose Gramma in the sea of people clogging the entrance to the baggage claim area. "*Now* let's go see Brander."

"Brander!" Jazz squeals and launches herself into his arms the moment we spot his rumpled cowlick and leather guitar case, but I hang back with Gramma. I'd love to clobber him with a hug of my own, but would that be weird? I've known him only a fraction of the time that Jazz has.

Besides, if he's seeing someone else in Nashville, maybe he wouldn't want a hug from me.

Go up there and tackle him, my heart yells as Jazz pulls away and reaches up to ruffle his cowlick—not too hard to do, since Jazz is almost as tall as he is—but I keep my composure and wait for Brander to step closer before greeting him.

"Hey." My voice sounds funny—hesitant, almost, and my smile feels shy as I lift my hand in a thumb-and-pinky wave.

"Hey, yourself." Brander's eyes—those deep, soulful eyes that never cease to remind me of the chocolate-covered almonds Mom used to munch on at night—focus on me. For a moment, it's as if I'm the only one in the crowded baggage claim.

And then someone pushes right in front of me.

Someone with a head of long, dark hair.

Someone wearing a curve-hugging crop top that I could only hope to pull off by the time I'm twenty-one...

Someone who looks a lot like Malia.

And, as she practically hops up and down in front of Brander, whose almond eyes have grown very, very round, I'm acutely reminded that Brander and I are far from alone.

"Hi, Malia." Brander's gaze bounces from me to Jazz, then back. "This is a surprise."

Malia giggles, loud enough for several passing families to turn and stare. Or maybe they're more interested in Brander. He's the celebrity after all. "Jazz mentioned you were flying in this morning. We spent the weekend with my *tutu* in Paia—it only made sense to come say *aloha* to the most famous singer on the island."

As if on cue, Malia's younger sister, Kanani, pushes through a crowd of people and hands Brander a haphazardly strung lei. "Aloha, Brander!" The little girl beams at Brander, then breaks into giggles.

Malia lets out a laugh of her own, then leans in close to Brander. "I think Kanani's starstruck."

Like you *aren't.* I tear my eyes from Malia and turn to wave at her parents, who are standing politely off to the side. They wave too, and Brander crosses over to greet them.

"You told Malia what time Brander's flight got in?" I pinch my lips together to keep from saying anything I'll end up regretting.

"Sorry." Jazz raises both hands, her eyebrows twitching. "We were talking after youth group. I didn't think she'd show up here."

"You don't say?" I huff as Brander takes a picture with Malia and a red-cheeked Kanani, who clings to Brander like he's a life-sized superhero figurine, before Malia's family makes their exit.

Brander's eyes quickly return to meet my own, but that rosy feeling of being the only one in the airport is long gone. Thanks to Malia and her fangirling, now all I feel is awkward.

"Was it a good flight?" I swallow against the dryness in my throat, and we walk with Brander as he searches for the right baggage carousel.

"The usual." He shrugs. "Except the label paid for me to fly first class, which was nice."

"Don't you always fly first class?" Given the size and style of the Delacroix residence, I'm surprised Brander's dad doesn't have his own private jet.

"Nope." Brander turns to face a rotating baggage carousel, his eyes hopping from one bag to the next as they circle around. "My mom's a cheapskate about some stuff. Especially airfare."

Brander's mom—the same woman who shows up for church wearing designer dresses that probably cost as much as Brander's Porsche—a cheapskate? Who would've thought?

After Brander grabs a polished leather duffle from the carousel, we head toward the exit. Gramma, Jazz, and I take turns peppering Brander with questions about Nashville and his time spent on tour, and a smile spreads over Brander's face as he details nights spent writing songs in a tour bus bunk.

That smile fades, however, the second a camera flashes somewhere in the not-too-far-off distance.

"Brander Delacroix?" A man sporting a particularly

greasy attempt at a mullet steps forward, chintzy-looking leather shoes squeaking on the floor, and sticks a small recording device in Brander's face. "I'm Mark, with the *West Maui Sun*. Would you be willing to answer a few questions?"

"Do I know you?" Brander takes a half-step back, nearly stumbling over his duffle.

"Not personally. My cousin works in PR for your parents' resort. He mentioned you'd be flying in today." The man grins, revealing a mouth of long, slightly pointed teeth—shark teeth.

"I'm sorry, Mark." Brander sticks his hands in his pockets, as though searching for something, then gives up and smooths a hand over his hair, pressing down his cowlick. "All interview requests need to be approved by my label."

"But I'm here right now." The man extends the arm holding the recorder. "Just a few questions? Off the record?"

Brander shakes his head. "I'm sorry. It's policy."

Mark's pearly whites vanish behind a sour frown. "Can't you at least introduce me to your friends? It seems to me you're pretty close." Mark's gaze darts from me to Jazz, as though he's trying to figure out which of us is the future Mrs. Delacroix.

Good luck, buddy. We're all still in high school.

Brander opens his mouth, but Gramma steps forward before he can speak. "Brander's been traveling for nearly twenty-four hours. I think it would be best for both of you if you conduct your interview another time."

Mark scowls at Gramma, who frowns right back, and he shoots Brander a final glare before stepping away. "I'll get in touch with your label, kid. Then we can talk."

The man's shiny shoes squeak as he stalks outside, and only when the sound is covered by the chatter of a group of tourists does Brander seem to relax. "I *told* my dad not to say anything about when I was getting home."

"I guess I shouldn't have said anything to Malia either.

Sorry." Jazz frowns and tugs at her braid as Brander kneels to unzip his carry-on.

"No biggie." He rummages around for a few moments, then closes the bag and stands, holding a University of Hawaii ball cap and a pair of cheap reflective glasses.

He slips on the strange semi-disguise as we head for the parking lot, and something in me winces. That cap is so obviously not his style, but I guess that's the point. The disguise seems to work too—no one gives Brander a second glance as we pile into Gramma's station wagon.

"Do you do that a lot?" I ask as Brander pulls off the getup and pats his hair into place. "Use a disguise?"

"It's not a disguise exactly. My cousin sent me the hat a few weeks ago. He's a sophomore at the Manoa campus. It's not my usual style, but it comes in handy." He ducks his head as Gramma pulls out of the parking lot. "You know nothing's changed, right? I'm still the same person I was before all this crazy stuff happened. Even if I have to wear an ugly hat sometimes."

"Tell that to the press." I cross my arms and scrunch my nose, and Brander frowns.

"I try. But people tend to only hear what they want to." Brander's usual smile wobbles, and he turns around in his seat as Gramma merges onto the highway. "I'm beat. Mind if I take a nap?"

"Go ahead." My spirits deflate as Brander settles back into his seat and closes his eyes. Sure—he's probably exhausted, but doesn't he want to catch up even a little bit?

Grams turns the radio down, and we ride along the highway in silence almost until we reach Lahaina, when Jazz clears her throat a decibel louder than necessary.

I turn to her, and she motions for me to scoot closer.

"What's up with Brander?" She frowns. "Jet lag?"

"Beats me. Do you think he's okay?"

"I hope so. But I think that magazine guy freaked him

out." Jazz nibbles on her lip. "That was so weird about Malia. I didn't tell her on purpose, you know."

"I know. But I hope most people won't act all starstruck like that." I fall against the seat as Gramma makes a sharp turn into Brander's neighborhood, but something in Jazz's expression keeps me from relaxing. "What?"

"Um, sorry to say, but I don't think you're going to get your wish." Jazz points out the window.

Gramma lets out a gasp as the car slows to a stop, and Brander stirs in the front seat.

There's a line of camera-clutching people—everyone from red-cheeked teen girls to official-looking reporters—stretched out across the massive Delacroix lawn.

"What's up?" Brander's voice is crackly with sleep, and he rubs his eyes and blinks before letting out a groan. "I told my parents not to let anything like this happen. Mom said she had it covered."

"Then what's going on?" Jazz's prosthesis hits my shin as she scoots over for a better view.

"I don't know, but I can't do this today." Brander ducks in his seat and pulls on the cap and glasses before anyone can storm the station wagon. "Can I hide out at your place for a while, *Tutu*? I'll text my parents and explain."

"That would probably be best." Gramma puts the car in drive and pulls away from the curb as fast as her rusty rig will take her. "No one should have to deal with the press after a red-eye flight."

"Agreed." Brander bends his head low over his phone to text his parents, and he keeps his disguise on until we reach Gramma's house.

Finally, once Gramma's parked in the driveway, Brander takes off the hat and sunglasses and moves to tuck them in his carry-on. And that's when I catch sight of one last person waiting.

But even though he isn't waiting for Brander so much as

for the rest of us, he makes me more nervous than the rest of the groupies combined.

After all, Dad and Brander have never met before.

This could get interesting.

Chapter Nineteen

BEFORE I CAN OFFER BRANDER A warning or any words of advice, he jumps out of the station wagon and sprints up the porch steps, nearly colliding with Dad on the landing.

From my spot in the car, I can't hear what's being said, but Brander seems too flustered to offer more than a passing apology before diving inside. The rest of us pile out and follow him, greeting Dad as we go.

"Brander?" Gramma leads us all into the living room where Brander is standing, his expression more than a bit shell-shocked. "Are you okay?"

"I am now." Brander drops the hat and glasses onto the couch. "Thanks for rescuing me, Bonnie."

"No problem. Would you like something to eat?" Gramma crosses to the kitchen before Brander even has a chance to answer. Other than Jesus, food is her solution to all of life's great crises.

"Are people crazy like that in Nashville too?" Jazz steps closer to Brander, concern edging her expression. "Shouldn't the label get you a bodyguard or something?"

"No way." For a second it looks like Brander's going to laugh, but he doesn't. I bet he would have—before he had to go off and get famous. "In Nashville, I'm a small fish in a very, very big pond."

"Did I miss something?" Dad steps forward, hands in his pockets, change jangling.

"Only about a million paparazzi swarming Brander's house. It was insane."

"Not a million. Let's not make this any worse than it

already is." Brander rolls his head back and groans. Is the lighting in here fooling me, or did I not notice the dark bags beneath his eyes earlier? "There were only five or six reporters. The rest were probably curiosity seekers. Mike told me to expect some excitement the first few days."

"So things will calm down?"

Brander nods. "This kind of thing blows over quickly. After a few days, I'll be old news. I hope."

An awkward quiet, punctuated only by the sound of Gramma clanging in the kitchen, falls over the living room. I take a few stifled breaths in the silence before turning to Dad. "Sorry for the weird introduction Dad. This is Brander. I've told you about him."

"Of course." Dad casts a long, discerning eye over Brander, like he's a student in his Psych 101 class.

So. He's playing the stern-professor card. Even after all the lengths I've gone to, trying to assure him that Brander and I are only friends.

"Nice to meet you, Brander." Dad offers his hand, and I send up a quick prayer that he'll soften his usual bone-crushing how-do-you-do squeeze.

Brander smiles and returns the shake, massaging his hand a bit after Dad releases it. "Nice to meet you, Mr. Galloway. Olive says you're a professor at Harvard? My aunt is a graduate of their law program."

This seems to impress Dad enough for him to drop a bit of his guard and smile, and we manage to make small talk until Gramma calls us all to lunch.

Thankfully Dad disappears upstairs after the meal, and Brander, Jazz, and I help Grams clean up before tromping outside to sit on the porch. Jazz and I take the swing, while Brander leans against the railing, the sunshine only accentuating the shadows beneath his eyes.

"So how are you? For real?" I ask once we're settled.

Brander shrugs and scrubs at his eyes like he's

transformed into a sleepy toddler. "Mike warned me there might be people hoping for a photo or interview, but I didn't buy it. I had it pretty good in Nashville, except—" he interrupts himself with a humongous yawn.

Except what? Though part of me is dying to ask him exactly that, the other part of me wants to see Brander get a solid eight hours of sleep before he says another word. "Are you sure you're up for talking right now?" My heart drops at the thought of *still* not getting to talk to Brander, but it's obvious he needs rest. "I bet Grams could make up a bed for you somewhere."

"I'm fine." He opens his mouth, as if to say more, but another yawn escapes instead. "Or maybe not. I think I'll text my mom and see if things have calmed down at home."

Before I know it, Mr. Delacroix has pulled in front of Gramma's—in Brander's beloved cherry-red Porsche—and whisked Brander away. Jazz and I sit, the tail of her long braid tickling my arm, as the Porsche's motor echoes in my ears as it disappears down the street.

"I've never seen him like that before." Jazz drops her chin in her hands and stares out at the water. "He's looked so happy on Instagram lately."

"He didn't look happy today."

Jazz nods. "It was probably jet lag, right?"

"Yeah."

"Then why don't I believe it?" Jazz stands and paces the porch.

"I don't know." But something tells me Brander's dealing with a lot more than jet lag, and I need to figure it out. Otherwise the joyful, happy-go-lucky Brander I used to know could slip away from all of us.

For good.

"It's that boy, isn't it?"

"Huh?" I lift my head and tear my eyes from my Bible to find Dad leaning on my bedroom doorframe later that afternoon.

"Brander. He's what's holding you back."

"You mean from Harvard?" I laugh. "If I went to Harvard, I'd be closer to Nashville than I am here, so no. Brander's not holding me back."

"Then what is?" Dad's voice rises, and he winces, as though realizing he won't get anywhere by pseudo-yelling. Thank goodness Macie's still playing at Alani's and Gramma is pruning the plumeria bushes outside. I don't need anyone else overhearing this.

"I don't know." It sounds like a flimsy answer, but it's the honest truth. "Ever since you told me about the scholarship, something hasn't felt right. I hate the thought of having to leave everything I know here."

"You haven't lived in Maui for more than a few months. Boston has been your home for sixteen years." Dad steps into the room and pinches the bridge of his nose. "Talk to me, Olive."

"I'm trying, but I don't know what else to say." *And I don't think you'd listen anyway.* "Until I pray about things more, I don't know anything about *anything.*"

"And why are you so sure God doesn't want you to go to Harvard? Do you have any idea how many people hope and pray to get accepted into that school?"

"I know." I shrug. "But Gramma's taught me a lot about God's will. I don't want to go against it just because."

Dad shakes his head so fast I can't tell if he's rolling his eyes or not—but something tells me he is. "Why won't you at least spend some more time working on the application? That due date's looming."

"Fine." I wince as I say it, and I clench my left hand in a fist. "I'll take another whack at it. But I'm not making any promises about whether or not I'll send it in."

"Good enough." Dad shuffles his feet, as though he's about to leave, but he doesn't. "About Brander. Where are you at in your relationship?"

"I thought we'd covered this before. We're friends. Good friends. Nothing else." *In fact, if you ask the Internet, he's seeing someone else.* "You don't need to worry about me, Dad. I don't have any plans to get myself stuck in something as messy as a relationship."

Dad wrinkles his brow.

"But you can talk to Grams about it, if you're still worried. She's known Brander a lot longer than I have."

Dad jerks his chin up and down in a nod. "I'll do that then."

"Good."

But as Dad heads downstairs and I turn to my Bible, I realize that nothing about this day feels *good.*

Jazz is out-of-sorts, Brander's acting like a different person, and Dad can't understand why I'm not jumping up and down at the idea of jetting off to Harvard. Life here sure hasn't settled down like I thought it would on New Year's Eve.

Is that a sign? A hint that I should go home—go to Harvard after all?

I slam the cover of my Bible shut and march over to my computer.

Maybe it *is* time to tackle a bit more of that application.

Chapter Twenty

"MALIA INVITED ME TO GO PADDLEBOARDING tonight. Wanna come?" The house is empty when Jazz pops the question during school the next morning, but I do a double take anyway.

"Huh?"

"Paddleboarding. Do you want to go?"

"Me? I thought you said I stunk."

"Well, you kind of do." Jazz softens her words with a smile. "But we're friends. And friends stick together."

"Then yeah—of course." I reach over and squeeze her arm. "Thanks."

"Cool." Jazz scribbles something in her notebook. "Wanna invite Brander?"

I open my mouth to say yes, but some part of me can't quite bear the thought of dealing with any more of Malia's fangirling—not yet, anyway. "I don't know. He seemed awfully tired."

"True. Just the three of us, then?"

"Yep." And maybe if we're lucky Malia will bail at the last minute.

Jazz narrows her eyes at me, almost like I spoke that last bit aloud, before she turns back to her schoolwork. But even though Jazz stays quiet, that little voice in my brain— the one that's so much wiser and kinder—won't shut up.

It's not fair to keep hating on Malia. So she's starstruck— who cares? She needs a friend as much as anyone else.

Maybe so, but am I the friend she's looking for? Or is she buddying up with us so she can get in good with the

Hawaiian Heartthrob?

Okay, maybe there are two voices in my head this morning, because this is seriously starting to sound like an argument.

Any advice, God?

I sit. Waiting. Listening.

But, other than Jazz's measured breathing, I don't hear anything.

So I crack open my science book and start to read—and that's when it comes.

Not a lightning bolt from heaven. Not even an audible voice.

Nothing more than a still, small *something* taking root in my chest, telling me that, no matter how weird it feels to be hanging out with Malia, something about it—at least for this moment in time—is *right.*

Okay, God. Whatever You say...

I'm nearly done with my math worksheet later that afternoon when Jazz bumps her foot against mine. "What's the latest on Harvard?"

"Harvard?" The word almost makes me choke. I stayed up way later than usual working on that application last night but now, sitting in a puddle of warm sunshine spilling into Gramma's comfy living room, I can't imagine going away.

"Is something wrong?" Jazz frowns.

I bite my lip. Should I tell her I've been working on the application? Better not. "Things are a real mess. I know most everyone thinks I should go, and part of me wants to. But the other part of me—the other part doesn't."

"Why don't you take a gap year or something?" Jazz runs a finger along the liner of her prosthesis. "I mean, no one else your age is going to college."

"Right?" I snort. "But..." I pitch my voice lower until it vaguely resembles Dad's. "This is an *incredible chance* to better myself. I can use this year to get ahead of the pack. It would be *absolutely foolhardy* of me to let the opportunity escape."

Jazz snickers, but her expression sobers quickly. "If it was up to me, you'd stay here. You know that, right?" Jazz scoots closer to me on the couch, as though keeping me near will ensure that I'll never leave.

"I know."

My phone buzzes before either of us can say anything more, and I dash out front before answering. On the off chance that it's Dad, I'd rather not have Jazz listening in while he rambles on about the glories of my soon-to-be new school. "Hello?"

"Hey." Though his voice is still tinged with tiredness, Brander sounds a lot more awake today. "I was wondering— are you free this afternoon? I have the day off from school, so I thought we could...I don't know. Catch up. Get a shave ice."

My chest warms at the thought of hanging out with Brander for real. We can eat shave ice, walk on the beach, ride around in his Porsche—like old times.

Except...

"Rats. I'm supposed to go paddleboarding with Jazz and Malia today." And, as much as I'd like to bail on them, I can't quite bear to give Jazz the opportunity to test-drive my replacement. "But why don't you come with us?" Hanging out with Brander and suffering through a potential round of fangirling is better than *not* hanging out with him.

Brander hums on the other line. "I don't know. I hate to butt in."

Before I can assure him that he wouldn't be a bother— more like a welcome addition—he clears his throat. "What about Thursday?"

"Thursday?" I almost drop the phone. I've barely seen Brander since he came back, and now he wants to wait until Thursday to hang out? "What about tomorrow? Or Wednesday?" Or, better yet, why don't I suck up my guts and bail on Jazz and Malia. What's the worst that could happen?

You don't want to know. Sheesh, that voice in my head sure is talkative today.

"Don't get me wrong." Brander's voice is thick. Sad. "I'd hang out with you every day if I could. But my schedule is a nightmare. That guy from the *West Maui Sun* is interviewing me tomorrow, and I probably won't even make it to youth group on Wednesday. All my aunties and tutus are flying in from the Big Island to visit."

"Oh." I swallow hard against the words echoing in my heart. *Tell Jazz and Malia you can't make it.* Brander might be here today, gone tomorrow.

But when he leaves, do I really want to be left with a best friend who decided to replace me?

"Are you and Jazz hanging out with Malia a lot now?" Brander's words, while not inherently suspicious, sound a bit cautious. As though he's afraid any time spent with Malia will turn me and Jazz into starstruck groupies.

"She and Jazz have the whole swim team thing in common, and Jazz is big on being a good friend to her. Since she's going through such a hard time and all."

Brander doesn't ask what I think of it all, and for that I'm grateful. Instead, we settle on a time to meet up this Thursday.

But as soon as we hang up, guilt pangs in my stomach. I hope Brander knows I'm not trying to brush him off. It's...

Stupid. That's what it is.

I nod and bow my head. No sense arguing with my conscience when I know it's dead right. I've got to get over this Malia business.

"Who was on the phone?" Jazz steps outside and leans on the porch railing, though her Cheshire-cat grin makes me suspect she has a pretty good idea who was on the other line.

"Brander. We're gonna grab a shave ice after school on Thursday."

"And you didn't invite me?" Jazz sticks out her lip and whimpers, but there's a good-natured sparkle in her eyes. "I guess I can suffer for the sake of romance."

"Romance? You're nuts." If I wasn't too far away, I'd smack some sense into Jazz right now. "It's *Brander*."

"Exactly." Jazz plays with the end of her fishtail braid. "Why would he only invite you unless—"

"He's not dating until he finds someone to marry," I protest. "Besides. It's not a date. All we're doing is getting shave ice. Catching up."

"On *Thursday*?" Jazz waggles her eyebrows at me. "Unless you forgot what day that is."

"I just said. It's Thursday."

"Yeah. Thursday the fourteenth."

"Of February?" I cover my mouth to smother a yelp. "*That's* not going to be awkward."

Jazz shrugs. "Don't blame me. You're the one who set the date. But *I* want to be the one to hear all about it as soon as you're home."

"Like there's going to be anything to hear. Brander might already be seeing someone in Nashville. Remember?"

Jazz stares at me, her eyes saying a million things she's too nice to utter aloud—all of them along the lines of *get a grip, girl.*

"Fine." I lift my hands. "I'll tell you everything. But don't come crying to me when there's nothing to tell."

Jazz nods, eyes still sparkling. "Deal."

"How's Brander doing?" The words fly out of Malia's mouth the second we join her in the water that evening. "He looked *so* tired yesterday." She widens her eyes and pooches her lips in a pout, and I swallow hard against the urge to gag.

"He's fine." The words come out a little shorter than I'd like, and I clear my throat to try again. "It sounds like he's a lot less jet-lagged today."

"Will he be at youth group?" Malia flicks a strand of shiny black hair over her shoulder and fixes her bikini strap, as though brushing up on her preening routine.

"I don't know." I shrug. "Why?"

Malia reddens and mutters something under her breath about getting his autograph.

Jazz's paddle slices through the water in swift, even strokes, and she pulls into the lead as we head up the coastline. Malia is close on her tail, and I—big surprise—bring up the rear.

For a while, I follow along in silence. Malia and Jazz seem to have plenty to talk about—swim team, youth group, and...*Brander.* Malia brings him up a grand total of five times in the time it takes us to paddle up the length of Kaanapali Beach. *Starstruck much?*

Jealous much? That annoying little voice in my head counters back almost immediately, and I know it's right.

We continue up the coastline, and I force myself to push my annoyance away with every stroke of my paddle. I'm feeling a lot lighter by the time Jazz and Malia exchange a glance and settle onto their boards. "Sit down, Olive." Jazz peeks over at me, a golden glow from the setting sun glinting off her almost white-blonde hair.

"Why?" I paddle closer, squeezing between her and Malia, before sitting cross-legged on my board.

"See that rock?" Malia extends a long-nailed finger in the direction of a rocky black peninsula jutting out into the ocean. "It's called Pu'u Keka'a."

"What about it?"

Jazz and Malia exchange another secret smile. "You'll see." They say it in unison, laughing as the ocean swells beneath us and sends our boards rocking.

We sit, watching the horizon in silence. A silence that even I can admit is remarkably less awkward than usual. Maybe Jazz is right. Maybe all Malia needs is a couple of good friends.

And maybe all *I* need is a fresh perspective.

A few last rays of sunlight skate over my board and dance over the rolling ocean waters. I dip my hand into the sea, trying to trace the strands of gold, but a breeze picks up and ripples the surface of the water, keeping the light barely out of reach.

Out of reach.

Like the answers I've been searching for—about Brander, about Malia…about college.

How can I leave this magical island I've come to call home?

How can I give up a scholarship in my mom's own name—a scholarship she'd be thrilled for me to have?

One way or the other, I have to make a decision.

But how?

"Olive." Jazz points to the beach.

I squint and focus in on the shore. We're far enough from land that I can't make out any individual people, but I do catch a glimpse of something—fire?—hovering above a mass of tourists. "Is that a tiki torch?"

But before either girl can answer my question, the torch *moves.*

And then, as the echo of Polynesian drums rumbles over the sea, the flame makes its way down the shoreline, headed straight for that big black rock. The flame picks up speed as it goes, until it seems to be climbing to the very top of the peninsula.

The drums grow louder, rumbling in my chest as a man's silhouette—holding onto the tiki torch—appears atop the rocks. He keeps running, reaching up to light several other torches as he goes, before coming to a stop at the tip of the peninsula.

Jazz reaches over to grip my hand as the figure tosses his torch into the water. Then he takes something off his neck—a lei?—and holds it up, as though offering it to the setting sun. He stands there, hands raised in a salute, before releasing the lei and letting it fall to the crashing waves below.

The drums go silent.

And then, even though I have a sneaking suspicion it's coming, I gasp along with Jazz and Malia as the man jumps off the cliff. He points his hands over his head in perfect form, then disappears into the dark ocean waters with barely a splash as the sun sinks below the horizon.

I can barely take a breath before the man bursts through the water, lifting his hands above his head and letting out a whoop. Jazz, Malia, and I echo his cheer and clap for him as he swims past us. The drums start up again, but they aren't loud enough to mask a smattering of applause from the onlookers gathered on the beach.

"And that was the cliff dive." Jazz's voice is hushed. When I look over at her, her expression is almost somber.

I'm about to ask more about it when Malia jumps to her feet. "Let's go." Her words cut through the intrigue of the moment, and we prepare to paddle down the shore to the rental stand.

I'm the last to rise—maybe because I'm new at the sport, maybe because I'm not quite ready to leave the allure of Pu'u Keka'a behind.

The air around me grows cooler as I follow Malia's lead, dipping my paddle into the water, now inky black in the growing darkness. Jazz and Malia chat off and on as we make our way to our starting point, but I stay quiet.

Something about the cliff dive—the way that guy jumped into the water so freely, so willingly, despite the waves pummeling the rocks below—won't erase itself from my mind.

I keep seeing him.

Jumping.

Diving.

He wasn't afraid to jump off that old, crumbling rock and into the tempestuous sea.

Or maybe he was, and he did it anyway.

Chapter Twenty-One

"YOU REALIZE…" DAD LOWERS HIS VOICE and sits next to me on the couch after Macie is tucked in bed Tuesday evening. "Macie's birthday is on Saturday."

I nod. I've been counting down the days—maybe not for the reason most good big sisters would—ever since Grams brought home a huge carload of puppy stuff, including a fluffy dog bed and half a pet store's worth of chew toys. "I told Gramma I'd help her make a cake."

Dad nods. "That's nice. But is that all? Wouldn't Macie like a party to go along with that cake?"

"Probably." I wince. I should've thought of that. Like, a few weeks ago. "I guess we should do something, huh? But it's awfully late notice now."

"Late notice?" Gramma steps into the room and squeezes onto the couch, sandwiching me in. "Not by island standards. Most everyone spends their Saturdays at the beach—we'll have the party at the park across the street. All we have to do is let Macie's little friends and their parents know we'll be providing some extra games and a cake this weekend. One of the ladies in my Bible study rents out bounce houses for *keiki* luaus. I'll call her up tomorrow and see if she can cut me a deal."

"Jazz and I could make invitations tomorrow, and Macie can hand them out with her Valentines on Thursday."

Dad clears his throat. "Tomorrow is a school day."

"*After* school." I focus extra-hard on Dad's chin—he forgot to shave again—to keep from rolling my eyes. "And I can help with the food, Grams."

Gramma waves a hand in the air. "No need. We'll make the cake, the rest will take care of itself."

"Huh?"

"I'll dig around upstairs and find some balloons, and I'll place a lei order at Safeway for party favors. Am I forgetting anything?"

"The puppy." I can't believe I'm saying it, but I still can't get the picture of that cliff dive guy out of my head—jumping headfirst into the unknown, trusting that he'll be okay.

Gramma does a double take, as though questioning her hearing, and I nod. "Believe it or not, I *do* want my little sister to be happy." I smile despite the churning and quivering in my stomach.

"Excellent." She reaches out to pat my hand. "Alex, I'll put you in charge of picking it up that morning. I want to keep it a surprise until the party's started."

Dad pulls out his phone to make a note. "Will do."

And that's that.

After school on Wednesday, Jazz and I settle onto the front steps with a stack of colored paper and a box of Gramma's crafting doodads.

"Thanks for helping." I grab a piece of turquoise paper and sketch a rough shape on it. "Macie's going to love these."

"No problem." Jazz adjusts her position, her prosthesis knocking the railing, and reaches for a piece of paper. "But what are we making exactly?" She bites her lip. "I'm not very artsy, you know."

"That's okay. I thought we could cut mermaid tails out of paper, throw some glitter on the front, and write the party info on the other side."

"Okay." Jazz lets out a breath. "I can manage that."

We get to work, scissors slicing through paper in counterpoint as the shadows grow longer.

Macie's bus pulls in front of the house after a while, and she hops off, taking a good moment to examine our progress before bouncing inside for a snack.

"How many have we made so far?" Jazz lays down her scissors and rubs her temples after an hour.

I do a quick count. "We only need to cut out three more tails."

"And decorate them? And write everything on the back?" Jazz moans and pretends to collapse against the steps. "It's getting late."

"Yeah, and we need to have these ready for Macie to take to school *tomorrow*." I poke Jazz with the blunt end of my scissors. "Come on."

"Fine, but at the rate we're going there's no way we'll make it to youth group."

I tighten my grip around the scissors and reach for another piece of paper. "Oh well. We can go next week with Brander. Like old times."

"But isn't Brander going tonight too?"

"I don't think so. His relatives are flying in for a visit. He didn't think his mom would let him escape."

"Oh." Jazz cuts out another mermaid tail, a sneaky smile spreading across her face. "I guess Malia won't get her autograph then."

"You mean you finally noticed her celebrity crush?"

Jazz gives me a look. "You'd have to spend five seconds around her to notice. She's starstruck. Bad."

"No kidding." And yet Jazz—sweet, loving Jazz—hasn't gotten sick enough of it to leave Malia in the lurch. "Good for you for being willing to put up with it. She's driving me crazy."

"This isn't unusual for her—obsessing over a celebrity, I mean. She'll get over it."

"I don't get why she'd bother getting all worked up to begin with." I pull out a jar of glitter, and we work together to coat the tails with a layer of shimmery purple sparkles.

I lift my head after a while. "How are you so good at getting along with people?"

"Anyone in particular?" Jazz waggles her eyebrows.

"I don't know why Malia's bugging me. She isn't *that* bad. I mean—you know what I mean." But even if Jazz isn't trying her on for size as a new best friend, something about Malia and her mini crush on Brander is seriously bugging me.

Jazz sets down her jar of glitter and runs a hand across her face, leaving a sparkly purple streak across her forehead like a unibrow. "It can be hard to get along with people who have, uh, strong personalities." Jazz sneezes and scratches her nose, leaving behind even more glitter. "But think about it—you weren't exactly Miss Congeniality when you showed up on *Tutu*'s doorstep last summer."

"Hey! Easy on the ego there." I brush glitter from my shirt, as though trying to stroke my wounded pride.

Jazz laughs, and I join in.

"Seriously, Olive. What I'm trying to say is that it's easy to judge people for their actions when we don't understand what's going on in their hearts. You know as well as I do that Malia's had a rough year. Maybe the reason she's so hung up on Brander is because she needs something special in her life. What could be more special than getting the inside scoop on a celebrity?"

"Maybe." I mean, I guess it makes sense. A little. "Where do you come up with this stuff?"

"*Tutu* was a great Sunday school teacher. She made everyone in that class wise beyond their years."

"I guess." I set down the glitter and cross my arms. "Maybe I should talk to her about all this."

"That definitely wouldn't be a bad idea."

"Hey, Olive." Brander greets me with a *shaka*-fisted wave and a huge smile when I open the front door on Thursday afternoon, a certain Valentine's Day card burning a hole in my front pocket. Should I pull it out and give it to him now? Should I wait?

Maybe I shouldn't give it to him at all. I definitely don't want him to think I've got the wrong idea. But at the same time...

"Olive?" Brander steps forward and waves a hand over my face. "Did I lose you?"

"Nope. Sorry." I step outside and pull on my worn pink high-tops. "Ready for shave ice?"

"More than." Brander pats his stomach, barely rumpling his crisp white button-down shirt. "Nashville might know how to do Southern food, but you can't get a decent shave ice to save your life."

"How'd you survive without it?" I slip one hand into my pocket to finger Brander's card as he walks me to his Porsche. "You had me convinced that it ran in your bloodstream."

Brander laughs, and he gives my arm a fleeting pat before cracking open the passenger's side door. "Hop in. This car's been lonely."

I do as I'm told, and before long we're winding along the road to the Shave Ice Shack.

"Thanks for making time to hang out." I look over at Brander, and he turns down the radio—playing his favorite classic rock—before returning the smile. "This is nice."

"Yeah, it is." Brander retrains his gaze on the road before I can smile back, but the corners of my mouth quirk up anyway. *Thank you, God, for bringing Brander home.* My heart does a jump-kick, and my hand finds its way into my pocket once more.

I should suck it up and give him the card—there isn't even a heart on it, for crying out loud—but I can still see his shocked expression when Malia showed up at the airport. I don't want him to think the entire female population of Maui has lost its mind.

Instead, as soon as Brander pulls into a parking space, I hop out of the car and lead the charge to the Shave Ice Shack. There's a line of course—mostly made up of hand-holding honeymooners. Guess love is in the air today.

I give the card in my pocket one last touch before turning to Brander. "How was dinner with the family last night?"

"Crazy. There were thirty of us all together, and Rosco got so excited he stole the whole roast snapper off the dining room table before my dad could finish praying." Brander laughs, and I join in before he breaks off. "Sorry. You probably aren't interested in hearing any dog stories, huh?"

I shrug. "Considering I'm going to be sharing the house with one starting Saturday, there could be worse things for me to think about."

Brander's almond eyes widen, and I fill him in on Macie's birthday surprise.

"Wow. You don't even seem that freaked out about it." We pause for a moment to place our orders before Brander speaks again. "It's amazing to see what you're letting God do."

"What do you mean?" I lean back on my heels as the girl behind the counter drizzles guava syrup over my cone of shave ice.

"You never would've stood for something like that last summer. This is a big step. I—I'm proud of you." Brander reaches out to squeeze my shoulder. Not a hug, per se, but definitely something.

A few minutes later, Brander and I head toward the

shoreline, loaded down with two extra-large cones of fluffy shave ice.

"Oh, man." Brander's expression slip-slides into euphoria after his first bite, and he sinks onto a bench near the water. "How did I go so long without this stuff?"

I shrug and sit on the bench next to him. "I ate enough of it for both of us."

"Thanks for that." Brander shovels in another mouthful. "What else have you been up to? Besides eating shave ice. I feel like we haven't talked in forever."

"That's 'cause we haven't," I point out before taking a bite of ice, perfectly saturated with not only syrup but also sweetened condensed milk—the local favorite. The sweetness melts over my tongue, highlighting the sour sting of my last words. I swallow hard. "Sorry. That didn't come out right. I know—"

"No. I get it." Brander takes another bite of ice, but even that can't keep the corners of his mouth from drooping. "I was out of the loop for way too long. There were nights I wanted to call so bad, but I felt like I shouldn't."

"What do you mean?" I reach out, as if to lay a hand on his arm, but stop myself. "You know what your mom says—'better to tell a friend than keep it all inside.' Isn't that what you told me last year?"

That brings a smile to his face. "Yeah, that's it."

"Well then?" I poke him with my elbow. "I'm a friend, aren't I?"

"Of course. Don't think I'm trying to keep anything from you." He sets down his half-finished treat and rests his head in his hands. "But I think God and I have some work to do before I should say anything."

My stomach twists, and it's definitely not from the shave ice. "Are you sure you're okay—like, for real?"

Brander shrugs.

"That's not an answer. Are. You. Okay?"

He nods. Barely.

"That's not much better."

"I'm fine." He meets my gaze, eyes wide-open and honest. "That's the truth. I'm fine."

"But?"

"Fine doesn't mean good. There's a lot of stuff piling up on me right now, and I don't know what God wants me to do with it. I—" He grabs his spoon and shovels in a bite of ice, as though to keep from saying something he'll regret. He swallows before continuing. "Ever since the tour, the label's been putting a lot of pressure on me. There are a lot of decisions for me to make. I keep waiting for God to give me an answer, but it's like I can't hear Him."

"Tell me about it." I stare out to sea. The waves roll in to shore in perfect intervals—measured precisely by the very creator of the universe. If God has so much care for the Pacific Ocean, He must be looking out for us too. Right? "Maybe when you finally hear from God you can tell me how He speaks, huh? Because I'm waiting for some answers too."

For once, Brander doesn't pry. Instead he scoots over and nudges my elbow. "You'll be the first I tell. And until then, know I'm praying for you."

"I'm praying for you too." I return the elbow-nudge, then lift my half-melted shave ice in a toast. He raises his in turn, and we tap them together. The plastic cones clunk together rather unceremoniously before we both take another bite.

"To unseen futures," Brander says after swallowing. "And to the One who sees them, even when we can't."

"Here, here." I lift another bite of shave ice to my mouth, but my hand trembles and I nearly drop my spoon. As if my body is suddenly manned by someone else—someone much braver and bolder than me—I set down my shave ice and reach deep into my pocket. My fingers brush slightly crumpled paper, and I pull out the envelope holding the Valentine I made for Brander. It's a little soggy from being stuck in my pocket on such a warm, humid day, but I can't let myself hesitate.

"This is for you." I keep my voice even and my arm steady as I hold the card out toward Brander. "Happy Valentine's Day. Not that you're my Valentine or anything. But...you know."

The corners of Brander's mouth turn up, and he slips one finger beneath the envelope flap.

"Wait!" I practically throw myself across the bench to keep him from opening it all the way. A blush spreads across my cheeks as easily as butter on a hot piece of banana bread. "I didn't mean for you to read it now. You should probably save it for later." *When I'm not around to die of mortification.*

Brander's smile fades, and his gaze flits to the envelope before he shrugs and slides it into his pants pocket. "Thanks, Olive."

"You're welcome." I offer a small smile, and it quiets some of the nerves jangling around in my stomach like dog tags.

What will Brander think when he reads it? I run over the words I wrote—the ones I inadvertently ended up committing to memory. I don't think there's anything too mushy.

But if Brander *did* find his future love in Nashville, will he take kindly to knowing exactly how much I care about him—that is, a lot?

I suck in a deep breath, catching a faint whisper of Brander's bergamot cologne mixed with sea-salted air.

One way or another, I gave him the card.

And he took it.

That has to count for something. Right?

Chapter Twenty-Two

"OLIVE!" FOOTSTEPS PITTER-PATTER ON THE floor as Macie darts into the kitchen on Saturday morning, less than an hour before her party is scheduled to kick off at the beach park across the street. "I can't find my mermaid swimsuit! It's supposed to be in the drawer, but it's gone."

"Don't worry, Mace." I run Gramma's fancy cake-frosting spatula over the top of Macie's blue-and-green-ombre frosted cake one last time, then take a lick of cream cheese frosting before turning around. "I laid it out on your bed earlier, remember?"

"Oh." Macie nods, but her forehead is scrunched up like a pug's.

"Is everything okay, squirt?" I stick the spatula in the dishwater and cross over to give Macie a squeeze, but she sidesteps just out of my reach.

"I don't want a birthday." Macie sniffles, and something wet drops from her eye. *Uh-oh.*

"Don't be silly." I step toward Macie and tip her chin up so I can look her in the eye, but my sister's somber expression doesn't waver. "Everyone wants to have a birthday."

"*I* don't." Macie crosses her arms.

I bite my lip and stand on my tiptoes to peek out the front window at Gramma, who's supervising the inflation of Macie's mermaid-queen bouncy house across the street. Jazz hasn't shown up yet, and Dad is still in the shower. *Where's backup when you need it?* "I thought you were excited about your party. Aren't you at least looking forward to jumping in the bouncy-house?"

"No. I don't want to have a birthday because…because of *Mommy*!" With that, Macie throws back her head and bursts into sobs. Fat tears spill onto her chubby cheeks, and she buries her wet face in my brand-new yellow sundress.

My heart pangs for Macie—and, okay, for me too. But now isn't the time to get sucked out to sea by the rip current called grief. "Macie, look at me." I drop to my knees in front of her and take her hands in mine. "I know this is rough. I felt like this at Christmastime. But what about this—do you think Mom would want you to spend your birthday crying?"

Macie shrugs. "Maybe."

"Come on. Now you're being ornery."

"*So?*" Macie scrunches her nose, but at least she isn't crying.

"Do you think Mom wants you to spend your life sitting around and moping?"

Macie blinks up at me. "No?"

"Was that a question?"

"No." She says it louder this time. "I guess she wouldn't."

"Right on, squirt." I give her curls a gentle tug and prepare to stand, but an *ahem* from the hall gives me pause.

"Everything okay in here?" Dad strides toward the kitchen, hair still damp from the shower. "Getting excited, Macie?"

Macie bites her lip and nods bravely. I give her one last squeeze before climbing to my feet and wandering down the hall. Best to give those two their daddy-daughter time.

Once I've dried Macie's tears from the front of my dress, Macie has Dad firmly entangled in a conversation about heaven. From the sound of it, now she's worried that Mom is jealous that we're having fun without her.

Which, to be honest, I've wondered about myself.

I'm lingering—okay, *eavesdropping*—in the hall when Gramma comes in, and she raises a brow at me. "Everything okay?"

"Hope so."

Gramma purses her lips and turns an ear toward the kitchen. "How long have they been talking? Alex is supposed to pick up the puppy now."

"Oh. Right." I peek at my watch. Only half an hour 'til party time. "Can't you go get it? I'll hold down the fort across the street."

"No. I still need to put the fondant mermaid tails on the cake—you got it frosted, right?"

"Yeah. But I'm sure I could decorate—"

Gramma raises a hand to quiet me. "Macie has a vision. So do I, for that matter."

"I won't mess it up."

Gramma cocks her head. "I don't know. Macie was very specific. We drew her idea out after school yesterday."

"Then why not have Alani's mom bring the dog when she drops off Alani?"

"Too risky. I hate to chance ruining the surprise."

"So I'll go talk to Macie about heaven while Dad gets the dog?" My whole insides shiver. Macie's already stirred up my emotions a bit too much for my liking. One more question and I might crack. "Or—I know. I can get Brander to come early and talk to her. That way Dad can get the dog, and Macie can get her answers."

Gramma's eyes light up. "Perfect."

"Great. I'll go call him." I start upstairs for my phone, but Gramma grabs hold of my arm.

"That's not what I meant. Macie needs to have this talk with her dad. It'll be good for both of them. But you and Brander can get the puppy." Gramma nods, almost to herself. "That's what you'll do."

"For real?" Some of that newfound bravery of mine

wavers. "Do I have to go with him?"

Gramma nods. "I haven't paid Alani's mom yet. Besides, this way you can pick out the puppy you think is least vicious." Her eyes twinkle in the morning light, and she grabs her purse from its hook by the door before rummaging through it. "Here." She hands me a wad of crumpled bills, and I give her as much of a smile as I can muster.

"Okay. Let me text Brander."

"How're you feeling?" Brander pulls in front of Alani's house and hops out onto the street. "This can't be easy."

"I'm fine, I guess. Let's get this over with." I march up the front walk, Brander close behind, and take a breath before ringing the bell. Almost instantly, a chorus of dog barks goes up from somewhere within the house. My gut clenches.

God, please don't let me lose it now.

As if he can sense my nerves, Brander moves closer and wraps an arm around me. "It's okay." His breath tickles my ear as he whispers to me, and I relax a bit.

"Thanks," I say right as the door swings open.

Brander drops his arm and waves as Alani's mom greets us with a smile.

"Aloha. Come in." She holds the door open wider, and Brander and I kick off our *slippas* before stepping inside. The house is bright and sunny, but I can't ignore the musty smell of dog. It grows stronger as Alani's mom leads us down the hall.

"The puppies are in the laundry room. They're getting a bit squirrelly, so watch out." She stops in front of a door and opens it, then unlatches a baby gate before motioning us inside. "We have four left."

Another whiff of dog hits me—square in the nose. I

hesitate before stepping into the room. I sweep my gaze over the room once—twice—before catching sight of a passel of white-and-gray puppies, all sacked out on top of each other. "That's them?" Not so squirrelly right now, thank goodness.

Alani's mom nods. "Yep. The two on top are little girls. Here." She stoops and grabs them—one in each hand. "You can each hold one."

My heart pounds in my ears as she nestles the tiny mutt into my arms, but the pup barely cracks an eye open. The little thing can't weigh more than a pound or two, and I can't keep the corners of my mouth from turning up.

"Pretty cute, right?" Brander steps closer to me and nods at his own bundle of gray-and-white fluff.

"Not bad. What kind of dog are they again?" I sneak a peek at the puppy snuggled in my arms. The thing's so fluffy it looks more cat than dog.

"Shih tzus." Alani's mom smiles. "They were once bred for Chinese royalty—the perfect puppy for a birthday princess."

At that, I can't help but smile as I turn to Brander. "Which one do you think Macie would like best?"

Brander reaches over to scratch the top of my puppy's head. "She'll be thrilled with either. Which would make *you* more comfortable?"

I sneak a peek at Alani's mom before answering. I bet it's not every day someone with a dog phobia drops by to pick out a puppy. "I guess we'll take this one." I nod at the puppy I'm holding. She doesn't seem the attack-dog type, and her gray spots are awfully cute.

"Great." The woman moves to re-open the baby gate before leading us to the front door. Alani peeks out from the living room and stares at us—or maybe at Brander—as we leave.

"See you soon." I wave to Alani, then press a finger to my lips to remind her that Macie's puppy needs to be kept secret. Last I heard, Gramma was planning on stashing the mutt somewhere for the first part of the party and bringing her out during Macie's requested party game of pin-the-tail-on-the-doggy.

"You did great in there." Brander peeks at me after we finish up business with Alani's mom and pile into his car.

"Thanks. I think I might be able to do this." I lay the puppy in my lap and wince as her sharp baby nails scrape my bare legs. "Or not. Ouch."

I duck my head to check my scratched leg for blood, but there's nothing, save for a nearly invisible white line. Poor pup. Maybe she didn't even mean to hurt me.

Because honestly, she reminds me more of my old kitten than a snarling pit bull.

We ride along the shoreline, and I pat the puppy's fluffy head with one hand as Brander sings along to one of those old-timey Fleetwood Mac songs. A few streets before Gramma's, though, he reaches over and switches off the radio. "Isn't it incredible how God gives us courage and peace when we need it?"

"You mean like with the dog?" I glance down at the bundle of gray-spotted fur and smile. This fluffy mutt could be a stuffed animal for as much trouble as she's causing. "Yeah. It's pretty great."

"Do you ever wonder? Like, does it ever make you nervous when God *doesn't* give you total peace about something?"

"What do you mean?"

"Maybe it's weird, but I have a hard time going along with stuff when I don't feel God's peace. Even if most people think it sounds like a dream come true."

"Is this about anything in particular?"

Brander ducks his head. "I'm not—I mean...never mind." He turns onto Gramma's street. "You have too much on your plate for me to unload my problems on you."

"That's not true." I squint to block out the bright sunshine as Brander parks along the curb. "I don't care how messed-up my life is. I still need to know what's going on in yours.

Brander kills the engine and sits a moment before turning to me and offering a sort of half-choked smile. "Thanks, Olive. That means a lot."

"And?"

"And—" A souped-up sports car pulls up behind Brander, its growling engine sending the puppy's head shooting up from my lap. The mutt yips, and I flinch.

"Here, let me take her." Brander jumps out of the car and moves to open my door. The puppy's nails scrape my leg again as Brander gathers her into his arms.

"Thanks." I follow Brander down to the beach, but while I'm grateful to be rescued from a puppy version of a temper tantrum, I can't ignore the fact that he still hasn't told me what's wrong.

Chapter Twenty-Three

"Is that the puppy?" Jazz practically swoons when she catches sight of Macie's squash-nosed little present, still tucked into Brander's arms, just minutes before party time.

I nod. "Keep it quiet. Macie should be out here any second, and we still need to hide this mutt somewhere."

"Oops." Jazz slaps a hand over her mouth. "Sorry."

"No problem. How long have you been here?"

"Only a few minutes. It looks great out here." Jazz motions to our patch of scrubby green grass in the oceanside park, and I nod.

"Gramma got up before dawn to make sure we could snag the tables." I motion to three balloon-marked picnic tables encircling the mermaid bounce house. Between the over-the-top decorations—Gramma insisted on stringing multicolored banners between the palm trees—and obvious beach theme, it's different than any birthday party I've ever been to. Macie will love it.

"I love it!" Macie's squeal echoes all the way down the beach as she and Gramma cross the street. My pulse kicks up a notch as Macie quickens her pace, making a beeline for the bouncy house.

"Quick, hide the mutt." I flap a hand at Brander, who dives behind a palm tree, then I run forward to meet Macie. "Are you ready to party?"

She nods, her head of corkscrew curls bobbing up and down like she's training to become a bobblehead. "This is perfect-ness." She spins in a circle, the sparkly blue fabric of her cover-up floating on the breeze as Gramma catches up, carefully balancing the cake in both hands.

"The others should be arriving any moment." Gramma smiles at Jazz as she sets the cake atop one table. "Where's Brander?"

"He's taking care of, um…things." I take a quick peek to make sure Macie isn't paying too much attention. Thankfully, she's too busy ogling that bounce-house to pay any attention to me and Grams. "He should be around any minute."

As if on cue, Brander steps out from behind the tree, now puppy-free and toting a foil-covered platter. "Sleeping in the backseat," he mouths, nodding in the direction of his car before offering Gramma the tray. "Anything I can do to help, *Tutu*? Dad sent some sushi from the restaurant."

"Wonderful." Gramma takes his offering and sets it next to the cake on what I guess is going to be the food table. "That was very generous of him. Make sure to thank him for me, all right?"

Brander nods, and I take a step closer to that platter. I saw the restaurant at Mr. Delacroix's fancy-pants resort once, but I've never eaten there. My stomach growls at the thought of finally getting a taste of the restaurant's sushi. But before I can sneak a piece, the other guests start arriving.

Gramma takes charge of greeting everyone and she puts me to work handing out leis. Before long the park is full of Macie's classmates. And their parents, siblings, *and* grandparents. Plus at least half the church congregation. It's like the whole island is here.

Which is cool and all, but we only made a small cake. And if Gramma is planning on ordering pizza like I'd figured, then the bill from Pirate Pete's will be more than a month's worth of groceries.

"What's wrong?" Brander leans in close after I finish

handing out construction-paper poodle tails for Macie's game of pin-the-tail-on-the-doggy.

"There are way more people here than I'd thought. How are we going to feed all of them?"

Brander laughs, then points behind me. "Haven't you seen the food table?"

I face in the direction he's pointing and gape. The recently empty picnic table is now groaning under the weight of what must be close to twenty different platters of food, plus Macie's cake and Brander's sushi contribution. "Where'd it all come from?"

Jazz trots up, prosthesis glinting in the harsh overhead light. "Everyone around here knows that *party* is a code word for *potluck*. Everyone brought something. But we can eat later—Brander, *Tutu* said it's time to get the puppy."

As Brander and Jazz trot off in the direction of Brander's car, the tang of barbecue sauce hits my nose, and I spot Dad presiding over a rib-laden grill. "Where'd all that come from?" My stomach lets out a happy groan as I walk over to the small barbecue.

"One of the men from church brought the meat—your grandmother asked me to do the honors." Dad's eyes grow wide behind his glasses, and he leans close to whisper to me. "I hope I'm cooking these right. It's been a while since I've done this."

Before I can say anything else, Gramma motions me over to join Macie and her friends as they finish their game.

"Birthday girl, you're up." Gramma ties a hibiscus-print scarf over Macie's eyes and hands her a puppy tail before spinning her around half a dozen times. "Now pin the tail on that puppy!"

Macie stumbles a bit before regaining her balance. She starts walking in a wavering line toward a tail-strewn puppy cutout taped to a palm tree. At the last minute, she veers slightly off-course. I hold my breath as Brander steps in front of her, the puppy clutched tightly in his arms.

Jazz appears at my side, and we share a secret smile as Macie's hands flail in the air, as if searching for something solid. She wobbles a moment and screws up her face as Brander darts out of reach, winking at the rest of us, before holding the puppy out toward Macie.

My sister's chubby hand connects with the puppy's soft, fluffy coat, and she lets out a squeal before dropping the paper tail.

"What was *that*?" She squeals again, then rips off the scarf and gasps. "My puppy!"

The adults all laugh as Macie grabs for the squirming ball of fluff, and Brander lays the mutt in her arms before stepping away.

"Hau`oli Lā Hānau, Macie," the entire crowd gathered in the park choruses—except for me. Instead, I murmur the words "happy birthday" under my breath, since I'm guessing that's what everyone else said.

Macie beckons her friends nearer to see her new pet, and melee ensues. The party game is abandoned as Macie prances around the park, hugging her puppy so tightly I'm afraid she might choke the poor thing.

"You're sure you're feeling good about this?" Brander makes his way over to talk to me and Jazz, and I nod.

"I'll manage." But there's a smile on my face as I say the words.

If the grin Macie's sporting is anything to go by, she's happier than she's been since Mom died. Besides, how can I be grouchy about something as sweet and fluffy as that puppy? "The little mutt is pretty cute. And she can't help it if she's a dog."

Brander's hand finds mine, and he gives it a squeeze as we stand together. Jazz shifts her weight, as though preparing to sneak off, but I hook my arm around hers before she can escape.

She angles her chin at my hand, which somehow intertwined itself with Brander's, as if questioning whether or not she's intruding.

I roll my eyes and give Jazz's own hand a squeeze. She squeezes back hard, and she doesn't let go.

The three of us stand there—fingers laced together, hearts equally as connected—for what feels like forever.

"A-*hem.*"

Enter Queen Malia.

"Great party, yeah?" Her voice comes from behind. "Olive, your *tutu* knows how to go all out."

"That she does." I smile, though it feels a bit like a grimace, as Brander releases my hand to offer Malia a *shaka.* How does this girl have such impeccably bad timing? "Have you had something to eat?"

"Yeah." Malia wrinkles her nose. "Thank goodness you brought sushi, Brander. The rest of that stuff is one-hundred-per-cent garbage. Can you imagine what my coach would say if I got caught eating ribs during swim season?" Malia gives an overdramatic shudder, then smiles.

Something in that smile curdles my gut, and a retort builds on the tip of my tongue. "I wouldn't call all that food junk, Malia. Last I saw, someone brought a family-size bag of barbecue potato chips. And I don't care how many grams of fat are in a serving—those chips are *not* garbage."

"No comment." Malia blinks at me like I've lost my mind, then turns to Brander. "The sushi was delicious, though—it went quick too. I was lucky to snag the last of it."

Of course you did. I try to keep that response tucked in my brain, but if the way Jazz's elbow hits my ribcage is anything to go by, it must show all over my face.

Without a word, Jazz hooks her arm tighter around my

own and drags me a few steps away from Malia and Brander. Once we're a safe distance away, she dips her head to whisper in my ear. "Remember. Empathy."

"Empathy. Right." I stare over at the now-empty sushi platter. "I'll try."

"That's the spirit." Jazz whacks me on the back so hard I'm afraid I might choke, then drags me over to the food table and grabs us each a plate. "Come on. Let's get some of these potato chips before they disappear too."

Chapter Twenty-Four

"I GOT A CALL." DAD STRIDES across the park as Gramma and I work together to untie the last few bunches of balloons from one of the picnic tables after the party.

For a second, I think he's talking to me, and I nearly lose my grip on the balloons. But for once, Dad's words appear to be directed at Gramma. I breathe a sigh of relief, but it catches in my throat when I spot a dark frown building on his face.

"Bad news?" I tighten my hold on the balloons—just in case.

"The professor who's been filling in for me is in the hospital. His wife is expecting twins, and it looks as if they're going to be born prematurely." Dad sticks one hand in his pocket, and the jingling of loose coins comes moments after. "There's no way he can continue to cover for me."

"Which means?" I practically kick myself for the sudden breath of hope blooming in my heart. I shouldn't be eager to put my dad on a one-way flight to Boston, but with all that's going on right now, that's exactly what I want to do.

Maybe he'll be so busy getting his class schedule organized that he'll forget all about the scholarship application. I can forget about it too, and I'll figure it all out next year. When I'm *supposed* to be thinking about that kind of stuff.

Dad's face is grim. "I knew I'd have to head home sooner or later. Quite honestly, it's been a matter of procrastination on my part. I suppose this is my wake-up call." His other hand sneaks into his pocket, and he shuffles his feet. "Macie is not going to be pleased."

As if on cue, all three of us turn to look at Macie. She's sacked out on a grassy patch in the shade, her puppy tucked under one chubby arm, a smile still on her face.

"At least she has the puppy to keep her company now." I shrug. "That's something, right?"

"I suppose." Dad's eyes meet my own, and he purses his lips. "I'm concerned about leaving you to finish that application on your own. You *have* been working on it, I hope."

"I'm on it. Honest." Whether I'll actually turn it in or not is another story.

Gramma takes a step closer to Dad. "We'll miss you, Alex."

"And I'll miss you." Dad stiffens slightly as Gramma wraps her arms around him, but he gives her a quick squeeze before she pulls away. "I suppose I should start packing. There's a flight leaving out of Kahului at eleven o'clock tonight."

Gramma's mouth falls open slightly. "Isn't that awfully short notice?"

"I'll barely get home in time to catch a few hours of sleep and prepare for my classes as it is. I wish there was another option, but I can't continue relying on my coworkers to sub for me." Dad removes one hand from his pocket and pinches the bridge of his nose. "I suppose I should tell Macie the news." He takes a step toward my sister, then stops. "Olive?"

"Yeah?"

"Don't go anywhere. I'd like you to help me pack."

"This is not how things were supposed to go." Dad tosses a stack of half-folded undershirts into his bag, then reaches for another pile of clothes. "I'd planned to stay with Bonnie until the end of winter term, at least."

"Well, plans change." I shrug, keeping one eye on Dad as I slide his laptop into its protective traveling case. *Don't ask about the application. Don't ask about the application. Don't ask—*

"But what about your scholarship application? The deadline is practically here, and we've barely worked through the preliminaries together. You haven't even touched the essay portion yet." Dad grabs a tired-looking polo shirt and plucks at a loose button. "It's the most important part of the process, and I know exactly what the other members of the board want to see. If you don't do it exactly—"

"Dad." I grab the shirt before he can start wringing it in his hands, then fold it and place it neatly in the suitcase. There. One small bit of order amid the mass chaos that has erupted in Gramma's tiny spare room. "It's all going to work out. Okay?"

And maybe that means me staying right here where I belong.

As if he can sense my thoughts, Dad takes a step forward. "Olive, I don't want you to let this slide. This could be the ticket to your dream. Don't allow yourself to get so caught up in all this shave ice and beach combing and youth group foolishness that you lose sight of what's important."

I toss a pair of socks in the bag. "Oh, I won't."

Dad's eyebrows shoot up—probably at my tone, which I'll admit was a little sarcastic—but his pocket buzzes before he can reprimand me. He whips out his phone and presses it to his ear.

By the time Dad's phone has been returned to his pocket, he's stirred up even more than he was already. It sounds like the university wants him to help cover the absentee professor's other classes.

By the time we finish packing, my own nerves are on high alert. Even though my heart is telling me one thing, another part of me can't ignore Dad's logic.

Am I willing to give up my dream in exchange for the life I've built here—especially when some parts of that life feel like they could start falling apart?

Gramma's rattling station wagon backfires, and Macie buries her head in her puppy's fuzzy coat and howls as Gramma and Dad pull out of the driveway later that evening.

I stand on the front porch and pat her back as she cries, my own heart feeling a little extra-raw. There's nothing quite worse than saying another goodbye—even if it's one I thought I'd be happy about. "It'll be okay, Mace. We can see Daddy again soon."

"But I wanted to go say goodbye at the airport." Macie sets her puppy down in its new bed—one of the many puppy-themed birthday presents Macie opened earlier today—and rubs her eyes.

"I know you did, but then you wouldn't have gotten home until way after your bedtime." I sneak a peek at my watch. "In fact, it's almost bedtime already."

"I don't wanna go to bed." Macie screws up her face, and I frown.

"Well then, let's at least go inside. I don't think the puppy should stay out here too long. She looks sleepy right now, but what would happen if she smells one of the neighbors' cats? We don't want her running off."

"Fine." Macie picks up the puppy and hugs her close as she follows me inside. "But can't you call Brander and have him take me in his fast car so I can say goodbye at the airport?"

"Macie. You already said goodbye." I shift my weight from one foot to the other. *Don't push it, sis.*

"But—"

"I have an idea." I duck into the hall and grab my phone from its charger, then dash back to the living room. "I'll call Jazz and see if she can come over."

"Jazzie?" Macie stares at me, long and hard. "Can she spend the night?"

"Maybe." I dial Jazz's number and hold the phone to my ear. "Can you come over?" I ask as soon as she answers. "We have a situation."

"A situation, huh?

"Yeah. Dad's gone—back to Boston." I tell her all about Macie's meltdown. "So, will you come?"

"Of course." *Thank goodness.* "Ruby's working the night shift today. I'll catch a ride with her."

"Jazz'll be here in a few minutes," I tell Macie after hanging up. It's not enough to bring a smile to her face, but her eyes give off the slightest bit of a twinkle, so I let myself relax. A breeze blows in through the open window, and I run my hands over my arms before putting my hand on Macie's back and pushing her toward the staircase.

"Come on, squirt. Let's get you in your pajamas."

"What are you going to name your puppy?" I ask after Macie has changed into her mermaid-print footie pajamas. Jazz hasn't shown up yet, and I need to come up with *something* to keep Macie's mind off the fact that Dad won't be coming home tonight.

Macie lays one finger alongside her chin and tilts her head, staring at the little mutt. "I don't know," she says after a while. "I want to make sure it's *perfect.*"

Oh, boy. I tilt my head way, way back. Considering the

snaillike pace at which my sister makes decisions, this poor pup could still be nameless by the time Macie has her next birthday.

I glance at the dog. She's a tiny little thing—mostly white, with a gray patch around her rump and a few on her face. With her curly tail and punched-in nose, the pup looks like something out of a storybook.

"What about Pepper?" I squat down to let the mutt sniff my hand. Her downy fur tickles my fingers, but I force myself to hold my hand steady.

"Pepper makes me sneeze. I think maybe Zuzu. Or Trixiebelle."

"Too prissy. What about Noodles?"

"Kiki."

"Jellybean."

"That one's not bad," Macie admits after a moment, but there's a knock on the door before she can say anything else. Macie runs to let Jazz in, and I stay sitting on the floor—alone with the pup for the first time. I reach out to give the dog a scratch between the ears, and that's how Jazz and Macie find us when they come into the living room a few moments later.

"Hey." Jazz sinks onto the couch above me, and she joins the puppy-naming committee until Macie starts coming up with more yawns than names.

"Want me to tuck you in tonight?" Jazz asks once my sister's eyelids have grown heavy. Macie nods, and Jazz half-carries her upstairs.

"Nighty-night, Puffinstuff." Macie's sleep-warmed voice drifts down from the stairwell, and I smile at her latest name idea.

Thank goodness Gramma wants to keep the little mutt tucked away in a crate until she's potty-trained. Brave as I might feel right now, I don't think I could fall asleep knowing the little mutt had full run of the house.

Supposedly Macie is going to help with the potty-training, but I'll believe that when I see it.

At least I didn't get stuck with that job—though I have a feeling it's going to be impossible to keep my distance completely. After all, someone's going to have to clean up after the pup when she has an accident. And Koa taught me that I can sop up piddle with the best of them.

"Thanks for coming tonight," I tell Jazz when she comes back. "You saved the day."

"No problem. You saved mine too."

"What? How come?"

"I called my mom today." Jazz's face grows grim.

"Need to talk about it?"

She shrugs. "Things are super weird."

"What kind of things?"

Jazz pinches her lips together. "You know how I said that you should be glad to have a dad, when so many people would kill to have one?"

"Yeah." I shudder. "Your mom didn't fall in love with some guy at the rehab center, did she?"

"Eww, no. What I'm trying to say is that I think I get it now. Why it's hard for you to be totally thankful for your dad."

"Wow." I blink. "What changed?"

"Nothing really. But she's driving me nuts." Jazz squeezes her stump. "I keep telling myself that some people—like you—would give anything to even have a mom. But—"

"But *what*?" My breath escapes me in a puff of frustration.

"Mom's getting...I don't know." Jazz picks at the liner of her prosthesis. "Bitter, I guess. The whole reason I called was to talk to her about the paddleboard race. She said she'd be out of rehab by then, so I invited her to watch. I should've kept my mouth shut."

"She doesn't want to come?"

"Not only that." Jazz keeps fiddling with her prosthesis. "She laughed."

"Laughed?" I grind my hand into a fist and press it into the sun-faded slipcover of Gramma's couch. Jazz doesn't deserve a mom like that. She deserves someone better—someone like *Mom.* "What would she laugh about?"

"The paddleboarding." Jazz's hand goes still, and she hunches up into a ball. "She made it sound like a big joke. Maybe it is."

"No way." I jump to my feet and throw myself onto the couch next to Jazz before giving her arm a squeeze. "Think about when we went out with Malia. Who was the bigger joke there—a one-legged wonder, or a sunburned mainlander trying to get her balance for the first time?"

"When you put it that way, I guess you *did* make me look pretty good." Jazz gives my arm a good-natured shove. "But honestly…" Her voice is tenuous. "All I'm trying to do is be nice and start some sort of a relationship with my mom, but she talks to me like I'm a walking failure. Like it was *my* idea to chop off my leg."

Heat rises in my chest, boiling up and into my mouth in the form of a handful of not-too-nice words. But calling Jazz's mom a bunch of ugly names won't make anyone feel better—not even me. "Maybe you should talk to Brander. He's smarter about this stuff than I am."

"Yeah, but I don't want to bug him. He's been so busy—doesn't he deserve a break?"

"Good point." I pluck at a loose thread on the couch. "Have you tried telling your mom that you don't like the way she talks to you? You're a brave person. You should tell her exactly how you feel."

"I don't know." Jazz squints at me. "How's it been working out for you?"

"What do you mean?"

"With your dad."

"Huh?"

"Didn't you talk to him about Harvard before he left? You know, about you're still not sure you want to go."

"Actually..."

"You mean you didn't? He still thinks you're going?"

I hold in an extra-deep breath, listening as Gramma's wall clock ticks away a good two dozen seconds.

"*Are* you?" Jazz's silvery eyes turn to frosted steel. She scoots away from me on the couch and wraps her arms around herself. "Did you change your mind and not tell me?"

"Um, not exactly."

"Did you lie to him then?"

"I didn't lie." Not technically. "I still don't know yet. We left things at that. For now, anyway." *That's got to make her feel better, right?*

"That's even worse."

Or not.

"If you're still deciding, that must mean that Harvard is sounding better and better. And the better Harvard sounds, the more you'll want to leave this place—leave *us.*"

"Whoa—slow down."

"You don't get it, Olive. I've never had a friend like you before. Someone I was close to. When I was little I never fit in. Then my leg did its thing, Brander and I started hanging out more and praying, and *Tutu* Bonnie started having me over. *And* you and Macie moved here." Jazz is rambling now, but I'm not about to stop her. "It's like I've finally found my *ohana.* I don't want to lose it."

"Who said you're going to? *Ohana* is forever."

Jazz's lip trembles. "Is it? For real? Because my *ohana* seems to be running out on me. Mom, Brander...you."

I wrap my pinky finger around and around the chain of my necklace as my heart aches for Jazz. The girl who's given so much of herself to others, never expecting a thing in return. The girl who was willing to be my friend despite everything going on in her own life. The girl whose own broken, messed-up pieces fit together with mine to form a friendship stronger than I ever could have hoped for.

How can I bear to give that up?

Jazz's chin quivers again, and I sling an arm around her. "I'm not going anywhere."

"What?" Her head perks up.

"Not now. Maybe never. So let's not think about it, okay?"

"Okay." Jazz plays with the tail of her braid. "But promise you won't stay for me. Or go because that's what your dad wants." She takes in a shuddery breath. "I'm being selfish about this whole thing, and I know it. Even if I want you to stay, you need to do what *God* wants you to do. Even if it's not the easiest thing."

"And how do I know what He wants me to do again?"

"Ask Him."

"What if He isn't answering?"

Jazz shrugs. "I guess you'll have to talk to Him about that."

"Yeah. Maybe I will."

And then, knowing Jazz won't mind a bit, I bow my head to do exactly that.

Chapter Twenty-Five

"ALOHA." MALIA'S VOICE IS SINGSONG-Y WHEN she struts up to the pew I'm sharing with Grams and Jazz next Sunday, and she's wearing a sundress that barely covers her hind end.

I return the Hawaiian greeting with a smile and stamp down the urge to elbow Jazz in surprise. Malia's outfit is more appropriate for a Vegas nightclub than a Sunday church service—even if said service is pretty much on the beach.

"Can I sit here?" Malia doesn't allow time for protest before she drops into the empty space next to Jazz. "Thanks."

I fold my arms over my chest and fight to keep a smile on my face. We'd been saving that spot for Brander. Things have calmed down a lot, but this'll be his first time back at church. Jazz and I figured that, if we could keep him busy enough, any autograph-seekers would leave him alone. Now Malia's spoiled that plan.

"What's up with Brander? I thought for sure he'd be at church today." Malia blinks at us, eyes wide and innocent, and flips her hair as the worship team takes the stage. Did she know that's who we were saving a spot for? Probably. "I wanted to ask him if—never mind. Whatever."

"What did you want to ask him?" Gramma peeks at Malia, and Malia's face turns bright red.

"I *said* never mind." Malia drops her gaze to the floor. "Seriously though, what's up with him? His Instagram has been dead since he left Nashville."

Thankfully the worship leader strums a chord before I

have to come up with a response. I stand with the others and sing, trying to focus on the music.

As we sit down in preparation to collect the tithe, I can't help peeking at the crowd gathered in the pavilion behind me. Brander is nowhere to be seen, and now I'm the one who's curious.

What *is* going on with him? Brander is never late, and especially not to church.

Jazz passes me the offering basket and waggles her brows. I wrinkle my nose in response, then turn to whisper to her after handing the basket off to Grams. "Did he say he wasn't coming?"

"Not that I heard." Jazz frowns. "There must be something going on—something he's not telling us."

"You're right."

And today—right after church—I'm going to find out what that *something* is.

I take a deep breath before knocking on the teak-paneled double doors that mark the entrance to the Delacroix mansion.

After church I told Jazz my plan and invited her to come, but she bowed out. Malia was making noises about going paddleboarding, and Jazz said it would be easier to get answers out of him if I went by myself.

Why she would think that—especially since she's known Brander a lot longer than I have—is beyond me, but whatever. At least Grams overheard and offered to drive me. But she dropped me off at the driveway, meaning I'm still here alone.

And feeling somewhat small standing in front of this massive front entrance, staring up at three layers of luxury craftsmanship and indoor-outdoor living.

I shuffle my flip-flops on the shiny porch tiles and lift my hand to knock again.

Before I can, the door swings open, and Brander's mother appears. "Yes?" She's dressed to the hilt in a linen pantsuit that probably costs more than my entire wardrobe. Maybe I shouldn't have changed out of my church dress before coming over.

"Do you need something?" Mrs. Delacroix lifts her nose—surprisingly sharp, now that it's only inches from my face—high in the air and peers at me as though I'm a pesky rodent. "Brander isn't expecting you."

"I know." I straighten my spine and flash my most becoming smile—if I have such a thing. "But he wasn't at church, and Jazz and I thought we should check on him."

Mrs. Delacroix's dark eyes brighten a bit. "Jazmine is here?"

I almost laugh at the usage of Jazz's real name—the one she'd never be caught dead answering to—but I keep my composure. "No. She had, um, other stuff to do."

Mrs. Delacroix raises her brows and holds the door open barely wide enough for me to step inside. "Brander is out by the pool. Try not to stay too long. I believe he is still rather jet-lagged."

"Jet-lagged. Right. Thanks, Mrs. Delacroix." I kick off my *slippas* and duck inside, booking it through the open-air living room and practically running out to the patio. I suck in a deep breath of plumeria-scented air and hold it in for a moment. The inside of the Delacroix mansion is so extravagant. I'm afraid I'll hurt something in it if I breathe a decibel too loud. But outside things are calmer—more tranquil.

I make my way toward the pool, warmth from the sun-speckled patio tiles soaking into my bare feet, Mrs. Delacroix's final words dancing a figure-eight in my mind.

Brander *must* be majorly jet-lagged to skip church to

hang out by the pool. Either that or he's hiding something.

"Olive?" Brander steps out from around a thick palm on the other side of the crystal-clear swimming pool. Even from here, his gaze seems heavy. "What are you doing here?"

"I hope it's okay that I ambushed you like this." I hold out my hands, palms up, as though presenting a peace offering. Maybe coming here wasn't such a good idea after all. "But Jazz and I were worried when you weren't at church. Your mom said you're still jet-lagged?"

"Kinda." Brander lifts a hand and runs it through his hair. "No. Why don't you sit down?"

"Um, sure." My gaze leaps over several expensive-looking teak loungers with pristine white cushions. They're all too beautiful—too perfect—to risk messing up. Instead I plop onto the ground and stick my feet in the pool.

Coolness washes over my legs, and I reach down to wave a hand through the crystalline water. Now *this* I could get used to.

Bare footsteps slap against the patio as Brander crosses over to sit next to me, but that's the only sound for several moments until a bird trills from a nearby tree and Brander finally opens his mouth. "Can I tell you something?" His words slice through the silence like an expert swimmer diving into the pool. Barely a ripple.

"Of course." My voice is soft too. So soft I'm afraid Brander doesn't hear me. "Of course," I say again. Louder. "You can tell me anything. And I won't tell anyone else, either."

"Thanks." Brander's gaze is so heavy, that one word so drenched in distress, that I can't help reaching out to squeeze his hand. My fingers barely brush his own, though, before something flickers to life in my brain.

What if he's about to tell me that he has a girlfriend waiting for him on the mainland? Brander has always been so loyal—to his parents, to Jazz...to God. I doubt he'd take kindly to having my hand on his while his true love is back in Nashville.

I yank my hand away so fast that Brander lowers his head and frowns, but I don't offer an explanation. Even if Jazz and Grams were right and that whole thing was a hoax, it's probably best to let Brander get whatever it is off his chest with as few distractions as possible.

"I'm sorry it's taken me so long to tell you this. I should have said something the minute you guys picked me up at the airport." He keeps his head down. Eyes focused on the sun-sparks flashing off the water below him.

Look at me, my heart begs, but of course he doesn't. Maybe he is seeing someone after all. I readjust my position and sit on my hands—just in case.

"The problem is, things are so great here. I love hanging out with you—and Jazz and *Tutu* Bonnie and everyone else. That's why I'm not sure if—" Brander peers past the pool and squints out at the horizon, the rippling ocean waters reflecting in his gaze. Whatever it is he has to tell me, it must be eating him alive. "I don't know if it's the best thing. For you, for me...for all of us."

I open my mouth, ready to tell him to spit it out already. But then, from somewhere deep within my brain, comes Mom's voice, urging me to have patience, to give Brander time to work things out on his own.

Brander laces his fingers together before placing his hands behind his head. He stares up at the sky for one long moment as the cry of a seabird echoes overhead. Then he lowers his head to look at me once more. "I don't know how to say it, so I guess I'll spit it out. Mike wants me to move to Nashville." Brander's eyes fall shut, his jaw locks in a grimace. "Permanently."

"Permanently?" Jazz yelps on the other line when I call her on my walk home. "You mean, like, for good?"

"Last I checked, that's what *permanently* means."

Jazz sputters like a worn-out boat engine. "But he barely got adjusted to this time zone!"

"I *know*. Wasn't it enough that he spent months on the mainland recording his single and touring with some of the greatest names in Christian music? Is he so special that they need him to live there? Forever?" I huff. "Don't answer that. I know he is. Special, I mean."

Because he's special to *me*—and to Jazz and Gramma and a whole bunch of other people in Lahaina. But does that mean he has to be that important to the rest of the world? "What is this island going to do without him?"

"Are you *sure* he's going to go? Maybe he'll decide that fifteen minutes of fame are long enough."

I shrug, but of course Jazz can't see me, so I force myself to answer aloud. "I guess he could do that. But I have a feeling—I mean, when the producer at one of Nashville's hottest Christian music labels tells you to get your butt back in the studio ASAP..."

"You listen?" Jazz's words seep through the phone line and creep into my gut, forming a heavy weight.

"Exactly."

"Not if you're Brander."

"What do you mean?" I kick at a fallen seed pod as I turn a corner.

"Brander only listens to one voice. And that voice belongs to God."

"But—"

"No buts." Jazz's voice is bolstered with conviction. "Brander will only go back if that's what he feels *God* wants him to do." She sounds so sure of herself that I hate to contradict her, but...

"What if God *does* want Brander to move to Nashville?"

Maybe, if that's what Brander decides, that would be God's way of telling me *I* should move to the mainland too. After all, Harvard's a lot closer to Nashville than Hawaii is. Not that any of that should matter.

Jazz hums on the other line. "But how would him going to Nashville work anyway? He has to finish school."

"There are high schools in Nashville. And online programs. And tutors and—"

"Okay, okay. Forget I said anything."

I laugh, almost able to picture Jazz waving her arms in the air, begging me to shut up. "I guess I'm getting ahead of myself."

"Kind of."

"Sorry." A fresh breeze greets me as I turn onto Gramma's street, and I slow my pace. "It's hard to think about another goodbye."

Jazz doesn't offer anything else, and I walk in silence for a few moments, phone still pressed to my ear, listening to Jazz breathe—in and out.

"Listen, I'd better go." I shift my phone to the other hand as I reach Gramma's house. "But I think we both need to be praying, okay?"

"Praying, yeah—but what exactly for?"

"Wisdom. Wisdom for Brander...and for me. For all of us." It's tough to admit, but I know I need as much help as Brander does. Hopefully God will give both of us an answer—preferably the same one. But even if He doesn't—if He sends me off to Harvard and keeps Brander here in Maui—I know I have to do what He says.

I can only hope that I'm strong enough.

Chapter Twenty-Six

"Need to talk?" Gramma's trouble-radar must be super-sensitive today, because she sidles up to me as I finish clearing the dinner table and tucks her arm around my shoulders before giving me a squeeze. "You seem a little down."

"Gee, I wonder why." The words leave my tongue fizzing with a bitter aftertaste. "Life is so confusing right now, Grams."

"Want to talk about it?"

"Thanks, but I think this is something between me and God." And *Brander* and God, for that matter. But I can't control that.

Thankfully Gramma seems to take the hint. She shoos me away as she lowers the stack of dinner dishes into a sink full of bubbly dishwater, blowing me a kiss as I go.

I wander into the living room, the gentle rush of ocean waves murmuring through the open window and settle onto the couch.

"God, help me. I don't know what to do." I mouth my plea, but even though my words aren't audible, there's something comforting about forming each one with my tongue. "Everything is so jumbled, with Brander and me and Nashville and Harvard. And then there's Jazz, and she's struggling too. It's all a lot to handle. I need *help*."

I close my eyes and rest my head in my hands. Waiting. *Come on, God. Can't You come down in a whirlwind and talk to me like You did in Bible times?*

Then again, back in those days God always seemed to

speak more in riddles than in actual advice.

Even still, I stay curled up on the couch like a pill bug, eyes closed, ears open—but the only thing I hear is the gentle *hum-swoosh* of Gramma's ceiling fan.

Until...

"I know it's hard, but sometimes you have to be brave and take the first step on your own."

"Huh?" I suck in a quick breath, and my eyes fly open at the words of wisdom, but my breathing slows as soon as I catch sight of Macie, standing in the entryway to the living room, beckoning to her puppy.

"Is everything okay?" I crane my neck to get a better peek at the bundle of fluff—which, Macie informed us all tonight, has been officially named Zuzu—but all I can see is the pouf of gray fur on top of her head.

"Yep. She's being silly. Come on, Zuzu." Macie slaps her leg and tries to whistle, but it comes out sounding more like a raspberry. She frowns and screws up her face in concentration as she tries again.

A few more attempts leave her red-faced and panting, so I do my duty as an older sister, pursing my lips and letting out a sharp, shrill whistle.

Zuzu's ears perk up, and she trots farther into view, which is when I realize why she was so hesitant to step forward in the first place.

"Macie, is Zuzu wearing *doll shoes*?" I squint at the sparkly pink ballerina slippers tied around the mutt's front paws and clap my hand over my mouth to keep from laughing when Macie nods.

"I thought maybe she'd want to play dress-up." Macie shrugs, then motions to her own ensemble. In place of her shorts, she's wearing a fake grass skirt, plus a seashell tiara from one of Hawaii's favorite ABC variety stores and a pair of mismatched mermaid-patterned socks. "But maybe she'd rather have a snack." My little sister licks her lips. Could she possibly have forgotten that we ate dinner less than an hour ago?

"Maybe Zuzu would like to play fetch." The mutt yips as if in agreement, then lifts a paw and chews at the ballet slipper tied to it. Poor thing. "Go find something to throw for her, okay?"

"Does that mean dress-up's over?" Macie doesn't wait for an answer before untying her hula skirt and letting it drop to the floor. Without a moment's hesitation, she runs down the hall toward the staircase. "Let me get a fetch-ball!" she hollers before disappearing upstairs.

"Put some pants on too!" I yell back before turning to roll my eyes at Zuzu. The poor mutt whines and buries her snout in one ballet-slipper-clad paw, as though embarrassed for my little sister.

"Here. Let me help you." I reach for one of the dog's curly-haired legs and pluck at the haphazard pink bow around her—do dogs have ankles?

My fingers fumble with the slippery, satiny ribbon, and I've only succeeded in making the knot in the bow even tighter when Macie slides into the room, a pair of shorts in one hand, a puppy-sized tennis ball in the other.

"I got my pants!" She spins in a circle on the floor.

"Well put them *on*." I give the ribbon another tug, but that only laces it tighter around Zuzu's leg. She lets out a groan, and I reach out to pat her head. "Sorry, mutt. Let's try something different."

This time, I start from the bottom, trying to work the pup's paw out of the tight-fitting slipper. "That's a good girl." I try to make my voice smooth like the silky satin slipper as I wiggle the shoe, pulling a little bit at a time. "Not much longer now."

The dog groans again, deeper this time, and I pause in my work to give her ears another ruffle before turning to Macie. "Next time, Mace—" I give the shoe another tug—

"Don't go putting doll clothes on your dog. The proportions aren't—" Something pokes my hand. "Ouch!"

Another low groan—more like a growl this time around—rattles the air.

That's when I feel it again.

Except this time, it's more than a tiny jab. It feels like a full-on bite.

And it's wet and slobbery too.

I know what I'll see even before I look down, but I scream anyway when I catch sight of the pup's mouth clamped around the fleshy part of my palm.

"Get off!" I let out another shriek and jump to my feet, narrowly avoiding knocking Zuzu right in the nose—not that she doesn't deserve it.

"Everything okay in there?" Gramma steps around the kitchen counter, drying her hands on a dishtowel, and cranes her neck toward the living room.

"No." I jump onto the couch and scoot as far away from the dog as possible as Gramma walks over. "That bratty little mutt bit me."

"Nu-hu." Macie shakes her head, curls flip-flopping everywhere. "She'd never do that."

"Well she did." I show Gramma my hand, two miniature beads of blood forming below my thumb. True, I've gotten worse scratches from a cat before, but this is different. "That puppy's going to grow up into a vicious mutt like the rest of them."

Everything that happened with Koa was a fluke. I knew it.

My hand burns where the mutt's teeth pierced through my skin, but what hurts worse is the realization that I was right all along.

No matter how cute a puppy might seem, dogs are nothing but a menace.

"You'd better sign that mutt up for obedience classes." I

jump from the couch and run upstairs, stopping in the bathroom to spray my hand with antibacterial solution before diving into my room and throwing the door shut.

Hard.

I pitch myself onto my bed, tears burning my throat, my eyes, my nose, but I won't let myself cry—I'm stronger than that. At least I should be.

It's only a nip. Should be healed in a couple of days.

But the tears keep coming, and I can't help but wonder if I'm crying about something more than a puppy bite.

I roll over and stare up at the ceiling, tears tickling my cheeks as they stream down my face. My breath comes in short gasps, but try as I might, I can't steady my breathing.

Is *this* my sign?

Is this what I've been waiting for?

Or am I overthinking all of this?

But God could've let Zuzu bite me. To remind me that life here is turning into a one-hundred-percent mess. To remind me that there's still a chance to change my path. To pack up and move to a place where I can live in a nice, safe, dog-free dorm.

Where I can do what Dad wants and become the person I always thought I'd be.

Where I can make my mom proud.

Applications are due tomorrow, but I still have time.

I push myself up to a sitting position, then slide off the bed and tiptoe across the floor to my desk, as if drawn by invisible strings.

My silver laptop sits atop a pile of school books, twinkling in the glow from the streetlights pouring in through the window. Beckoning to me.

Something stirs in my chest as I sit down. Whether it's excitement or fear, I can't tell. Maybe it's both. Who knows?

What I *do* know is, for the first time in a long while, I know what I have to do.

My heart pounds in my ears as I log onto my computer and pull up the half-finished application.

What about Jazz? I cringe.

What about Gramma and Macie and Brander?

My heart pinches at the thought of saying more goodbyes. Especially since the words in my head sound suspiciously like something Mom would say. She always wanted me to make friends.

But no. Mom would want me at Harvard. The scholarship is in her name after all.

I pull up a new window and copy and paste my grade transcript into the required space in the application document, my stomach churning more and more with each tap of my finger.

What will Jazz think of this? Another person leaving her. And not just anyone, but her best friend.

And Gramma and Brander—will they *really* understand? I'm not even sure if I do.

My finger hovers over the backspace key, and my breathing grows even faster. Can this be right? After all I've been through on this island, how can I even consider leaving?

I drop my gaze to my lap, but I can't help catching a glimpse of the bite on my hand. *Was that You, God?*

I close my eyes and rest my head in my hands, the gentle creaking of Gramma's house settling down for the night echoing in my ears as I wait.

But it seems that God has gone silent once more.

I lift my head and brush hair out of my eyes. Maybe He's staying quiet now to test my faithfulness. Like Abraham and Isaac in the Old Testament—maybe I need to show Him I'm willing to do what it takes to do His will.

Even if it's hard.

And if this *isn't* what God wants from me?

I bring my hands to the keyboard once more and take a breath.

Maybe I don't have to worry about that right now. If God does have strong feelings about whether or not I should go to Harvard, He'll make it plenty clear which path I should take.

But until then, I guess I'd better keep working.

"Hey, Dad?" My voice is crackly with exhaustion when I call Dad later that night—at midnight, actually. I snuck downstairs as soon as Macie drifted off to dreamland, and I've been hard at work on the application ever since. But now I've reached the hardest part. The personal essay.

And I'm stuck.

The prompt wants me to write about my biggest inspiration, and it's obvious who I'll choose—no one inspires me more than Mom—but as for how I'll actually *write* the essay, I'm stumped.

"Olive." Dad's voice is still thick with sleep. I must have caught him before his alarm did. "What are you doing up? Tomorrow is a school—"

"I'm doing it." I take a deep breath, the admission filling my chest with a mix of hope and heartache. But then my gaze lands on the framed photo of Mom hanging in the hall, illuminated by the living-room lamp. Her eyes twinkle in the reflected light, and she smiles encouragingly at me.

Go for it, sweetheart.

"*What* are you doing?" Dad's voice, tinged with aggravation, breaks through my fog of hesitation.

"I'm going through with the application."

"You're..." There's a sharp intake of breath on the other line. "You are?"

Words catch in my throat, so I nod. But Dad can't see me of course, so I swallow hard and open my mouth. "I know it's short notice."

"I'll say. The deadline is tomorrow." Dad huffs.

"I *know*." My voice creeps up, and I wince. I've got to keep my voice low. No sense waking up Grams and Macie over what very well could turn out to be nothing. I might not even *get* the scholarship. I might finish too late to send it in. I might finish in time, then decide not to send it in after all. God could tell me I made a mistake—that I misheard him.

Or I could be leaving. Who knows?

"Olive?" Dad hums on the other line.

"Right. Sorry. I'm all done except for the essay. You said that you'd help me with that when I was ready."

"I assumed *ready* would be at a normal hour in the day. You know I don't endorse procrastination." There's distant clacking on Dad's end of the phone, like he's pulling something up on his computer. "But I suppose I can make an exception this time around. I have a few hours before my first class. Let's get to work."

My breath leaves me in a whoosh of relief. "Thanks, Dad. That means a lot to me."

"Of course. But what, may I ask, changed your mind? I was under the impression that you were going to let the whole thing slide."

"I think God finally spoke to me." Maybe. Will I ever know for sure if this is right? But how could it be wrong?

Dad feels good about this, and Mom would be thrilled. So what is there to be nervous about?

God, if this isn't right, You'd better speak up—and sooner, please, rather than later.

Dad coughs on the line, interrupting my prayer. "Are you ready?"

I sweep my hair over my shoulders, as if brushing aside my apprehension. "Ready." My breath catches on the word. I can almost see Dad, glasses on the end of his nose, a determined smile creasing his face. "Are you?"

"Absolutely. And we don't have much time. Let's get going."

Chapter Twenty-Seven

"UH-OH. WHAT'D YOU DO?" JAZZ'S EYES flicker to life the second I answer the door Monday morning, and I duck my head.

"What do you mean?" I fix my eyes on Jazz's bare feet and choke back a yawn. Maybe if I can keep from meeting her gaze, Jazz won't see the dark circles under my eyes until I'm ready to tell her about my decision

Somehow, I ended up finishing the entire application last night—this morning, actually. It was after four o'clock before I finally sent the whole thing off and tumbled into bed, but it was worth it. Dad was thrilled, of course. Mom would've been too. If she was...here.

The thought of Mom smiling down on me soothes my tiredness as I hold the door open wide for Jazz to come in.

"You look like you got hit by a truck." Jazz's words are machete sharp as she tromps inside. Guess eight o'clock is too early for tact. "Is this about Brander and the record deal?"

"No."

"Then what's up?" Jazz casts her gaze over me as we get settled in the living room. "Is everything okay with Tutu? Macie?"

I nod.

"Then what gives?" Jazz bounces on the couch cushion, her wide eyes giving her the appearance of a too-curious cat.

And we all know what curiosity did to that poor cat.

I open my mouth to offer a watered-down explanation that's more about Macie's maniac puppy then my decision to send in the application, but the words escape me, leaving my throat rough and dry.

"It's the application, isn't it?" Jazz's eyes turn to silver dollars. "Did you decide to send it in after all?"

Something in Jazz's voice sends a trickle of guilt down my spine, but I shrug it off and nod. "There's nothing wrong with exploring my options. And Harvard is a good one."

"But—" Jazz snaps her mouth shut. Tugs on her braid. "What made you decide?"

I tell her about my prayers for myself *and* Brander, then about the drama with Macie's puppy. About how excited Dad was when I told him I'd decided to go through with it after all. How I know my choice will make Mom proud.

"Olive, your mom is *dead.*" Jazz's words slice through my heart and I wince. *Definitely* too early for tact. "And if she was alive, do you think this is what she'd want? To see you run away because life here isn't picture-perfect?"

"I'm not running away. Mom went to Harvard, and she knew it was my dream school." Somehow, in the bright light of morning, that sounds like an awfully flimsy excuse.

"So? You know God has a different plan for each one of us. Unless you've always happened to miss church on the weeks they give that sermon." Jazz's feathery eyebrows bristle before her face freezes over completely. "You had one bad night—week, month, whatever. Does that mean you should give up?"

"Maybe—"

"Nope." Jazz tosses her head, her braid flying out to hit the back of the couch. "It doesn't work that way. If I'd decided to give up on everything when life got hard, I'd be dead."

My mouth flies open, but Jazz fixes me with a look that stops any words from escaping me.

"Olive Galloway, I love you to death. You're the best friend I've ever had." Jazz draws in a shuddery breath. "If

God wants you to go to Boston to chase your dreams, then I'm all for it. But I think this sounds like you're taking the easy way out of a tough situation. And I don't like it one bit."

I open and close my mouth a good half-dozen times, feeling strangely like a floundering fish. This is a Jazz I've never seen before. I don't know whether to be impressed or terrified.

"I don't know what to say, Jazz. The application's already been sent in." I raise my arms, as if in defeat. Because, much as my pride hates to admit it, she has a point. A good one. "What do you *want* me to say?"

Jazz's gaze grows even colder, if such a thing is possible. "I don't want you to say anything. To me. But I think you'd better spend a whole lot more time talking to God unless you want to end up making a decision you're going to regret."

The rest of the day passes at the pace of an overweight sea slug. By the time Gramma brings Macie home from school and Ruby swings by to pick Jazz up, it feels like it should be midnight. At least.

Part of me wants to call Brander and tell him all about the puppy, my decision, and Jazz's reaction. I wonder if *he* thinks I heard right. But another part of me...

Another part of me yawns. Big and loud and long.

The world beyond Gramma's big front porch—a world of sand and sun and surf and the clouds hanging over the outlying islands—shimmers before me, and my eyelids grow heavy as I relax into the warm, fuzzy embrace of a doze.

In this half-awake trance, I can see Mom as clear as day, beaming at my accomplishments. "I'm so proud of you."

It's almost like she's right here next to me, whispering those words in my ear.

"Proud of your choice...Jazz and Brander..." Though they're delivered in my mom's own crystal-bell tone, the words are fuzzy.

Like I can almost hear, almost understand.

But not quite.

What are you saying, Mom? The voice in my head is screaming, begging to be let out. To talk to my mom face to face. But it's like my mouth is wired shut. I can't speak. All I can do is listen.

"You don't need to say your words out loud for me to understand, Olive. I'm your mom...I can see straight through to your heart. Just like Jesus can."

And then, as suddenly as she was here, Mom is gone. Vanished. And now all I can see is Jazz—her eyes ice cold like they were today—and Brander, his cowlick drooping. I try to say something, assure them everything will work out, but still the words refuse to come.

I swallow hard to try again, but before I can even open my mouth, Jazz and Brander are gone. Vanished. And I'm left all alone, waiting for something—but I don't know what.

If this is a dream, it's one of the weirdest I've ever had. And if it's not...I don't get this—any of this.

Please, God, let me understand.

"Are you okay?" A few minutes—hours?—later, Macie climbs onto the couch next to me and buries her head in my arm. "Were you sleeping?"

"Just daydreaming," I reply, but my voice is crackly. Maybe I did fall asleep after all. "How was school?"

Macie shrugs and grabs my hand, squinting as she inspects the spot where I got bit last night. "There isn't any blood."

"It wasn't a very bad bite." I stare down at my palm. If I

didn't know better, I'd never be able to tell that I'd gotten nipped the night before. "I guess I'll always be a baby when it comes to dogs."

The corners of Macie's mouth droop, and even her peppy curls seem to sag. "I wanted you to get along. Zuzu doesn't like being locked in the backyard all day. She wants to play with the neighbor's dog, but Grammy says she can't until we give her all her shots."

"I'm sorry, Mace. I wanted us to get along too." I stroke Macie's hair with my good hand, and she nestles deeper into me. Like I used to do with Mom. A strange warmth fills my chest at that thought, but it's only there a moment before it turns into a deep, sharp ache.

One reminding me that, once I head off for the mainland this fall, moments like these between me and Macie will be few and far between.

"Do you think you could give her another chance?" Macie tugs on my arm, her grip surprisingly firm. "It's hot outside. Zuzu wants to come inside and sit under the fan. And she wants to give you an I'm-sorry kiss."

"She does?" My insides quiver at the thought of letting that mutt's mouth come anywhere near me, but I nod anyway. After all, the little mutt isn't going anywhere. I've got to make peace with her at some point. "I guess I could let her do that."

"For real?" Macie clasps her hands over her chest.

"Sure." After all, how afraid am I of that nippy little mutt? Not too much, considering all the other stuff I have to worry about.

Stuff like college and God's plan and...

Saying goodbye.

"I'm coming, Zuzu!" Macie jumps up to rescue her pup, accidentally kicking my shin as she lands on the floor, but I barely flinch. I'm too numb, struggling against the waves made by my own decision last night.

My heart hums, as though overpowered by the realization of all I'll lose when I leave this place. A ray of light creeps over the couch, coming to rest on me, and a lump rises in my throat.

I'll miss this crazy island, where it's summer even in February.

I'll miss the people at church.

I'll miss Gramma and Jazz and—

My pocket buzzes.

Brander. The name on the screen brings a smile to my face despite the unease whirling in my mind, and I tap to answer the call.

"Hey." My voice cracks as the word comes out. "What're you up to?"

"Thinking hard about a lot of things." Brander chuckles, but his tone is heavy, like he's bearing the weight of the world on his vocal chords. "How are you?"

"Pretty good." The fib rolls off my tongue all too easily. If I was Pinocchio, my nose would stretch all the way from here to Kaanapali Beach. I should know better—I do, actually. "Let me say that again. I still have no idea what I'm going to end up doing with myself, but I did send in the application. Stayed up all night to do it, too."

"Oh." Brander's voice falls flat on that word. "Okay. What changed your mind?"

"God did." That answer sounds more and more fishy every time I use it. Was it God who spoke to me, or was it— you know—*me*?

"Hmm." I can almost see Brander stroking his cowlick, lost in thought, but before he can say anything else, a buzz comes through from his end of the phone.

"What was that?"

"Someone's beeping in. Give me a sec."

"Okay." I drum my fingers atop my knee and watch the palm trees outside sway as I wait.

"Sorry about that." Brander's voice sounds even duller when he finally comes back on the line. "That was Mike. He's all worked up and wants me to call him right back. Can we talk later?"

"Yeah." My heart deflates a little, though I can't blame Brander for wanting to talk to Mike. It must be exciting to have the head of one of Christian music's biggest record labels begging to talk to you. "Call me later?"

"Actually, I was thinking we could get together tomorrow. Go somewhere fun, talk in person instead of on the phone."

"That'd be great." We firm up the details, and Brander wishes me good night before we hang up.

And then my phone buzzes. Guess I'm popular tonight.

"Olive?" Dad's voice is clear and strong on the other end. "How are you?"

"Great." I throw as much optimism into my voice as I can. "Thanks for all your help last night. It meant a lot to me."

"It meant a lot to *me*." Dad's voice grows strangely thick. "Of course, your mother would've been a better one to help you—she was the family wordsmith after all. Olive...she would have been so proud."

"You think so?" A smile tickles my lips. For a moment— just a moment—I lose sight of everything I'll lose when I leave this place and all I can think of is Mom, beaming down at me from Heaven. Maybe Grandpa's standing up there with her right now.

"Have you told your grandmother yet about your decision?" Dad's voice chases away the vision of Mom, and my own smile fades a bit as reality sinks in again.

"Not yet. She's been at the gallery all day, and now she's making dinner." Though, knowing her *Tutu*'s intuition, she probably figured it out for herself the second she saw my bleary eyes across the breakfast bar this morning.

"Oh." A brisk breeze blows over Dad's tone. Like my reluctance to share my decision with Grams is a hint that I'm having second thoughts.

"I told Jazz, though. First thing this morning." Actually, she pried it out of me, but still...

"Was she excited?"

"You could say that." *But not in the way you're thinking.* I bite my lip. "But it'll be a big adjustment for her. Like it will be for me."

"An adjustment? Of course. But there are webcams and postcards and messaging apps. You two can talk whenever you want. Besides, you'll be so busy you'll barely have time to think about her."

I flinch at those words. Even if they are true, there's not a chance in the world that Jazz won't miss *me.* But Dad's too far gone for me to argue with him.

Instead, he spends a good hour telling me all about the classes I can take in the fall. Psych 101, advanced bio, and a bunch of other courses that he's sure I'll love. And maybe I will. But none of them—not even any of the literature classes—sound like enough to keep me from missing *here.*

By the time I get off the phone and wash up for dinner, my head is spinning.

If Gramma notices I'm feeling off, she doesn't let on. She simply offers her usual soft, sweet smile as I slide into my chair and asks Macie to pray for the food before we dig in.

"Anything exciting happen today?" Gramma asks us both the question, but her gaze is dead set on me as she spoons a helping of deli-made chicken curry salad— Foodland's finest—onto my plate.

I shove a forkful into my mouth and chew as long as possible to keep from answering. Thankfully Macie quickly comes up with a story of her own to tell, and I'm off the hook.

It's not that I don't want to tell Grams about the application, but if it's going to upset her as much as it upset

Jazz, I'd rather spare her the heartache.

At least for a little while.

Until I double-check with God and make sure this whole thing *is* His will after all.

Chapter Twenty-Eight

"YOU'RE IN FOR A TREAT TODAY." Brander's smile is brighter than I've seen in a long time when he shows up on the front porch Tuesday afternoon, and he ushers me into his car with a gentle touch to my arm.

"What do you mean? Aren't we going to the Shave Ice Shack?" I relax into the soft leather seat of Brander's Porsche, and the wind plays with tendrils of my hair as Brander hops into the driver's seat.

"Nope." Light winks in the corners of his chocolatey, almond-shaped eyes as he pulls away from the curb. "Have you had a Hawaiian donut yet?"

"No." The word *donut* makes my mouth water. "I can't remember the last time I had a donut, actually."

"Then you're in for a real treat. Hawaii does donuts better than anywhere else."

"Really?" I roll an elastic off my wrist and throw my hair into a ponytail as Brander zips down the road toward Front Street.

"Really. They're so good they barely even deserve to be called donuts."

"They're not, like, filled with poi or anything. Are they?" I shudder at the thought of poi, a wobbly, gelatinized version of mashed potatoes—if you consider a taro root to be anything like a potato. Which I don't.

"Wait and see." Brander laughs, then turns his head toward me, the corners of his mouth quirked up.

I return the smile before Brander turns his gaze on the road, and for a moment everything in the world feels *right*.

The wind whistles in my ears as we drive down the road, the ocean flying by on my right, Brander on my left, bobbing his head to the beat of the song on the radio. When we pull onto Front Street, though, he presses a button, and the radio goes silent. Brander turns to face me again. "You know...I need to tell you something." He pulls into a parking place and puts the car in park before reaching over to squeeze my hand. "I'm sorry."

"Huh?" I laugh and shake his hand off. "Where did that come from?"

He shrugs. "I was thinking about you leaving—about how much I'll miss you. And how I let you down."

"Let me down? How?"

"With the calendar. By now, we were supposed to have watched the sunrise at Haleakala *and* driven the road to Hana. I haven't been a good friend lately. And I'm sorry."

"Whoa, quit it." This time, *I* grab Brander's hand—even if he does have a girlfriend hidden somewhere back in Nashville, I can't let him struggle alone. "I don't care about the calendar. I care about *you*. You're not usually so..."

"Distant? Reclusive? I guess you're right." He scoffs, and I flinch. Brander isn't the scoffing type—that's always been my job.

But maybe it's finally time for me to step things up and be a friend to Brander instead of expecting him to swoop in and save me from my own problems.

"Don't be so hard on yourself. You've had a lot going on, and it's been a big adjustment for all of us."

"I guess."

"And I'm here to talk." I give his hand one last squeeze before letting go. "If you want to, I mean."

"Yeah. I do." He opens his car door and jumps outside, then motions for me to do the same. "Let's go."

I follow him as he leads the way down Front Street to a tiny stand across the road from a strange, scrubby-looking forest.

"That's the Great Banyan Tree." Brander must catch me staring at the misplaced jungle. "Haven't you seen it before?"

I shrug. "I guess I've never paid much attention to it."

Brander smiles. "People come here from all over to see it—it's the most famous tree on Maui."

I take another look at the tree as we get in line at the donut stand. The most famous tree on Maui, and it's not even a palm tree. Just a crazy thing with enough trunks and hanging branches to make it look like something out of a Tarzan movie.

I examine the banyan tree a moment longer, then turn and crane my neck to see inside the little donut stand. It's similar to the Shave Ice Shack, except even smaller. But the line's almost twice as long. A few people elbow each other and point at Brander. I shuffle my feet, growing warm from more than the sunshine blazing overhead. "So, now that we're here, are you going to tell me what's so special about a Hawaiian donut?"

"It's a surprise. Wait and see."

Thankfully I don't have too long to wait—the line moves fast, and soon Brander is placing an order for two strawberry lemonades and half a dozen donuts, except he calls them something else. *Malasadas.*

"What's a malasada? And why did you order half a dozen of them?" I shake my head at Brander as we move to the side to wait for our order.

"A malasada is what every donut wishes it could be." Brander swallows hard, as if he can already taste the sweet pastry. "And trust me. You'll wish we'd ordered twice as many."

By the time we collect our drinks and a bright yellow, grease-spotted bag from the stand, my stomach is growling and I'm dying for a peek at these famous malasadas.

Brander leads me past the banyan tree before motioning

for us to sit on the seawall. I tuck my dress under me and settle down next to him, letting my legs dangle above the surf.

"Here you go." He reaches into the bag and hands me a malasada—a strange, uneven dough ball crusted with sugar. "Cheers." He lifts his own in the air and bumps it against mine before taking a bite.

I do the same, then close my eyes and tilt back my head. "That's good." I take another bite, bigger this time, and groan as the crackly sugar crust gives way to the delicious doughiness of the malasada. I finish it in another few bites. "That's *really* good."

"I thought you'd like it." Brander wipes a bit of sugar from his chin before taking another bite. "They also come with fillings—coconut, guava, that kind of thing—but I like them best as is."

"I don't blame you." I take a sip of lemonade. "Thanks for this. It feels good to get out."

"Yeah" Brander ducks his head and fiddles with his paper straw.

I stare out at the water, at the glimmering crystalline blue waves and the palm trees that run down to meet the shore at the north end of Front Street. It's beautiful—perfect, even. I might have grown up by the Massachusetts Bay, but I never knew the ocean could be so blue until I came here.

The thought of going back to seeing a gray harbor instead of these magical waters makes my stomach twist. Keeping my eyes fixed on the ocean, I grab another malasada and nibble on it, letting the sugar sweeten my mood.

But even a malasada isn't enough to keep my mind off of everything that's going on with Brander and me. We haven't had much time to talk lately, and I need to know where he's at. "Have you decided about the record deal yet?"

I must catch Brander mid-swallow, because he hiccups, then coughs like he has something down the wrong pipe.

"Sorry." I thunk him on the back a few times to get him to stop, but he keeps on sputtering like a dying boat motor. "Good grief. I didn't mean to startle you."

"It's okay." He sets down his half-eaten malasada and turns toward me. "And no. I haven't decided. I keep praying about it, but I don't feel like I hear anything. Part of me wonders…"

"What?"

"I don't know. But I'm starting to think that God wants me to make the right decision on my own."

"How does that work? Isn't God supposed to tell you what the right decision even is?"

"Sometimes." Brander tilts his head to the side, as though wondering how to explain things to me so they'll make sense. Am I seriously that dense? Maybe so. "Other times, I think God allows us to exercise free will. He didn't create us to sit around, waiting for Him to pull some sort of heavenly strings that will put us all in the right place at the right time. He wants us to study the Bible and use it to help us decide which way we should go."

"Okay." I nod, like I get what Brander's saying. And to some degree, I do. "But isn't that a lot of responsibility for God to put on us humans? I mean, I have a hard time deciding what shave ice flavor to get, let alone what to do with my life."

Brander cracks a smile. "I didn't say it was easy, but each decision we make is an opportunity for God to grow our faith in indescribable ways."

"Let me guess. Gramma taught you that."

"I'm telling you. Your *tutu* is smarter than she looks."

"True." A supersized wave crops up and crashes onto the seawall, dousing my legs with saltwater. "But about the Nashville thing. If God isn't going to come down and tell you what to do, then what *are* you going to do?"

"I don't know. I thought I did." He shrugs. "Now I'm not sure. I need to make a decision soon though, or else it won't be mine to make."

"What do you mean?"

"Since I've been gone, Mike's started hounding my parents, reminding them what a great opportunity this is for me. If I don't decide something soon, I'm afraid my parents will *make* me go back."

"Seriously?"

"Yeah. Mike could convince half the people on the island to buy a parka. He's a good talker and an even better salesman. And I've heard enough of my parents' side of the conversation to know that he has them hooked on the idea. Not that he doesn't have a point. After all, there aren't many people who get an opportunity like this."

"True." Another wave splashes up, and a seabird cries overhead as I take a drink of lemonade. "Can I give you my two cents?"

"Please."

"For someone who has a bright and glorious future waiting for them in Nashville, you don't seem too excited about it. If you're that afraid that your parents will *make* you go back...then I don't think you should."

Brander stares down at his hands, calloused fingers knotted together, and gnaws on his lip. "Can I tell you something?"

"You can tell me anything." My hand twitches, and it's all I can do to keep from reaching out to give him a hug. A few months ago, I probably would've, but now that he's semi-famous, something about it feels wrong. Like I should ask permission first or something. And that seems even stranger than just hugging him in the first place. So, instead, I pop the rest of the malasada in my mouth and reach for another.

Brander hasn't even opened his mouth to talk, though, when a squeal rings out from behind me. "Aloha guys!" Brander and I turn in time to watch Malia jog halfway across the grassy oceanside park and plop down on Brander's other side, almost squashing the rest of our malasadas. "What's up?" She pushes her sunglasses onto her head. "Brander, I'm surprised you aren't, like, swarmed by fans. Everyone keeps looking over at you."

"Rats." Brander ducks his head. "I was hoping people were starting to get over it."

"Not a chance." Malia swings her legs over the surf. "Why would you want them to forget about you, anyway?"

"Because there's nothing special about me to begin with." Brander twirls his straw around in his lemonade. "Besides, I'd rather stay quiet and enjoy the view. And the malasadas."

"Malasadas?" Malia wrinkles her nose like *malasadas* is a dirty word. "Better watch out or they'll head right for your hips." She juts her chin in the direction of my third donut.

And then—just to torque her—I lift it to my mouth, take the biggest bite I can, and chew, making *mmm-mmm* noises the entire time. "Want a bite?" I ask once I've swallowed.

Malia's eyes practically jump out of their sockets. "You're crazy." She spits the words in my direction before scooting closer to Brander, her arm almost brushing his. "I meant Olive, of course. She should know by now that I shouldn't eat anything like that if I want to stay in shape for swim team."

Brander chuckles nervously and scoots across the seawall too. *Away* from Malia. "Is the swim team headed to state this year?"

"Of course." Malia prattles on for a minute about their last meet. "Coach says I could get a full-ride scholarship next year if I practice hard over the summer. But that's pretty boring compared to everything you've got going on.

Hey, when you were over in Nashville, did you meet any of the big stars?"

Brander politely offers a CliffsNotes version of the celebrities he's spotted in Nashville—all of them very recognizable names—and Malia practically falls at his feet.

"Did you ever actually talk to any of them?" Her voice is hushed, almost awed—like she can hardly stand the excitement of being in the presence of someone who was in the same room as a handful of Grammy nominees.

Brander goes on to tell her about a run-in he had with a particularly rude country artist, and Malia hangs on his every word. When he's done, she laughs extra-long, and my stomach twists. This girl seriously needs to get a grip soon, or I'm afraid Brander will get used to her fawning.

"That is *so* cool," she says for what must be the millionth time. "It must be so cool to be famous."

Brander smiles, like Malia's kidding, but I have a sinking suspicion that she's all too serious.

There's something deeper in her gaze too. Something she doesn't offer aloud, but something that makes me raise my eyebrows all the same. Her hand drifts to her pants pocket, and she hesitates one long moment, mouth half-open, before jumping to her feet and waving. "Nice talk, you two, but I've gotta go. See ya around?"

She barely waits for me and Brander to smile and nod before she takes off in a jog, one hand in her pocket, long legs carrying her across the park in only a handful of strides.

I lift my lemonade glass to my mouth and take a long drink. "You actually met all those people?"

"Yeah." Brander's brow creases. "But it doesn't matter. They're like you said—*people.* No one special."

"Right." I press my fingertips to my temples. If only I could get Malia's words out of my ears. Words that remind me that Brander is not only my friend, but also a *star.*

"Before Malia showed up...you were going to tell me something?"

"Right." Brander takes a deep breath, as if bracing himself for the words he's about to speak.

That picture—the one everyone else thought was fake—flashes into my mind, and my heart twists. What if Brander's whole point with this is to tell me that he's otherwise attached? That we can't be friends anymore?

But if so, why would he bother getting me a lemonade? He could've dropped the bombshell on Gramma's front porch and run off. Or put it up on Instagram for the world to see, for that matter.

"Do you remember that guy at the airport when I flew in?"

"From the West Maui Sun?" I shudder. "He didn't put out a bad article about you or anything. Did he?"

Brander laughs. "No. But he's a lot like the paparazzi in Nashville." He clamps his mouth shut, almost as though cutting himself off. "This isn't coming out right."

"It's okay. Just say it however you need to."

"Fine." Brander lets out a massive breath. "When I was on tour, I spent some time during intermission praying with people. I'd invite anyone in the audience who needed prayer to come up to the stage."

"That's nice of you."

"Thanks." Brander smiles, but it seems awfully feeble. "Usually the guys backing me up stayed and prayed for people too, but I was doing an acoustic gig one night, so I went down by myself. This girl came up, and..."

This is it. He's going to tell me to back off. We're done being friends. I never should've given him that Valentine. What was I thinking? And why on earth did he take this long to tell me?

"Olive?" Brander waves a hand in front of my face. "Did you get all that?"

"Yeah." My voice catches, and I blush even harder. Brander and I never even went on an official date. Why does this hurt so bad?

Maybe because he's one of my closest friends.

Ever.

"I get it. It'll be hard keeping my distance, but I know you need to be loyal. I'll still be cheering you on, though. From afar."

"Afar? No, no, no." Brander reaches out to grab my shoulders. "I'm explaining this all wrong."

"Huh?"

He releases his grasp on me and brings his hands back to cover his face. "I knew I should've put this in a letter."

"No. I get it. Honest." It's tearing me up inside, but I do understand. If I was his girlfriend, I'd hate the thought of him hanging out with some other girl. Especially a girl who gives him Valentines.

"It's not that we can't hang out anymore, but I have to be more careful. Mike doesn't want the paparazzi to make any more sensation stories out of me for a long time—forever, ideally."

"No, I totally...wait." I blink at him. "Sensation stories?"

"Weren't you listening?" Brander tilts his head back and groans.

"Not much, I guess. But I know this is about your girlfriend. I totally—"

"Girlfriend? No! You weren't listening, were you?"

"Maybe you'd better say it all again. Just to be safe."

"The girl wanted to ask Jesus into her heart for the first time. I prayed with her, but it was super loud in the room, so I leaned in close for her to hear better. Someone must've been watching, and they snapped a photo at a bad time. It showed up on a couple of gossip sites. Not enough to make it a big deal, but it got Mike on high alert. He wants me to be more careful about the paparazzi from here on out."

Relief bubbles up in my chest, and I laugh. "You mean you're not seeing someone in Nashville?"

"What? No! Why would you think I was? I took you out on Valentine's Day, after all." His cheeks flush red. "Not like that was a date or anything but still..."

"Yeah. Right." My feeling of relief dissolves into the realization that I am the world's biggest idiot. Why didn't I trust that Grams and Jazz knew what they were talking about? They've known Brander a million times longer than I have anyway.

"You seriously thought I was dating someone in Nashville?"

"Yeah." I open my mouth to say more, but I can't quite make myself admit that I was checking him out on a bunch of dumb gossip sites. Plus, he probably can figure out that much from the look on my face. "I guess it was kind of a stupid thought, huh?"

"For sure. The only reason I even told you about the girl is because I don't want you to think I'm avoiding you. Sometimes I might not look like myself."

"Like when we picked you up at the airport?"

Brander nods. "Mike's being pretty OCD right now. He doesn't want the press to catch so much as a glimpse of me, let alone spin anything the wrong way."

"That's fine." I take a breath of sea air, holding it in a second longer than usual. "I understand."

"You do?"

"Of course." I reach out to squeeze his hand, to make sure he gets it, then freeze. "Guess I shouldn't do that, huh?"

"Not here. But maybe when we get to Tutu's house, I could give you a hug?" He lowers his eyes. "That sounded weird. Didn't it?"

"Not to me." I stand and brush sugar from my fingers. "We're friends. Good friends. And friends hug."

"Yeah." A smile reappears on Brander's face. "They do."

Chapter Twenty-Nine

I CAN STILL HALF-FEEL BRANDER'S warm, strong arms around me as Jazz and I walk to youth group the next evening, and the sensation makes me smile. There's something about a hug—especially one from someone like Brander—that can convince a person that all is right in the world.

"I told you it was fake." Jazz laughs at me when I finish telling her the whole story. "Did you honestly think Brander would fall in love with someone he barely knows? In Nashville?"

"What was I to think when every teen magazine in the US ran with the story?" I kick at a half-flattened seed pod on the sidewalk. "It's terrible that Brander has to deal with stuff like that. Why can't he live his life like a normal person?"

Jazz shrugs. "Guess it comes with the territory."

"Then maybe he's in the wrong territory."

Jazz twines the tail of her braid around her finger. "I've been praying super hard that he'll make the right choice." She doesn't need to say it out loud for me to know—the *right choice* is for Brander to stay *right here.*

"I've been praying for you too." Jazz turns her head to the side, as if to admire the rose-tinted evening sky, but I have a feeling her main goal is to avoid meeting my gaze. "I know you don't believe me, but I think God wants you to stay in Lahaina. At least, *I* want you here."

"I know." I pluck a stray plumeria as we pass by a bush loaded with the sweet-smelling blooms and breathe in deep before handing the flower to Jazz. "Part of me wants to stay here too."

"Then *stay*." Jazz lifts the flower to her nose. "I don't get why you're making this so complicated."

I fish around in my sea of thought for a concrete answer, catching a whiff of plumeria as Jazz tucks it into her braid. Suddenly I'm six years old and wrapped in Mom's arms, breathing in her sweet-smelling perfume. Hearing her voice when I told her I was one of the first kids in my class to read aloud for the teacher.

I'm so proud of you.

How often did I long to hear those words? To know that what I did was enough.

Maybe that's it—why this whole choice is as hard for me as it is.

"I want to make my mom proud. She went to Harvard, and Dad started this scholarship in honor of her. It would be a slap in both their faces for me to reject it."

Jazz crinkles her nose. "So you'd rather go off and live a life you don't even want? Just to make them proud?"

"Maybe I do want it and I'm scared. That night Zuzu bit me, I was sure I knew what God wanted me to do." I catch another hint of plumeria from Jazz's braid, but the flower's calming sweetness is turning bitter—it reminds me of too much.

Too much joy.

Too much heartache.

Too many memories—memories made, memories forgotten, and memories I wish I could forget.

"Why do you think God wants you in Boston?" Jazz's words soar through the air and burst open right in my face.

"Um, I don't know." And that's the honest truth. I don't know—because I haven't asked. Sure, I've asked God where I should go and what I should, but have I ever asked Him *why*?

When I came here last summer, all I *could* do was ask God why—why He had to take Mom, why He wanted me here, why I couldn't go to Boston. And He answered me. He brought me Jazz and Brander. He helped me discover a place—an *ohana*—where I belonged.

But now I have to make the biggest decision of my life, and I've been going about it all wrong.

Why I can't tell Jazz is beyond me, but instead my own stupid pride heaps a half-baked, half-true answer on the tip of my tongue. It tumbles out before I can stop to think twice.

"God has to want me in Boston. Why else would everything happen the way it did? I mean, would things here be such a mess if He wasn't telling me I need to take this opportunity?"

Jazz tilts her head to the side. "For one, I'm having an awfully hard time seeing how things are 'such a mess.'" She lifts her hand to make air quotes. "Sure, Malia's being a pain—what's new? And your sister got a harmless little puppy. What else?"

What else? Um...

Thankfully Jazz opens her mouth before I have to respond. "Even if life here is as hard as you say, why would God want you to run from it? Wouldn't He rather have you stick it out and see things through?"

"Then why did I hear—"

"I don't know what you heard. Or if you heard anything other than a few runaway thoughts in your own head." Jazz keeps her gaze focused on the path ahead. "But that's what I think. You're making way too big a deal out of nothing, especially when there are real problems on this island that don't involve Olive Galloway."

Uh-oh. "Is something wrong?"

"No."

"Could've fooled me."

"Okay, fine." Jazz lowers her voice as we turn another corner. The church pavilion comes into view at the end of the road. "Mom gets out of rehab on Saturday."

"What? Seriously?"

Jazz nods. "Ruby told me this afternoon."

"Nice of her to give you advance notice."

"It's best this way. I'd rather not have it hanging over my head any longer than necessary. Mom's going to be staying at Ruby's, and I'm afraid she'll laugh in my face the first time I take off to go paddleboarding with Malia."

"She wouldn't do that. She couldn't."

"You don't know my mom." Jazz wags her head from side to side. "She's not like a real mom. She has no problem calling things exactly the way she sees them."

"Then she should be proud of you. You're doing something many two-legged people aren't strong enough to do. Myself included."

Jazz shrugs. "She doesn't see it that way. As far as I've ever heard her say, I'm an idiot." She slows her pace as we draw nearer to the church. "Maybe I am."

"You are not." I sling a protective arm around her waist. "You're the strongest, bravest person I know. And if your mom can't see that, then she's a fool."

"I agree." A voice comes from behind, and I turn to find Malia walking behind us, smiling and flashing a *shaka* like eavesdropping on private, personal conversations is a perfectly natural thing for her to do. I open my mouth to tell Malia to mind her own business, but she cuts me off. "You won't hear me admit this very often, but Olive's right. You're amazing, Jazz. If your mom doesn't think so, then *she's* the idiot." Malia slings her arm around Jazz too and squeezes tight.

I nearly trip over my own feet as I stare at this strange person that looks like Malia and sounds like Malia yet is acting nothing like the Malia I know. She must catch me gawking, because she angles her face toward me and offers a strange, close-mouthed smile. "Why're you looking at me like that? I'm not all bad." A wicked gleam floods her eyes.

"Just mostly."

A laugh slips out before I can stop myself, and I return Malia's smile, though mine feels a little stiff. "I never said you were."

"You don't have to use words to get your point across." Malia's smile deepens until it's almost...genuine. If not for her over-the-top fangirling lately, I'd think the stuff Jonah's been preaching at youth group was starting to break through.

Jazz squints at Malia and me. "You two are acting super weird."

"We are?" Malia and I say it at the same time, and it's enough to break the tension altogether. The two of us lock eyes and laugh, and in that moment a flicker of forgiveness lightens my heart. Malia can't help it if she's clueless, over-the-top, and more than a bit starstruck. But what if, somewhere deep inside, she wants to be a true friend? To change?

Maybe all she needs is someone to show her how that's done—and I can't think of someone more experienced than yours truly.

"Hey!" Malia perks up, and every part of her seems to go into fangirl mode as soon as we help Jazz up the final step to the church pavilion. "Brander's here."

"Sure enough." I follow Malia's gaze to where Brander is talking to a group of giggling younger girls and absently running his fingers over his guitar strings.

"Is he doing worship tonight?" Malia seems to take an extra-long stare at Brander before turning to Jazz and me.

Jazz shrugs. "He didn't mention it to me."

"Yeah, I thought he'd still be hiding out." A bit of my good mood fizzles as Malia takes a good look at Brander.

"I'm going to say hi." Malia takes a step toward Brander, then stops. She turns and motions for Jazz and me to come closer. "Can I ask you something real quick? It's kind of embarrassing."

"Sure." Jazz hooks her arm through mine and pulls me forward.

"You guys know Brander so much better than I do. I was wondering...do you have any idea how he'd react to something?"

Jazz shrug. "Depends on what the something is."

Malia dips her chin. "I've been wanting to ask him ever since we saw him at the airport, but I don't want to be a total dork. See, my little sister has this huge obsession with Brander. Like, huge. She thinks he's the best thing that happened to this island since shave ice."

Must run in the family.

Malia's cheeks flush a sunset red, almost as if she heard me. She lowers her head even more, letting her silken hair fall over her face in a cascading waterfall. "I know I've been acting all starstruck lately, but the thing is, I need to get this signed." Malia whips out a copy of the photo she took that day at the airport.

"You *need* it signed? Why? I mean, that's a bit much, isn't it?" The words leap out before I can stop them, and I'm met with a jab in my side from Jazz's elbow before I can even close my mouth.

Malia stares at me for one painful second, eyes wide, something whirling beneath her gaze. *Uh-oh.*

Jazz squares her shoulders, as though preparing for battle.

And then...

Malia laughs.

The sound of it is enough to make me join in. We stand there giggling at each other with Jazz looking at us like our coconuts have both officially cracked. Which maybe they have, seeing as I don't even know what exactly I'm laughing about.

"What's going on?" Jazz steps back and stares at us, eyebrow crooked. "I don't get it."

"Me neither." I let one more giggle slip out.

Malia rolls her eyes. "I'm more than happy to explain, but not here. It's kind of—"

A chord strums over the loudspeaker, and Malia snaps her mouth shut as Brander steps up to the microphone. "Aloha everyone."

Shouts of "*e komo mai*"—*welcome*—and "Brander *no ka oi*"—*Brander's the best*, I think that means—fill the pavilion and spill out onto the beach beyond. Brander ducks his head, cowlick bobbing.

"Mahalo, you guys. Thank you. I've missed this—a lot." Brander shuffles his feet. "I know a lot has changed since the last time I was up here, but tonight I want to focus on the fact that our God doesn't change. His love always stays the same. No matter what storms come our way, He will always be beside us. Right?"

A chorus of agreement rises from the gathered crowd, and I join in.

Brander starts the intro for his first song, the rest of the worship team following his lead. A breeze wafts over us, and the music swells in my chest as Brander sings about God's unending, unfailing love. The song's upbeat tempo buoys my heart and fills my chest with hope.

My voice reaches up to join the voices of the others. The sound twines together in a ribbon of song, reaching up, up, up...until the melody nearly bursts through the roof.

Normally I'm not so bold, but today—with Jazz and Malia beside me and Brander onstage where he belongs—I belt out every word of every song.

I sing for friends. Old friends and new, and the ones who might have been misunderstood all along.

I sing for everything that's gone wrong these last few months, and for all the things that've gone right.

I sing for who I was, who I am, and who I'm hoping God will let me become.

I sing for all of it. Because even though my life is nothing like I'd expected it would be, I'm glad for it.

I don't know what my future holds. But whether I'll be living in Boston or standing right here in Lahaina come this time next year, I do know that what Brander said is true.

No matter what, God will always be here. And He will *always* be the same.

Right after worship ends, my phone buzzes with a text. I pull it out. Dad.

Big news! Call me ASAP.

My breath hitches.

At youth group. Talk later?

Probably not the response he was hoping for. He responds with a thumbs-up that makes my spine tingle as I pocket my phone.

Good thing God never changes, because I have a feeling everything else is going to.

Chapter Thirty

"YOU THINK I HAVE A THING for Brander. Don't you?" Malia corners me as soon as I've piled my plate with this evening's dinner offering—none other than good ol' Pirate Pete's Pizza—after worship.

She doesn't even give me time to answer before her hand closes around my free arm. "Hey!" My pizza slip-slides on my plate as she drags me over to a deserted table overlooking the church parking lot.

"Guys, wait up." Jazz trails after us, juggling a plate of pizza and another plate piled with deep fried potato wedges—or, as Pirate Pete's likes to call them, buried treasure. "Can't we sit by the water?"

"No." Malia cuts her eyes at Jazz before plunking her purse down on the table. "If you want to know what I was laughing about earlier, we need to do it here. Where no one's around to eavesdrop."

I settle down next to Malia and stare out at the handful of cars scattered around the lot. Nothing like a change of scenery to make me appreciate our usual table overlooking the bay. "This'd better be good."

"You have no idea." Malia stares at me, like she can barely believe what a doofus I am. "Listen, I'll admit I was pretty awkward at the airport that day."

Ha! I knew it.

"Maybe I'm still a little starstruck." Malia dips her head and pokes at her salad. "I never knew Brander very well before he went off and got all"—she waves her hand—"famous."

"He's no different than he was before." Jazz opens her mouth to take a ginormous bite of pizza.

"How should I know that? I've never met a celebrity before. But Olive, you need to know—the picture I want him to sign...it's not for me. It's for Kanani."

"Kanani?" My mind takes a slow trek down memory lane until I'm standing back in my spot at the airport, watching Kanani freak out all over Brander. "I guess that makes sense."

"I'm telling you, she's obsessed. I caught her one day at the park with my phone, playing Brander's song on repeat. She had such a huge grin on her face." Malia sets down her fork and twines a strand of hair around her finger. "Ever since we lost the house, she's been a different kid. So have I."

A teeny part of my heart grows warm and gooey, like the cheese dripping from my slice of pizza. Maybe Malia's *not* exactly who I thought she was.

I reach across the table to give her hand a supportive squeeze, but she stops me with one coal-eyed glare.

"Don't you dare go all mushy on me." Malia's voice is hard, but it softens on the next sentence. "Thing is, I want to make my sister smile. Even a little. I thought if I could get Brander to sign this picture for her, then she'd have something special. Something cool to show the kids in her class."

"Then why didn't you have him sign it for you weeks ago, instead of showing up and bugging him about Nashville all the time?" I poke at my pizza, but Malia's story has put my appetite on hold.

"I'm embarrassed, okay?" Her words snap and splinter like brittle driftwood. "Brander's, like, famous and super-rich and...I don't know. It seems dumb, the homeless girl going up to him and begging him for a favor. It's way easier to ask him questions about Nashville and stuff. That way I can go home and tell Kanani all about what he has to say."

"Brander wouldn't think any less of you if you asked for his autograph." Jazz wipes her hands on a greasy napkin. "He loves everyone, and he'd be happy to help you."

"You think so?" Something shimmers in the corner of Malia's eye. A tear? "I want to do this for Kanani. She's been so out of sorts ever since—never mind."

"What?" Jazz shoves another piece of pizza in her mouth. "You can tell us, you know."

"I know. But I'd also like to stay alive in the process." Malia's gaze cuts over to me.

"What are you looking at me for?" My voice swoops higher than I'd expected, and Malia is quick to shush me.

"Keep it down." She wags one thin finger in my face. "And I'll tell you, but you have to promise not to flip."

"I promise." Why would she think that I would? Then again, I haven't been the best example of a calm, compassionate person since Malia started hanging out with us.

"Remember—you promised." Malia scrapes her hair out of her eyes. "Truth is, Kanani's been a beast ever since Macie's birthday party. She's wanted a dog for years. We were finally planning to adopt one right before Dad got laid off. Now that Macie has a brand-new puppy, Kanani's pretty jealous."

"That makes sense." Jazz lifts her can of passionfruit juice but doesn't take a sip. "I felt that way a lot when I was little. Everyone else in my class always threw these super-cool luaus and birthday parties. I was lucky to get invited, let alone have a celebration like that on my birthday."

"Ouch." Malia's gaze darts away—was she one of those girls who didn't invite Jazz? "I never thought about that."

"It was pretty rough. But it definitely helped build my character."

"You are *way* too optimistic." Malia rolls her eyes, but

the shove she gives Jazz is a good-natured one. "I kind of like it though."

"Wait a minute." I blink at Malia as her words swirl across my brain like storm clouds during a squall. Impossible to focus on, yet strangely steady all the same. "You haven't been hanging around us to get in good with Brander? I mean, as more than a friend?"

Malia scoffs. "No. I mean, yeah I was hoping you could help me with the picture thing, but that's it. He's a cool guy, and he's super cute, but I'm not—I mean, I don't think we're each other's type. Unfortunately."

At that, all I can feel is guilt—guilt that rolls over me like a tidal wave, sucking me in and promising to not let me come up for a very long time. "What an idiot I am." I can hear my words, but they're murky. Almost like I'm underwater. "I shouldn't have assumed that you...I mean, even though we have different personalities that doesn't mean..." I snap my trap shut before I can keep rambling, but Jazz seems to understand what I'm getting at.

"Friends?" Jazz's face is bright and clear, her expression as inviting as an empty hammock on a lazy Sunday.

"Friends." Malia nods. "To be honest, I could use some. School this year stinks, thanks to my...um...housing situation. But you guys treat me differently. Like I'm a person, not a charity case. Thanks for that."

"You're welcome." Jazz is quick with a response, but my mouth stays stapled shut. I have a lot of work to do before I catch up with Jazz in the friendship department.

Hard work. The kind that's never come easy to me. But work I'm willing to do.

Work that, right now, seems a lot more appealing than any college course at Harvard.

"I can't believe he signed it for me!" Malia lets out a tiny squeal and clutches the picture—now signed—to her chest before Jonah begins the night's sermon later that evening. "Kanani's gonna flip."

I smile before turning my attention to the stage. Something tells me Malia's still a little more starstruck than she lets on, but for once I don't care. After all, I feel the same way around Brander sometimes.

Before anyone can say anything else, Jonah swings himself onto the stage—ignoring the perfectly good staircase—and perches on the end of it, his wild surfer-dude hair falling onto his neck in damp ringlets. "Time to get started." He lets out a piercing wolf-whistle, and a hush blankets the room.

"First of all, can we give another huge *mahalo* to Brander for that awesome worship set?" Jonah claps his hands together, and we all join in. Brander acknowledges the praise with a wave of his hand and a duck of his head— and is that a blush I see spreading across his face? Poor guy.

"He doesn't seem too comfortable, does he?" Jazz leans over to whisper in my ear.

"Not at all." If I didn't know any better, I'd think he was miserable. But being a music star has been his dream for so long—this must be what he wants. Right?

Thankfully there's no more time for me to dwell on that thought before Jonah launches into his sermon.

"Today we're going to talk about Jonah," he says after leading us in one more prayer. "Not this Jonah." He jabs his thumb at himself, and about half the room groans. "But the Jonah in the Bible. See, God had big things planned for him. And Jonah didn't like them. Not at all."

"Doesn't everyone know this story?" Malia groans under her breath and nudges Jazz in the side. "I mean, Jonah doesn't do what God wants, so he gets eaten by a whale. The end. Don't do bad things, kiddos."

"Shh." Jazz and I hiss in unison before turning our eyes on Jonah.

But, as Jonah takes us on a journey through his eponym's book of the Bible, even I feel as though I'm hearing parts of the story for the very first time.

"God gave Jonah a choice." Jonah stops reading right after the part where the big fish comes and swallows Jonah. "He could do what he was asked—share the news with the people of Ninevah—or he could 'go his own way.'" Jonah pauses to hum a few bars of the old Fleetwood Mac song, and a few people laugh.

"Seriously though, God wanted Jonah to make the choice on his own. He wasn't forcing Jonah to go one way or another. He gave him the ability to choose what he thought was best. And, like we all are sometimes, Jonah was stubborn. He was sure he had it right—that his way would lead to a happily ever after."

"Big whoops." Jazz laughs under her breath, but I keep my eyes fixed on Jonah. If the sudden pounding in my chest is anything to go by, this is something I need to hear.

"So many times, we can be tempted to examine our circumstances and make our own decisions based on our emotions. And that isn't right." Jonah jumps to his feet and paces, his flip-flops *phwaping* against the stage. "When we rely on our emotions, we're wrong ninety-nine percent of the time.

"What should we rely on then?" Jonah stops mid-stride, plants his feet on the stage, and lifts a finger toward the heavens. "We should rely on the Lord. Even when He doesn't speak to us audibly or put a road sign in the middle of our life, He has a plan for us. God doesn't want to treat us like a roomful of puppets, but He does know what's best for us. And when we ask, He *will* give us guidance."

A chill runs down my spine, though I'm not exactly sure why. It's not like I've been hearing much from the Lord lately.

Jonah's eyes roam the group, until they stop right on me—or so it seems. "The question is, when God does speak, will you be willing to listen?"

Chapter Thirty-One

"THAT WAS A GREAT MESSAGE." JAZZ sticks close to my side as we tromp through the sand to the Shave Ice Shack with Brander after youth group. "Good worship too." She elbows Brander, then backs away. "Oops. Hands off, right? Don't want the paparazzi going after me."

She means it as a joke, if the way the tiki torches reflect in her eyes like mini fireworks is anything to go by, but Brander doesn't seem to take it that way. He shrugs and keeps his head down as we get in line to place our orders.

By the time we collect our treats—Brander gets his for free, thanks to a selfie, an autograph, and one very starstruck girl working the counter—a strange silence has settled between the three of us. Not awkward, exactly, but hesitant. As though each one of us is afraid of saying something to spoil the mood.

"Sorry I'm so quiet, guys." Brander lifts a spoonful of shave ice to his mouth as we walk toward the shoreline, but he doesn't take a bite. "I've got a lot on my mind."

"Like that sermon?" I dip my spoon into my own shave ice before it can melt in the balmy evening. The sun might be down, but the darkness is like a warm, fuzzy sweater around my bare shoulders. "That was enough to chew on for a month."

"I know." Brander finally takes a bite. "And I think I need to. I don't want to end up like Jonah—Bible Jonah, I mean."

"You read my mind." A wave crashes far offshore and crawls forward to lick my toes, the foamy water sending the sand beneath my feet shifting one way, then another. "I thought I knew what I had to do, but what Jonah said is making me wonder."

Jazz offers me a sympathetic smile in the semidarkness, but she stays quiet. As much as my mind is staggering under the weight of my own troubles, a special part of my heart aches for Jazz.

Not only does she have her own stuff with her mom to deal with, but she also has to worry about her two best friends picking up and moving to the mainland for good. If I were in her shoes, I'd be about to croak.

I take another bite of shave ice, as if the sweetness can make everything right in my world. For one second, before the ice melts on my tongue, it does—and then another wave breaks, closer to shore this time, and I'm returned to my current reality.

Here I am on one of the most beautiful beaches in the world, with two of the most incredible people I've ever met, and I'm honestly considering giving it all up? For real?

My heart picks up speed, pumping and pumping until I can hear little more than the sound of blood rushing in my ears.

Because I *know*.

Maybe God isn't speaking audibly to me, but He's speaking all the same. He has been this entire time—through Gramma and Jazz and Macie and even that annoying little voice in my head.

I want to stay. No, I *have to*.

There's no way I can pull a Jonah and run away to a new life simply because things in Maui have been rocky. Even if Brander decides to go to Nashville. Even if Macie's puppy gives my sanity a run for its money. Even if it means hanging out with Malia more than I'd like.

God wants me here.

I'm *needed* here.

Don't ask me why, because I have no idea.

But all I know is right here, under a sky speckled with stars, surrounded by salt-kissed air, and wrapped in the tradewinds' loving embrace…this is where I'm meant to be.

Brander leans over to nudge me as he walks me to the front door after our shave ice trip. Jazz's leg started hurting halfway back to the church, and Brander—gentleman that he is—couldn't resist a chance to drive us home in his cherry-red chariot. We dropped Jazz off first, which means now it's just him and me.

"You're quiet tonight." Brander keeps his voice low. I can barely hear it beneath the drone of a million crickets. "Big thoughts?"

"Bigger than you can imagine." I mount the porch steps and lean on the railing. Brander does the same.

"Need to talk about it?"

"Not yet." First, I need to tell Dad that I've changed my mind. "But soon. What about you?"

"Same. Maybe I should go talk to Jonah."

A hush wraps around us, punctuated only by the crashing of waves, but the silence between us is sweet. Comfortable. Knots in my stomach—knots I didn't even know I had—seem to loosen as we stand in the darkening evening.

For the first time in what feels like forever, our silence is peaceful.

Hopeful.

Yet, all too soon, it's broken by a yawn from Brander. He chuckles, as if embarrassed, and moves to leave with a smile and *shaka.* "See you soon. Maybe we can finally drive the road to Hana this weekend—if I can convince my mom to let me out of her sight for that long. I think she's afraid the paparazzi have a tracking device imbedded in my sunglasses."

We share a laugh as he heads down the walk to his car. I stay on the porch as he pulls away, hand raised in a wave, then cross over to sit on the swing.

An unusual coolness spreads through my chest. Is it peace—the knowledge that I've finally made my choice—or is it fear? Goosebumps prick at my arms, and it's not because of the cool breeze blowing across the porch.

Mom's face materializes in my mind, her features clear as day, her expression murky. Is she proud of me for making my decision, or is she sad? Disappointed that I won't be following in her footsteps?

Maybe I'll never know.

I stand and head inside, the image of Mom haunting me as I pad down the dark hallway and come to a stop in front of Gramma's bedroom door. It's late—she might be asleep—but I have to talk to her.

I knock, the time-worn doorframe scraping my knuckles, and cock my ear toward the door.

Nothing.

I try again, but I'm rewarded with nothing more than a low snore. Guess I'll have to catch her in the morning.

So, for now, I head upstairs, my room beckoning like a lighthouse calling a ship in from the sea. I change into my pajamas and smile as I slip into bed. Even though no one knows I've made my choice, my heart is light with the knowledge that this place will be my home for many more years to come.

But then, right when my eyes have grown heavy and fuzzy with sleep, a single thought snakes its way into my mind and sends me jolting upright in bed, clutching the covers to my chest despite the stuffy warmth of the room.

I was supposed to text Dad.

My chest grows lava-hot, then icy cold as I peek at my

phone. It's the middle of the night in Boston. If I call, I'll either wake him up—and I know how much he hates that—or get sent straight to his voicemail.

Oh well. I can call him tomorrow.

And with that, I hunker back into my blankets, fluff my pillow once for good measure, and go to sleep.

Except I don't.

Because now Dad's text is playing on a continual loop through my brain, and something tells me that whatever he has to say is going to get me in capital-T-style trouble.

Chapter Thirty-Two

"GRAMMA?" I POKE MY HEAD OUT of the upstairs window the next morning at the sound of her car engine starting up. I'm half-dressed, still wearing my cat-print pajama bottoms beneath my green sundress, but I race down the stairs and run barefoot onto the porch as her car rolls toward the street. I've got to catch her before she takes off. She should know about the application—and my decision. Especially because I'm counting on her to help me pick up the pieces after I get hit by whatever bombshell Dad wants to drop on me.

"Gramma!" I lean over the porch and wave my arms at her, but she has her neck craned, her head tilted over her shoulder as she backs out of the driveway. And while the temptation to run after her is strong, I'm not about to let the neighbors see me running after a rattletrap station wagon in my pajama pants.

Her old car groans and pops as she makes her way along the street, and I cross my fingers. Maybe she's going on a coffee run.

Except Gramma always makes her coffee at home.

"What are you doing?" Macie's voice comes from the doorway, and I turn to find her staring at me, Zuzu tucked under her arm like a fluffy gray-and-white purse. "And why are you still wearing your jammies?"

"I was trying to catch Gramma." I step inside, giving Zuzu's ears a ruffle before closing the door and peeling off my pajama bottoms. "Do you know where she's going?"

"Art gallery." Macie sticks a curl in her mouth and

chews.

I yank it right back out.

"No bad habits." I hold onto her curl a split second longer, then something tickles my arm. Something *alive.*

I look down, right as Zuzu's wet nose bumps my elbow. She nuzzles me again, then opens her mouth, her teeth brushing my bare skin.

I yelp, jerking away as fast as I can, heart pounding. To my surprise, Macie's lip puckers, and even the puppy squirms like she's concerned.

"You're over-reaction-ing." Macie lifts her chin, as if proud of using such a grandiose—though made-up—word.

"Over*reacting.*" I can't help correcting her, even as my cheeks grow hot. "And yeah, I am." I glance at the poor pup and lift my hand to give her a pat, but the landline shrieks at us before I can do anything.

"Yeouch!" Macie nearly drops her puppy in an effort to cover her ears, and I hurry to answer the phone.

"Hello?" The phone's kinky cord wraps around my arm. Why on earth hasn't Grams tossed this thing and bought a cell phone? Or at least something cordless?

"You're home?" It's Dad. "Then why are you ignoring me?"

"Ignoring you?" I wave a hand at Macie, shooing her off to finish getting ready for school. "What do you mean?"

"I've called your cell phone at least ten times in the last hour. And if your memory is serving you correctly, you know you were supposed to call me last night."

"Sorry." I swallow a lump in my throat. "I forgot."

Dad huffs. "That much is obvious."

I huff right back. "You should be glad my thumbs aren't glued to my phone. What's going on, anyway?"

"Can you keep something confidential?"

Confidential? I peek behind me to make sure Macie's not within earshot. That girl knows no secrets. "Is everything okay?"

"Of course. Better than okay, actually." Dad's voice changes from craggy and grouchy to light and lilting. The way it used to be...*Before.* "The scholarship committee got together yesterday to make a decision. You're in."

In?

I'm shot with an instant dose of adrenaline, and I nearly drop the phone. *No, no, no. Not now. Not when I've finally made my choice.* My mouth opens of its own accord, about to say a million things Dad won't want to hear.

I have to stop. Keep the words from coming out.

Deep breath.

"I'm...in?" It comes out sounding shaky. Feeble. Not the excited, jump-up-and-down reaction I'm sure Dad was hoping for. "For real? There's no way they'll change their minds?"

"Not a chance. The only thing left is for the board to put out the official announcement, but that won't be for a few weeks." Dad's voice is tinged with pride. "I knew you'd do it. That essay was a masterwork. Blew everyone else away, like it did me. Writing about your mother like you did, reliving all those memories—that took courage."

"Courage?" I'll need more courage than it took to write that essay if I'm going to burst Dad's shiny bubble of excitement. My confidence feels weaker than my voice as I open my mouth to explain things before Dad can get too carried away. I try to form the words with my tongue, but it feels thick. Clumsy.

God, help. I know what I want—no, what You want. But how can I tell that to Dad?

I can't.

The realization hits me dead in the chest as Dad goes on about how much everyone loved my essay. He sounds so happy, so proud, that I let him ramble. I can't kill his excitement. Not now.

But still…

"It's not my dream." It escapes before I even know I'm going to say it, and instantly I'm scrambling. Fighting. Trying to yank the words back and bury them deep in my throat before Dad can hear them.

"What was that?" Dad laughs. "Of course it's your dream—has been since you were a little girl."

"I know." But now the thought of leaving this island and saying goodbye to all I've come to hold dear sounds less like a dream and more like a nightmare. "It's one thing when it's a dream. It's different when it's real."

"Huh?"

I clear my throat. I've got to make this right—keep from hurting his feelings and painting myself as the most ungrateful kid in the world.

That way, when I back out for good, I won't be starting on already-shaky ground. "What I mean is, college—Harvard—is closer than I ever imagined it could be. And I…uh…" The words seize in my throat, and I almost choke.

Dad's chuckle on the other line is like a squirt of lime juice in a paper cut, and I grit my teeth as he starts rambling about how Harvard is the perfect place for me. How Mom would've been so proud.

Because somewhere inside of me, I know that it's true. I *would* love Harvard, a place where I might finally fit in with more than a few straggling nerds. Mom *would* be proud of me for catching my dream.

But…

A faint tendril of Mom's voice tickles the nape of my neck as Dad and I say goodbye. Her soft, smooth tone stays with me as I replace the phone in its cradle, shoo Macie off to the bus stop, and settle onto the porch swing.

It's only when I close my eyes to pray that her words become clear.

I'll always be proud of you, sweet girl. But you know

what makes me prouder than any scholarship? Your character. Your willingness to follow God wherever He leads.

It's not always easy, but the blessings that come from following His plan are worth more than a thousand scholarships.

Trust Him.

The faint echo of Mom's voice rings in my ears along with the trill of a bird perched in Gramma's hibiscus bush. I reach into the cool morning air, as if to grasp the words before they can disappear. To hold onto them. Forever.

Because even though it sounds like Mom speaking, something tells me that the words planted in my heart come straight from God.

Which means I was wrong all this time. And now I have to dig myself out of a practically bottomless pit. A bottomless pit named Dad.

Chapter Thirty-Three

LATE THAT AFTERNOON, AS JAZZ AND I are putting the finishing touches on our World War II essays, a gust of wind pushes through the open window, ruffling the pages of my history book.

"Wow." Jazz lifts her head from her notebook and shivers. "Must be a squall coming in."

I nod and dip my head lower over my laptop, not about to acknowledge the fact that Jazz's words are accurate in more ways than one.

And, if the rocking and churning in my gut is anything to go by, my internal turmoil has the potential to be a lot more devastating than any storm that'll roll through Lahaina this evening.

My heart creeps into my throat. I have to tell Dad that I've changed my mind—that I'm not going to Harvard after all—or I'll end up on a one-way flight to Boston at the end of the summer.

For all I know, he could've bought me a plane ticket already. As far as he's concerned, my biggest dream in life has come true.

Except it's *not* my dream anymore—and he'll never know that if I don't speak up.

Fast.

I have to call him. Right now, before things can get out of hand. Except it's closing in on midnight his time, and Dad's always been a believer in getting in a firm eight hours' sleep on a school night.

Still, it would be worth waking him up to tell him the

truth.

Wouldn't it?

Why did Gramma have to pick today of all days to cover her friend's late shift at the gallery? *Come home, Grams. I need you.*

The pumping of my heart rushes in my ears, coming faster and louder until I can barely hear.

The rumbling of the ocean, the howl of the wind, even the incessant whir of the ceiling fan—all of them are muted beneath the commotion in my own mind.

"You okay?" A voice cuts through the deafening confusion in my head, and a hand pats my back.

I turn, expecting to see Jazz but instead finding Macie. She stares at me with wide eyes, then points to my computer. "You were glaring at it."

"I was?"

Macie nods, and her curls jiggle. "Is your homework hard? I had to write a story in class today all by myself. It was hard."

"It is hard, squirt." I pat the couch for her to sit next to me. Little does Macie know that this particular brand of *hard* stems from a particular college scholarship, not a yawn-inducing essay on the international impact of the Doolittle Raid.

"Hard?" Jazz shakes her head at me over the screen of her dented laptop. "At least you have a computer that wasn't made on the same day God created the heavens and the earth." She rolls her eyes and whacks the side of her behemoth laptop. "My screen's frozen."

"Want to use mine? I'm done anyway." I quickly upload my paper into the student portal before offering the computer to Jazz. "Your stuff's saved to the cloud, right?"

She nods in answer before the keys start clacking. "Thanks."

"No problem." I settle against the couch cushions and

tuck an arm around Macie. A gray cloud rolls across the skyline outside, and I shiver. What will Dad think when I tell him?

"I'm hungry." Macie scratches her nose, then buries her head in my shoulder as another gust of wind bursts across the room. "And cold. I don't like it when it gets cold here."

"I won't argue with that." I hop off the couch and shut the window before any more chilly air can blow inside. "Gramma should be home from the gallery soon to start dinner. You're staying, right, Jazz?"

I turn in time to catch Jazz's thumbs-up over the laptop screen, then motion for Macie to step into the hall with me. "Let's give Jazz some privacy." I squat until I'm eye level with Macie and keep my voice low. "She's working on a monster essay."

Macie's smile sags. "But I wanted to play with her."

"You can play with me." I put on a smile that, surprisingly, chases away a bit of the tempest in my heart.

"You wouldn't want to play." Macie crosses her arms and glares down at the floor. "We were going to play with Zuzu."

"Oh." A tendril of embarrassment finds its way into my stomach, tangling with the mass of anxiety already there to create a nasty knot of tension. Tension that, one way or another, has got to go.

I might not be brave enough to wake Dad up and tackle the scholarship mess, but there could be worse things in life than spending the afternoon with a pint-sized pup like Zuzu. "I'll play with you both."

"Yay!" Macie does a little two-step dance in the hallway before she grabs my arm and practically drags me outside to where Zuzu has been hanging out in the yard.

Another gust of wind sweeps through the yard as Macie throws herself onto the grass next to her puppy and ruffles the mutt's fluffy head—guess she forgot about being cold.

But I sure didn't. "Why don't you bring Zuzu inside? We can hang out upstairs."

"No. She wants to play fetch, and you have to play fetch outside."

"Give me a minute then." I run inside for a sweater, ignoring the buzzing of my phone on the kitchen counter as I grab an old Pacific Whale Foundation hoodie of Gramma's from a hook in the front hall. A storm is rolling in, and Macie has a lot of wiggles to get out before the weather turns nasty. Whoever's calling will have to wait.

As much as I hurry though, I'm not fast enough.

The second I step outside, another gust of wind sends raindrops dancing across the deck.

A droplet of wet spatters on my nose, and Macie squeals like she's been tackled by a tsunami. "Everybody in!" She bellows the command like an army sergeant and dashes inside, Zuzu yipping at her heels.

I follow suit, stepping inside right as the front door slams shut. "I'm home." Gramma's voice seems to fill every corner of the house as she bustles into the kitchen, balancing two overflowing brown grocery bags on her hip. "How is everyone?"

"Good now." Jazz slides the laptop onto the coffee table and ambles into the kitchen, moving a little slower on her prosthesis, like she usually does after therapy. "But that history essay totally had it out for me. I hope I can pull off a B or it'll kill my grade."

"I'm sure you did a great job." Gramma lends Jazz a smile, then reaches into one of the bags to withdraw a stack of brown takeout boxes, each with a different name scrawled on it. "I grabbed some sandwiches from that new deli by Island Grocery on my way home."

"Goodie!" Macie stands on her tiptoes to find her box, then hugs it to her chest as she runs to take a seat at the dining room table.

The rest of us move a bit slower, collecting silverware and napkins before joining her, but soon we're all gathered around the table.

Rain drums overhead and the tantalizingly nutty aroma of freshly toasted bread wafts through the air as Gramma offers a quick blessing. As soon as she sends up an *amen*, I open my eyes and take a second to admire the scene before me—Gramma's feathery smile, Jazz's catlike grin, and Macie's chubby face, already stuffed with a bite of her sandwich.

As I unbox my pastrami sandwich, I feel another rush of assurance that this island bungalow truly is *home*. I'm making the right choice in staying. I know it.

My heart spins in my chest, and a sudden rush of tears threatens to escape. How could I have ever thought about giving up my one and only *ohana*? It would've been impossible.

As impossible as telling Dad I've changed my mind.

My mouth goes dry as I take a bite of my sandwich. If not for a particularly delicious honey-mustard sauce, I might not be able to swallow. The drumming of rain pounds beyond the half-open dining room window as my brain gears up for another spin in the blender of anxiety.

Not only do I have to cough up the courage to tell Dad *no,* but I also have everyone else to think about.

What if Gramma asks about the scholarship? Or Jazz? I can't lie to them, but how can I admit the truth? Like it or not, I have a full-ride scholarship to Harvard.

Fortunately, Macie monopolizes Gramma and Jazz for the first part of dinner. But when I reach for the second half of my sandwich, a lull hits the conversation.

And that's when the other—more dangerous—squall finally hits.

"Olive, do you know when you'll hear about the scholarship? It's been a while since you turned it in."

Gramma sets down her sandwich—a sort of lobster roll, from the looks of it—and blots a dab of avocado from her upper lip.

"It hasn't been *that* long." The words stick in my throat, and I reach for my water glass. "They probably won't announce who won for another couple of weeks." My chest shudders even though nothing I said was a lie. After all, Dad asked me to keep everything confidential.

Not that a little thing like confidentiality has kept me from sharing stuff with Grams or Jazz before.

"Anyway, I don't even want to go." The hammering in my chest stills as I release those words—words that have been dying to leave my mouth for way too long.

"Then what will you do if you get the scholarship?" Jazz's brow knits. She sets down her sky-high chicken club sandwich. "You wouldn't change your mind, right?"

"No." I shake my head so hard my brain feels like it's stuck in a food processor, but it's worth it when I hear Jazz's deep breath of reassurance.

"Good." Her eyes are soft. Trusting. I can't let her down.

"You're staying here? For sure?" Macie bounces up from her seat and runs to give me a mayonnaise-smeared hug. "With me and Jazz and Grammy and Zuzu?" She huffs out a breath. "Good. I was gonna miss you."

I smile at Gramma over Macie's mop-top, then at Jazz, who lifts her hand in a *shaka*. She takes a supersized bite of her sandwich, then looks at me again. "I know this year probably hasn't gone the way you were expecting, but I think you'll be glad you stuck it out with us."

"I think so too." I peel Macie off me with a pat to her back. "Go finish your dinner, squirt."

Macie nods her agreement and pops into her seat before tearing into her meal once more. I pick up my sandwich to do the same, but the weight of all I have to do keeps me from taking a bite.

I know better than anyone that two half-truths make a whole lie. Meaning that, right now, I'm caught in the most tangled web I've ever woven.

I have to get out before it's too late.

Chapter Thirty-Four

THE SECOND JAZZ LEAVES AFTER DINNER, I grab my phone and run upstairs to call Dad. Who cares that it's still the middle of the night in Boston? Something important like this shouldn't have to wait.

I enter my passcode, finger hovering over my address book, when a notification pops up. I have a voicemail.

"Aloha." Brander's voice greets me as I play the message, and I can't help but smile. He sounds better than I've heard him in a long time. Maybe he finally made his decision too. "I know it's kind of short notice, but I was wondering if you and Jazz were free this Saturday. It's time for me to start making up for all those adventures we missed. Let me know."

The message ends, and I hurry to text Jazz.

Brander says he has a surprise for us on Saturday. You in?

I throw on a pair of pajamas and flop onto my bed, crossing my fingers that Jazz will reply soon. A few minutes later, my phone buzzes, but it's not a text—it's a phone call.

"I got your message." Jazz sounds breathless on the other line. "It sounds fun, but don't you remember? Saturday's when Mom gets out of rehab."

"Oh. Right." My excitement is snuffed out like a solitary birthday candle. "Sorry. I forgot."

"It's okay. Just go have fun. We can do something together later."

"No way." My heart aches for Jazz, always willing to make a sacrifice for the people she loves. "I haven't been the best support for you lately, and I want to change that."

"Thanks. But what is there for you to do? You can't help fix my mom like you can help buy me a leg. People are...complicated."

"Tell me about it." Dad's face flashes in my mind, and a nervous laugh slips out before I can stop it.

"What do you mean?" From the sound of it, Jazz's intuition radar shot up. Way up.

Whoops.

"Nothing. Never mind." If only I could tell Jazz exactly what's going on, I know she'd have some advice for me. But I'd hate to get her wrapped up in my tangled web before I've talked things through with Dad.

Until then, maybe it's my chance to show her some support. "Hey, why don't I come with you to the rehab center. When are you guys leaving?"

"Early. And the rehab center's in Paia—it's a long drive. Trust me, you wouldn't want to come."

"Paia? Oof." The only time I met Jazz's mom, she was raving drunk, but I have a feeling she's not the kind of person you'd want to spend a long car ride with even when she's sober. Though that's beside the point.

Jazz needs to know I'm here for her. That I care. An involuntary shudder travels up my spine and zaps the base of my neck as I open my mouth. "You're sure you don't want me to ride along? I'd be happy to. And I can't speak for Brander, but I bet he'd be down for it."

Jazz's breath catches. "For real?"

"Of course." Hopefully I don't sound as apprehensive about it as I feel. "I'll text him."

"That'd be great." Jazz's breath quivers on the other line. "But I want you to think about it before you make your final choice. It's going to be awkward. You'd probably rather do something with Brander."

"I know, but I *want* to go with you." I grip the phone. If

only Jazz was here. I'd give her the biggest hug in the world. "I'll call Brander. You go ask your aunt what time you're leaving and text me, okay?"

We hang up, and I get right on the phone with Brander. "I know it'd be a lot more fun to do whatever you had planned," I finish once I've explained my idea, "but this is important to Jazz. I haven't been the best friend lately, and this is a way I can make it up to her. If you don't want to though, I totally get it."

"Of course I'll go." Brander sounds a lot more enthusiastic about the idea than I feel, even though it was my suggestion in the first place. "Maybe afterwards we can do something fun to take Jazz's mind off of things."

"Good idea."

"Hey." Brander coughs on the other end before I can say goodbye. "Since I have your ear, can I tell you something?"

"Sure. What—is something wrong?"

"A lot of people think there is." Brander takes a deep breath. "I turned down the record deal."

"Wait, really?" My heart gives a kick, and I jump up and walk back and forth across the space between my bed and Macie's. "What made you decide?"

"The same thing that helped you, probably."

"Huh? How do you know *I* made a decision? For all you know, I still could be waffling back and forth."

"But you aren't." Brander's voice is uncharacteristically smug, and I have to laugh. "Waffling, I mean. Jonah's sermon packed a punch."

"You're right. As usual. And it sounds like God gave us the same answer."

"What?" Brander almost yelps, then laughs. I laugh as well, relishing the sudden lightness in my chest. Who knew God's plan could make a person this happy?

Neither of us say anything for a moment, and I breathe in the sweet relief of knowing that, sooner or later, things are going to return to normal.

Someone says something on Brander's end of the phone, and there's a rustling noise. "I'm fine, Mom. Just happy." His voice is fuzzy, like he put his thumb over the phone's mic, before it becomes clear again. "Sorry about that. I think Mom's afraid the paparazzi are going to attack me one night in the backyard. I've been out by the pool with Rosco."

I shiver at the name of Brander's German shepherd, but my heart isn't in it. Usually I'd be well on my way to a minor heart attack at the thought of that crazy guard dog, but tonight all I feel is peace.

Peace that, despite all the messiness of the past few months, things are finally *right*.

Or at least they will be.

Soon.

Friday flies by in a blur so fast that I wouldn't have time to call Dad and tell him about my decision even if I wanted to. By the time Brander and I walk up to Jazz's front door on Saturday, the thought of going to school at Harvard has become a faint memory—a daydream from another lifetime.

I know I still have to suck up my guts and tell Dad, but right now everything in me is focused on Jazz. On being a *friend*.

Even when it's hard.

Brander raises his fist to knock on the door, his other hand finding mine and giving it a quick squeeze before Ruby hollers for Jazz to get the door.

"Coming!" Even at this early hour in the day, Jazz's voice is crisp and clear. Barely uneven footsteps sound from within before Jazz throws open the rickety front door. "Aloha." She smiles as bright as always, though maybe a bit forced, and turns to beckon Ruby forward.

"Good morning." Brander lifts his hand—the same one that was squeezing mine moments ago—in a *shaka*, not even raising a brow at the new tattoo scrolling across Ruby's collarbone. I straighten up and do the same, and Ruby offers a wave in return.

"Ready to go?" She motions with her keys to a rattletrap minivan parked on the side of the road, and I force my chin up and down. Let's hope that today's adventure won't result in any more dents in that van.

Jazz must sense what I'm thinking, because she leans over to whisper to me as we make our way through the overgrown front yard to the car. "Don't worry. Ruby's not a bad driver. Parking around here is extra tight."

"*Right.*" I swallow hard, and Jazz and Brander laugh, but that doesn't keep me from shooting up a quick prayer as the three of us pile into the backseat—Jazz in the middle, resting her prosthesis against the hump on the floor.

Ruby's road-trip soundtrack of choice pours out of the speakers—a heavy metal CD that will likely have my ears bleeding by the time we get to Paia—and I fire up another prayer.

Because as freaky as it is to be soaring along Ho'onakapi Highway with Ruby at the helm, inside I'm staring down something a lot more frightening.

God, give me the courage to face Dad and tell him what's best for me—what You want for me. And help me do it soon. Amen.

"This is it." Jazz grips my fingers, her knuckles turning white, as Ruby pulls off the main road. She turns onto a long, winding path flanked by towering palms, and my pulse quickens.

Brander's jaw is locked tight, his eyes fixed straight

ahead. Even Ruby seems to straighten up. She switches off her Metallica CD as she drives around the final bend, coming to a stop in front of a sprawling one-story building.

We pile out of the car in silence, the air thick and still but for a slight breeze, and walk single file toward the front entrance. Ruby presses a large button marked *Intercom*, and a speaker crackles and pops before a voice tells us to state our business.

As if in unspoken agreement, Ruby steps aside and Jazz leans forward to talk. "I'm here to get my mom. Ronnie Whitaker." Her voice is soft yet powerful. Not without fear but filled with a current of something stronger.

Something I'd like to have.

There's a sharp buzz, and Brander and I jump almost simultaneously. We share a swift smile before the speaker crackles. "Door's unlocked now. Come in."

None of us move for a long second, but I'm not surprised when Jazz takes charge and pushes the door open. We follow her lead, crowding into a stark white room. The space is well-furnished but empty, save for the receptionist at the desk, and something tickles the space between my shoulders.

This is like the hospital where we said Goodbye to Mom—a place for sick people to get better...except some never do.

Right then, a door on the far side of the room swings open and a tall woman who shares Jazz's blonde hair steps out. Jazz stiffens, and it's as though the air in the room gets siphoned out. All I want to do is throw my arms around my friend and give her a squeeze, but now's not the time.

Instead, I watch as Jazz's mom walks toward us. Her jaw is sharp, her nose crooked, and her eyes make her look like she could tell stories I'd rather not hear. Yet something about her composure—her raised chin, maybe—makes it obvious that she and Jazz are related.

Jazz is the first to step toward the woman. "Hi, Mom." Her voice comes out as a croak, like her throat has gone dry.

"Looks like you brought a whole party." Ms. Whitaker adjusts the fraying duffle slung over her shoulder. She runs her gaze over each of us, but her eyes seem to linger on me the longest. Does she remember me from the last time we met? My spine quivers, but I keep my head up and meet her gaze.

Brander is the next to come forward. "Nice to see you, Ms. Whitaker." He offers his hand. "I don't know if you remember me or not, but I'm—"

"Familiar." Ms. Whitaker takes Brander's hand and squeezes. Hard. Brander doesn't flinch, but he steps aside and massages his hand once Jazz's mom releases it. "You're on the radio here sometimes."

Brander's cheeks flush. "I guess I probably am."

"Why aren't you in Hollywood or somewhere?"

"It's a long story." Brander motions toward the door. "You'd probably like to get going, huh?"

"I guess." Ms. Whitaker's eyes flick over to Ruby, and she nods. "Thanks for picking me up, sis, but I'm beat. Think we can hit the road?"

Ruby's chin jerks up in what I guess is a nod, and we fall into line, making a strange, silent procession as we walk to the van.

"What's new with you, Jazz?" Ms. Whitaker glances back at the three of us once Ruby has pulled onto the highway. "You're not still doing that surfing thing, I hope."

Jazz's usual healthy tan pales all the way up to her hairline. "It's paddleboarding, and yeah. I am, actually. In fact, Olive and Malia and I are all going out to practice after church tomorrow."

"Jazz is doing great," Brander pipes up. "I can't wait to watch her in the race next weekend."

"Why, Jazz?" Ms. Whitaker flops back against her seat.

"Why would you put yourself out there to be humiliated like that? Don't you think our family has enough of a bad name as it is? Half-cracked mom, one-legged daughter. A family of failures." She snorts, and Jazz flinches beside me.

My heart pangs in my chest, and I squeeze her hand in a silent show of support. Glancing across the row at Brander, I search his eyes for something—some clue as to what I should do or say—but he looks as lost as I am.

For all the times Jazz mentioned her mom's attitude, I wasn't expecting this.

And, as much as it makes me ache for Jazz, another part of it leads me to wonder...

How will my own dad feel when I end up failing *him*?

Chapter Thirty-Five

"YOU NEED A SHAVE ICE." BRANDER points a finger at Jazz's chest once Ms. Whitaker has disappeared into the spare room at Ruby's house to get settled.

"No, I don't." Jazz sinks onto a sagging couch with a faded palm frond print and hangs her head.

"Who are you and what have you done with Jazz Whitaker?" The joke barely serves to draw a smile out of her. Maybe I should try another tactic. "Seriously, Jazz. Shave ice is a cure-all. Someone taught me that last year."

"I don't think even shave ice could cure what's going on in here." Jazz places one hand over her heart. "*Maybe* a key lime pie, but that'd be a stretch."

Brander's eyes flick over to meet mine, and I shoot him a thumbs-up before ducking out into the front yard. A few minutes later, Grams has a pie half-ready for the oven, and Brander is leading Jazz down the front porch steps.

"I'm doing this for the pie, just so you know." Jazz sticks her tongue out at me as we climb into Brander's car, but she softens it with a wink.

"Don't worry. I don't expect you to be in a good mood right now." I push my hair behind my ears, cuff and uncuff my turquoise shorts—anything to keep my hands from balling into angry fists. It's all I can do to keep from jumping out of the car, marching right into that darkened crypt, and giving Jazz's mom a serious piece of my mind.

Thankfully, Brander starts the engine before I can do anything I'll regret, and by the time he pulls up in front of Gramma's house my anger has fizzled a bit.

Gramma is waiting out front for us, and she greets Jazz with open arms and a peck on her head. "You can stay here as long as you'd like," I hear her whisper in Jazz's ear as Brander and I pass into the entry. "Whatever will make the adjustment easier."

"Thanks, Bonnie." Jazz doesn't pull away for a long moment, and when she does there are tears in her eyes. "I might stay the night, if you're sure you won't mind." "Not at all." Gramma gives Jazz a pat, then scuttles away into the kitchen—probably to check on her pie. "By the way," she calls, "don't worry about Macie disturbing you. I saw her off to the beach with Kanani and her family this morning."

Macie is hanging out with Malia and her little sister? I nearly laugh at the irony, but my face falls when I catch another glimpse of Jazz's grim expression.

"Do you want to talk?" Brander peers at Jazz as we settle onto the couch in the living room. "You know everything your mom's saying isn't about you, right? She's dealing with a lot of her own problems right now."

"Yeah." I clear my throat. I'm definitely not the best person to be offering relationship advice, but who else is there? Grams is busy in the kitchen with her Mixmaster, and Brander, well...he's a guy. "If your mom is anything like me, she doesn't have it out for *you*. More like the world at large."

"And I happen to be at the center of it." Jazz snorts, and in that moment, I see what she could become—a younger, harder version of her mom. What she's always resisted before. Through tragedy and amputation and healing, she's never lost her spark. Until now.

My chest burns. "What your mom says can't define you." I squeeze Jazz's arm, and the solid set of her face grows wobbly. Almost like she's about to cry. "You don't deserve to hear what she has to say. You're brave and bold and caring and…don't listen to her, okay?"

"'Kay." Jazz's voice wavers, but her expression smooths out before tears can turn her face into a soggy swamp of depression. "Thanks, you guys."

"Do you want to do anything to take your mind off of it all?" Brander clasps and unclasps his hands.

"Yeah." Jazz takes her braid and twines it through her fingers. "I want to pray."

"Let's do it." Brander takes Jazz's hand, and Jazz takes mine. We bow our heads almost simultaneously, and Jazz starts. Brander goes next, and when it's my turn to pray, there are few words left to be said. But I open my mouth all the same. *Please, let me find the right words.*

Before I can come up with any, Gramma's landline lets out its characteristic shriek. My head pops up, and I stiffen as Gramma answers it.

"Olive?" Jazz opens her eyes. "What's wrong?"

"Nothing." And that's the truth—Grams could be talking to a telemarketer for all I know. But still, something about the call has my hair standing on end.

For good reason too, because a moment later Gramma's gaze darts over to me. "The scholarship?" She's speaking at a perfectly normal volume, but her words boom in my ears like she's yelling through a megaphone.

No.

I clench my hands into fists, forgetting I'm holding hands with Jazz and Brander until Jazz lets out a small yelp. "That's attached," she whimpers. I pull away, my palms growing sweaty.

Dad can't tell Gramma. Because if he tells her and she tells Jazz…

Suddenly the clamminess isn't constrained to my palms. It spreads throughout my entire body, and my face burns hot while the rest of my blood runs colder than a freshly made shave ice.

If Gramma tells Jazz, she'll know me for who I am—a two-faced coward, too afraid to stand up for myself.

God, what have I done?

My mind races too fast for me to hear an answer as I begin concocting excuses. Explanations. *I was going to tell him. Really. But things have been so crazy busy lately...*

One glance at Jazz and my defense dies in my brain. She won't buy it. Why should she?

"What's the matter?" Brander looks over at me, his eyes wide and kind.

I turn my head to the side and stand, but not before his expression gets burned into my mind.

Gramma continues her conversation, her eyes growing wider by the second, but I can't hear a thing as my heart pounds in my chest.

"Olive?" Someone lays a hand on my back, and I nearly jump. I whirl around to find Jazz staring at me, her silvery eyes swirling with unasked questions.

"I'm sorry. So sorry." I bury my face in my hands. "I can explain, I promise."

Jazz squints at me. "What are you talking about?"

"You'll see." The words fall out of my mouth like a coconut dropping from a palm tree as Gramma finishes her conversation and walks over to me.

"Congratulations, Olive." Gramma's words are measured. Cautious. "Your father said you got the scholarship. That's—"

"I know." I stare down at my clasped hands. There's no point in hiding anymore. Time to let the truth come out. "Dad told me a few days ago. I didn't tell you guys because—"

"Because you're going, aren't you?" Jazz's eyes grow wide, the tears I thought she'd pushed away returning to flood both her gaze and her voice. "Does that mean you lied to me? To us?"

"Wait. You *are* going to Harvard?" Brander's gaze darts between me and Jazz like he's trying to decide who to believe.

Even Gramma knits her brow. "You sounded so certain that God wanted you to stay here."

"It was a lie. It must've been." Jazz's face grows cold and hard, the way it looked at the rehab place. "I can't believe you'd pull something like this on us. I thought we were *ohana*."

"We *are*." I fix my gaze on Gramma, then Brander. They have to understand. Don't they? "I'm not leaving. But telling Dad I've changed my mind will crush him. Total destruction. I haven't been able to make myself do it." *Yet.*

"Wait, I don't get it." Brander's forehead creases his head. "Are you going to Boston after all?"

I open my mouth to tell him no when Jazz bursts out with a sob.

"Look at her face. Of course she's going." Jazz stalks to the front entryway. "I shouldn't have gotten my hopes up. After all, why would she want to stay here with a one-hit wonder and a pathetic peg-legged pirate when she could have *Harvard*."

I open my mouth, choking on my own words, but every explanation dies in my throat as Jazz lifts her chin and throws open the door.

She steps outside, then as quickly, she pops inside once more and pins her eyes on me. "Oh—Olive? Don't come paddleboarding tomorrow. If you're leaving, then there's no point in us getting any closer before the inevitable has to happen."

With that, she's gone, slamming the door behind her so hard the photo of Mom hanging in the hallway rattles against the wall.

My breath catches as the frame drops from its hook, falling toward the floor in what seems like slow-motion.

"No!" I race to catch it, but I'm too late. The frame hits the ground and shatters right as I step into the hallway, sending glass flying in every direction—including my bare feet.

Shards prick at me as I drop to my knees, but the pain doesn't have room to register amid the aching sadness spreading out from my chest.

I reach out for the frame, as if to touch Mom's comforting smile, as tears coat my throat.

"What have I done, Mom?"

What have I done?

Chapter Thirty-Six

WE CLEAN UP THE MESS, BRANDER humming under his breath like he's trying to fill the awkward silence between me and Grams.

Once the glass has been swept away and I've cleaned up my bloodied knees, I hobble downstairs like a prisoner walking to her execution.

Gramma pats the couch for me to sit, but instead I stand in the middle of the living room, head down, eyes watering. If only Brander would take pity on me and leave, but I know him too well. He'll want to stay. To help.

Except this time there's nothing he can do.

"Where do you want me to start?" I clasp my hands in front of me and lift my head for a moment, but the confusion in Gramma and Brander's gazes sends my gaze hurtling toward the floor.

"Why not with the truth?" Brander's voice is soft, his words measured. Cautious.

"Truth sounds good." Hands still clasped, I sink to the floor, sitting crisscross.

"Why don't you sit up here?" Gramma interrupts me before I can even start. Once again, she pats the empty space next to her on the plumeria-slipcovered couch.

Pins and needles stab at my foot, but I don't even blink in the direction of the sofa. "I'd rather have you two looking down on me." Usually this line would be delivered with a wry smile or mocking laugh, but I've suddenly run out of emotional energy. Instead I whisper a prayer, then begin.

"When I sent in my application, I honestly thought I

should go to Harvard. Things here were hard. Running away sounded easy."

Gramma nods like she understands, but her gaze is unnaturally shallow—like the beach at low tide. It must hurt that I kept all this from her.

My heart pangs, but I press on. "Then when Jonah talked about hiding from God, I knew that's what I was doing. I decided that night that to stay in Maui."

"But it was too late." Brander's words are hushed, almost pained. I sneak a peek at him, but he doesn't lift his gaze from his linen shorts.

"No. That's exactly it. I've been planning on backing out of it—*honest*. But...I haven't gotten the nerve up yet to tell Dad."

Brander perks up at that. "That's not so bad then."

"Actually..." Gramma stands and crosses over to rest a hand on my shoulder. "Olive, your father was calling with some news."

My heart hiccups as I stare up at her. "What kind of news?"

"Upon the approval of your scholarship application, you were also guaranteed enrollment into Harvard."

"Yeah. So?"

Gramma takes a long breath, as though preparing herself for my reaction. This can't be good. "Your father called to tell me—to tell *you*—that he expedited the enrollment process. You are officially a student at Harvard University, starting this fall."

Gramma says more, but her voice seems to fade away.

It's as though the four sturdy walls of the living room fall away as a great behemoth rises from the depths of the ocean to swallow me.

Whole.

"Dad, I am *not* going to Harvard."

I square my shoulders and lift my chin, delivering the statement with every ounce of bravado I have in me—which, unfortunately, isn't very much.

My reflection in the bedroom mirror scowls at me. *Stop rehearsing and call him already. Before you lose your nerve.*

"You're right." I stick my tongue out at myself and reach in my pocket for my phone. Might as well get it over with.

Besides, all of this talking to myself is making me go a little crazy.

I punch in Dad's number and hold the phone to my ear, waiting.

Waiting...

"Olive, there you are!" Dad's voice is breathless on the other line. "I hope I didn't make things awkward with your grandmother. I'd assumed you'd told everyone."

"You told me not to. That it was confidential. *Remember?*"

Dad laughs. "I meant for you not to shout it from the rooftops of social media—certainly I expected you to tell Jazz and Bonnie and that boy of yours."

I open my mouth to correct Dad about my relationship with Brander, then snap it shut. If I go off on a tangent now, I'll never find the courage to get back on track.

A lump rises in my throat, as if trying to keep me from saying the words that I need to, but I swallow hard and press on. "I have something to tell you. You probably won't like it." I take a shuddering breath. "In fact, you're going to hate it. It'll ruin all your plans."

"What? Have you decided to change your major? That's no problem. There's still plenty of time to alter your schedule. Bonnie must have told you about the early enrollment. I'm sorry it was so sudden, but I had a spare moment and knew I could expedite things this way and—"

"Dad. You're rambling." I'd bet anything that the change in his pockets is jangling right now. "Besides, this isn't about my major. This is about Harvard *period.*"

"Still feeling nervous?" Dad laughs again, but it sounds more uncomfortable this time around. "Don't worry. I was terrified my first semester, but it got easier. The nerves do go away."

"It's not that. I—Dad, I'm sorry." My voice breaks. Maybe this is going to be harder than I'd thought. "I can't go to Harvard. It's not where God wants me."

"But you have to go." He says it so simply, so matter of fact. But he's wrong.

"You don't get it, Dad. I *can't* go. It's not right. I wish I had a different way of explaining it, but I don't. All I know is I'm not going to Harvard."

"Olive, I don't—you can't..." Dad sighs and I sigh right back.

"Listen, you're probably mad. Thinking you wasted your time putting in all that work to help me with the scholarship application, but it wasn't for nothing. Didn't we have fun writing that essay? Aren't you proud of me?" Now I'm the one who's rambling, but I hardly care. "Aren't I...enough?"

Silence.

Silence that echoes in my ears.

Silence that makes my heart pound.

Silence so bleak, for so long, that I have to check to make sure Dad didn't hang up on me. When he speaks again, his voice is tenuous. "Olive...you will *always* be enough. You're my smart, talented, beautiful, *brilliant* daughter. I'm so proud. Your mother—she'd be even more proud than I am, if such a thing could be possible."

My heart swells, and his words—words I thought I'd never hear from him—warm my chest. "You mean that?"

"With all that I have in me I do." His voice wraps me in a woolen blanket, hugging me tight and acting as a balm to the slice in my heart that's been there ever since that night in the hospital after Mom died. "I haven't been the best father lately. I never have been. But I am nothing less than proud of my amazing, incredible daughter. Nothing could ever change that."

"You mean...you're not mad? That I don't want to go to Harvard, I mean."

"Not mad. Disappointed, perhaps." Dad takes a breath. "But even more so, I'm disappointed for you."

"What?" I grip the phone. "Why?"

"You've been officially enrolled." Dad's words drip with remorse—an emotion I've never heard from him before. "I understand why you'd want to back out, but at this stage in the application process...you can't. It's simply not done."

"What?" I nearly drop the phone. "It has to be done." It's *going* to be done if I have my way about it.

"I'm sorry, Olive, but there are school statutes in play. My own reputation as a member of the faculty to be considered. You are officially a student at Harvard University."

"No. There has to be another way."

"Take it from someone who's on the board of trustees. There's not."

My heart sinks past my toes, into the living room below. This can't be the end. Not when I've finally found the courage to make Dad understand.

I say a hasty goodbye, hang up, and toss the phone on the bed before leaning on the tacky mirrored closet door. I stare at myself, forehead pressed against the glass, my own two eyes looking back in disbelief.

Of all the messes I've made in my life—and there've been a lot of them—this is by far the worst one ever.

All of the memories I have here, all the joy and pain I've

experienced on this island…soon they'll all be swept away, like footprints in the sand at high tide.

How will I learn to live a *new* new life—one not only without Mom but also void of Gramma, Jazz, Brander, and Macie? Who will help Brander outrun the paparazzi until they get tired of him? Who will play fetch with Macie and Zuzu in the evenings? Who will help Jazz with her schoolwork?

School.

That's how this whole mess started, anyway. With school. Why did I have to get so far ahead in my classes? Why did people have to invent school anyway? Why can't I be in two places at one time? That way I could make Dad happy *and* do whatever-it-is that God wants me to do here on this island.

And…

What if I could?

My heart kicks at my chest, an idea forming in my mind. I meet my own gaze once more, something sparking deep beneath the surface of my eyes, before pushing away and grabbing my phone.

Maybe there is another way after all.

Chapter Thirty-Seven

I SHOW UP AT THE BEACH after church on Sunday, exactly like Jazz told me not to. I can't help it. The sun is shining, the water's glistening blue...and I really, really need to apologize.

Unfortunately, Jazz and Malia are already in the water when I walk down to the shoreline. Hot sand burns my bare feet as I jog up the beach to a board rental place, pay my fee, and drag one of the dinged-up paddleboards down to the water.

It's heavier than I remembered, and I struggle to push it into the surf on my own. The waves crash over my knees as I hold it steady and hop on, my neck already roasting in the bright afternoon sunlight.

Why didn't I talk to Dad sooner? Then this whole mess wouldn't have ever happened.

But I'm here now. And, thanks to my second talk with Dad yesterday, at least things aren't as messy as they seemed at first.

A wave crops up, nearly pitching me off my board, and I tighten my grip on my paddle as I make my way out past the surf. By the time I've made it past the break, Jazz and Malia are way ahead of me. I'll never catch up.

Instead, I stand, cupping my hands around my mouth to holler. "Hey! Wait for me!" If I'm lucky, they're not out of earshot yet.

It takes a moment, but Jazz finally glances over her shoulder, her braid cutting through the air like a whip. But she keeps paddling. *Away* from me.

Even from here, I can feel resentment rolling off her in

waves more powerful than anything crashing onshore today.

Kneeling on the board, I balance my paddle across my knees and bow my head. *God, help. I know I've messed up—big time—but I'm trying to make things right. Please let Jazz understand. Please let her forgive me. Please, will you forgive me?*

Staying on my knees, I dip my paddle into the surf, putting every bit of energy I have into my strokes. The sun shimmers, bouncing off the surface of the water and nearly blinding me. I squint against the harsh light and keep paddling.

By the time I'm within shouting distance of Jazz and Malia again, my arms are burning both inside and out—guess I should've put on sunscreen.

"What are you doing?" Malia's voice carries over the waves, and she switches directions to paddle closer to me. "Jazz said you weren't coming."

"That's what she thought." I climb to my feet. "But I don't let other people make my decisions for me. I wanted to go paddleboarding, so here I am."

Malia squints at me. "She said you didn't *want* to come."

"She did, huh?" I shift my gaze to Jazz, who's turned her board so her back is to me. She's still a good distance away, but I drop my voice to make certain she can't overhear. "That would be her mistake—*she* was the one who didn't want me to come."

"Then what gives? I kind of doubt you decided to come out here for fun if Jazz told you to stay home. All you ever do is slow us down."

A million different rebuttals flit through my brain, and a few even gather on my tongue before I swallow them back. Now's not the time to get into a tiff with Malia—not when she's the only link connecting me to Jazz. "I'd tell you, but it's a long story. And you and Jazz probably want to get to work. *Without* me slowing you down." A wry smile slips onto my face as the last words leave my mouth.

"Yeah. There are only a few weeks left before the race, and"—Malia drops her voice—"I'm starting to get nervous. I've gotta work on my stroke if I want to beat Jazz. But if you need to talk, I guess we could do it afterwards."

"For real?"

"Sure. Why not?"

I arch a brow. Malia doesn't strike me as the heart-to-heart type. Still, she's been spending a decent amount of time with Jazz lately. Maybe she *could* help me out. "Meet me at the Shave Ice Shack when you're done."

"Okay." Malia nods, then heads toward Jazz. I sink onto my board and watch them talk for a moment before taking off. Jazz never even twitches in my direction.

My chest aches as I start toward shore to return my board and put on my cover-up, but a tiny part of my heart knows I deserve every bit of the cold shoulder Jazz is shoving in my face.

My only hope is that I can find a way to fix things between us before it's too late.

True to her word, Malia meets me at the Shave Ice Shack, skin glowing after her paddleboarding session. Ignoring the array of tempting shave ice flavors, she throws her glossy ebony hair into a ponytail before buying a bottle of water. I take that as my cue to order a cone that's twice the size I usually get—just in case Malia decides she wants some after all.

Malia stays quiet as we walk over to a shaded picnic table, but she lays into me before I can take my first bite of shave ice. "What gives? Jazz has been a crab pot all day. I thought it was because of that stuff with her mom, but you made it sound like it was *your* fault."

"It is." Guilt swirls around me, and I hang my head. Yesterday was hard enough on Jazz—why did I have to go and make it even worse? I quickly explain about the scholarship mess, leaving out the part about my maybe-solution, and wait for Malia's reaction.

"So?" Malia shrugs and takes a long gulp of water. I should've known not to hold my breath. "She's mad at you. Big deal. Sounds like you deserve it."

I snort. "Hope you're not planning on getting a job as a counselor."

"Sorry." Malia's cheeks redden beneath her tan. "But seriously. You messed up. Go apologize—and understand if she needs time to get over it."

"I don't *have* time!" My voice creeps up to a near-dramatic volume, and the guy who'd been working the counter at the Shave Ice Shack raises a brow at us as he schleps through the sand to the parking lot—must be the end of his shift. I turn to Malia. "I can't spend every day knowing Jazz is hurting. I have to make things right. Now."

"Sorry, but you said it first. I'm not good with this stuff."

"How come you wanted to talk to me then?"

"Because." Malia lets out a strange half-snort, half-sigh. "You looked like you needed a friend. You and Jazz are good for me. My whole family thinks so. I thought I'd try and return the favor. Lot of good *that* did me."

"Olive? Malia?" A voice comes from behind, and I turn to find Brander walking through the sand, jangling a loaded keyring. "What's up?"

I swing my legs over the picnic bench and spin around to face him. "Just trying to figure out a way to apologize to Jazz. What're you up to?"

"Work." There's a hint of pride in Brander's voice, and I examine that keyring. There are far too many keys on it for it to belong to Brander. It's not like he's rich and famous enough to have an entire *fleet* of Porsches, after all. Plus, that one key looks sort of familiar. "You mean—"

"Now that I know I'll be staying around, I figured I should start working where I belong. I was going to tell you and Jazz yesterday, but then things got crazy."

"Yeah. Crazy." I scuff at the sand. "Are you free to talk?"

Brander nods. "Sure. This is a slow part of the afternoon—it would be nice to have some company."

I smile, then turn to Malia, but I don't even have to say anything before Malia stands and skirts around the picnic table, barely looking at Brander. "Don't worry, I get it. Brander's probably a lot better at this counseling stuff than I am. But hey, at least I tried."

"Exactly. And I'm grateful for it." I meet Malia's eyes and we exchange a real, true smile.

She heads off after that, waving over her shoulder and choking out a somewhat bashful goodbye to Brander, who watches as she sashays away. "She's changed a lot." He rubs his chin. "You and Jazz are good for her."

I nod, the words *you and Jazz* lumping together in my throat. If I can't fix this mess between us, there might not be a *me and Jazz* anymore. Ever. "Are you sure you have time to hang out here and talk? Shouldn't you get inside the stand?"

"Good idea. Come on."

"But I—"

"You're fine."

"Fine?" I laugh. "I remember that manager. He was tough."

"Yeah, but you're not an employee this time around. If he puts anyone on probation, it'll be me." Brander presses his hand to my back, gently but firmly ushering me into the cool, dark shack and closing the door behind us. In all these months, it hasn't changed a bit. If I close my eyes, breathe in the smell of sea salt mixed with fresh-made syrup, I can almost imagine we time-traveled back to last summer.

I float in my sea of memories—my first shave ice, visiting Jazz in the hospital, selling bracelets with Brander—for only a moment more before I snap back to the present.

Brander stands inches from me, eyes wide, lips parted slightly. His gaze is focused on me, like he wants to say something but doesn't have the words.

"What?" I cross my arms. "Do I have syrup on my chin or something?"

Brander flinches, as though caught, and takes a clumsy step away. "No. Not at all. You're perfect."

"Um, thanks?" I squint at him. I thought Brander was going to counsel me, not lose his ever-loving marbles. "What gives?"

"Sorry." He runs his hands through his hair before slinging a ratty apron around his neck. "Just thinking. How are you? You seemed pretty shook up yesterday."

"I still am. Majorly." I close my eyes and pinch the bridge of my nose. Exactly like Dad always does. I haven't even stepped foot in a Harvard classroom and I'm already turning into him. Not good. "Jazz doesn't want to talk to me, and I don't blame her, but I have to apologize."

"What about school? Did you talk to your dad?"

"Yeah. It's too late. I'm officially a student at Harvard." There might be a loophole, but I'm not about to get Brander's—or my own—hopes up."

Brander bites his lip. "Maybe you could transfer to UH after a semester."

"And miss out on four years' worth of paid schooling? Dad would have a fit. He says he understands why I want to stay here, but part of me wonders if that's only because he knows it's technically impossible. I'm stuck."

"So you're going there for all four years, huh?" Brander's jaunty cowlick seems to sag, and I don't think it's because of the humidity. "Wow. That's...that stinks."

"Tell me about it." *Please, God, let there be another way.*

"But at least I have months before classes start."

"I guess. It's still a major bummer."

"I know." I lean on the counter—still as cracked and stained as it was last summer. As much of a business as this place does, you'd think they'd put part of their profits into a renovation. "But a lot can happen in a few months." *Like a magic loophole working out, maybe?* My hand strays to my cover-up pocket, and I clench my teeth against the urge to pull out my phone. Maybe Dad has called or texted. Maybe he talked to the board about my idea. Maybe—

"Maybe I should've gone to Nashville after all."

"Huh?" I nearly collapse onto the counter. "What do you mean?"

"I honestly thought God wanted me in Maui to keep ministering to people. Jazz, Malia—*you.* Now that you're going off to Boston, I don't know."

"You're being ridiculous. There are tons of people for you to minister to here, even if I'm not around. Besides, Nashville and Boston are a long way away from each other."

"Not as far away as Boston and Lahaina. I'll miss you."

I'll miss you too. But there's still a chance—one last, feathery breath of hope left in my heart. And until it's gone, I can't bring myself to act like I'm seriously going to leave. So instead I take a deep breath and lift my chin. *Be strong.* "I don't want to focus on that right now. I'm more concerned about Jazz."

"I get that." A gaggle of middle-aged ladies dressed like twenty-somethings walk by, but none of them get in line for a snack, so Brander keeps talking. "Have you tried apologizing to her yet?"

"No. And I'm kind of afraid to. I've never seen her mad like she was yesterday."

"Me neither. But she usually gets over things pretty fast. You should go over to her house."

"I doubt she'd open the door. She saw me out on the

water trying to catch up with her and Malia today—she could've said hi if she wanted to."

Brander shrugs. "The least you can do is try."

"You think it'd help?"

Brander nods. "I know it would."

"Okay." I steel my spine. "I'll go over right now."

"Good." Brander adjusts his apron straps, then straightens to attention as someone approaches the stand. "Call and let me know how it goes, okay?"

I shoot him a thumbs-up as the customer places their order—asking for an autograph too. Go figure. Brander scrawls his signature across their half-full punch card before flipping on the ice-shaving machine.

I'm almost to the door when the ice-shaver stops whirring and Brander calls my name. "One last thing."

"Yeah?" I turn to face him.

He offers a smile, one sweeter than the bottle of passion fruit syrup in his hand.

"I'll be praying for you."

Chapter Thirty-Eight

A STIFF BREEZE USHERS ME ONTO Ruby's street. My still-damp swimsuit clings to me beneath my cover-up as I jog down the sidewalk. I've nearly reached Ruby's house when my phone chimes in my cover-up pocket.

"Dad?" I press the phone to my ear and slow my pace. "Have you heard from your friend yet? What did he—"

"Not Dad—Gramma." Gramma's voice smooths over my tangle of nerves, and suddenly all I want is to be ensconced in her embrace. "Brander called and said you were going to visit Jazz."

"Yeah. I'm about to knock on her door." And pray that she'll be willing to let me in.

"Okay, then I'll keep this short." Gramma's voice quavers. "Right now that scholarship you won is making a bit of a mess out of things, but I want you to know that I'm still proud of you for getting it. You are a bright, strong, talented young lady and—"

"Thanks, Grams." I laugh, but it catches awkwardly in my throat. "You don't have to say all that to make me feel better."

"I'm not." Gramma's words are firm. "Take it from someone who knew your mother better than most anyone else on this earth. Sophie would've been so proud of you— she already was. But she'd be even more proud of you for being willing to do what's right in God's eyes."

"I don't know about that." My voice breaks, and I clear my throat to keep from sounding like a total baby. "You know that's all I've wanted this whole time—to do her proud.

But I kind of blew that, with all the secrets and lies and stuff."

"Perhaps. But your mother had a huge heart, one filled with much forgiveness. She would be proud of you no matter what. I know I am."

"Really?"

"Of course." Gramma's words are round and full. True. "Now go make things right with Jazz before either of you let this stretch on longer than you need to."

"Okay." My stomach churns a bit. What if Jazz isn't as forgiving as Mom—as Gramma? "Thanks, Grams."

I move to hang up, but before I can end the call, Gramma clears her throat on the other line. "You know you're never alone, right? Your mom is with you exactly like the Lord is with us. Those we love the most never leave our hearts. Look inside—you'll find her there."

"If you say so, Grams." I roll my eyes, but I can't help smiling, and as I finish my call with Gramma and start toward Ruby's, it's almost as though I can feel Mom walking right alongside me, squeezing my hand and whispering in my ear.

"Everything's going to be all right."

"What do you want?" Jazz narrows her eyes at me immediately after she swings open the front door. "And why are you following me everywhere?"

"Hey." I lift my hands, palms up. "It's a small island."

"Don't play dumb. I told you to give me some space, so stop stalking me." She makes a move to swing the door closed, but I leap inside before she can.

"You never told me to give you space, you said I didn't need to go paddleboarding this afternoon. But I *wanted* to go, so I did."

"Then why aren't you still out there?"

"Because I *care* about you." I stomp across Ruby's living room and throw myself onto the dilapidated couch. It creaks and groans in protest as I collapse against one broken-down arm, but I ignore it and get comfortable. Something tells me I'm going to be here a while. "Listen, Jazz. I'm a coward. I probably always will be. But I'm not a liar."

"You could've fooled me yesterday." Jazz clomps over to me, dragging her prosthesis a little. "If you're not a liar, what *are* you then?"

"Um, a truth-stretcher?"

She glares. "That's the same thing."

"Fine. It is. I'll admit it." I pat the cushion next to me for Jazz to sit. She does, leaning so far against the opposite arm of the couch she might as well be sitting across the room. "But you need to face the fact that I came here to apologize, and I'm not going to leave until you let me."

"Go ahead then." Jazz snaps her mouth shut and crosses her arms, as though she can't wait for me to say my piece so she can kick me out onto the street. "But make it quick."

"Fine. Here goes. I wasn't lying to you when I told you I wanted to stay. Yeah, I knew about the scholarship by then, but I was honestly planning on telling Dad that I was backing out."

"Then why didn't you?"

"I got scared. But the point is..." What *is* the point of all this? "Listen, I'm not happy about how I handled things. All I know is I came here to say I'm sorry. And I've spent so much time rambling that I haven't even done that yet."

A tiny smile appears on Jazz's face. "Actually, I think you just did."

"Maybe so." My palms grow damp. I've never before doubted Jazz's forgiving spirit, but today... "I need to know, Jazz—will you forgive me?"

Ruby's wall clock ticks away almost a minute's worth of my agony until Jazz clears her throat, making a small pinprick of noise amid the roaring silence.

"I forgive you." Her voice trembles, and she doesn't meet my gaze. "But that doesn't undo any of this."

"Does that mean we're not friends anymore?"

"Of course not, silly." She smiles, but the smile doesn't quite reach her voice. "But you'll be gone before we both know it, and who's to say you'll ever come back?"

"Of course I'll come back." In fact, if my plan works, I might not have to leave at all.

"That's what my dad told my mom too. Before he ran off for good."

Ouch. "I'm not your dad, Jazz."

"I know." She rests her chin in her hands. "But you *are* leaving. It's hard."

"It's hard for me too, you know." I reach for her hand and squeeze once. Twice. Three times.

Jazz stiffens. "What was that for?"

"I don't know." I scuff my bare foot against Ruby's grungy carpet. "Me being weird, I guess."

"Oh." Jazz hangs her head. "I—I don't know why I thought..."

"What?"

"My mom used to squeeze my hand like that." Jazz lowers her voice. "When she was, you know...normal. And then I'd squeeze back. Three squeezes meant 'I love you'. Four was 'I love you too.'"

My heart hiccups in my chest. "Mom and I did that too. Before."

Jazz meets my eyes, her chin quivering. She's not going to cry, is she? I could count on a closed fist the number of times I've seen Jazz really, truly cry since I moved here in the fall. Usually she only gets teary-eyed over happy stuff, like dog movies.

God, help me. What do I do?

But then, suddenly Jazz is tackling me with a hug and something wet is dribbling onto my arm, and I don't need an answer anymore. "I love you, Olive." She squeezes me so hard I can barely breathe. "You're the first real friend I've ever had. Besides *Tutu* and Brander, I mean. And I don't know how I'm going to say goodbye in the fall. I'll miss you. So much."

Tears swell up and shimmer in my eyes, and I hug Jazz back every bit as tight. "Me too."

Because as far as I know, I really am destined for life back on the mainland. Unless Dad manages to come through for me.

And maybe he will.

Chapter Thirty-Nine

One week later

"GO, JAZZIE, GO!" MACIE JUMPS UP and down as a group of paddleboarders appear at the far end of the shore, ready to paddle to the death on this final leg of the race. We saw Jazz off at the starting line at the northern tip of Ka'anapali beach, then headed over to set up a picnic blanket down the shore a ways from the finish line.

Our spot on the beach is too far away for me to see clearly, but there seems to be a clear break between the first three racers and the rest of the pack. *Please, please, let one of them be Jazz.*

The racers paddle closer, and I crane my neck to get a better view. Does that one near the front have a blonde braid?

She does!

My pulse kicks up, and I wave the poster that Macie helped me make in the air. "You can do it, Jazz!" My voice gets lost in the fray as dozens of other onlookers shout their own words of encouragement, but I hardly care. I let out another whoop, then turn to Brander. He smiles at me, almond-shaped eyes crinkling at the edges.

"Olive." Macie tugs on the cuff of my shorts and sniffs. "I can't *see.*" She thumbs her nose at a paunchy boy of about ten who somehow managed to sneak in front of our blanket.

"Here, let me." Brander swings Macie into the air and perches her on his shoulders. He and I have seen a lot of each other lately, since I finally managed to convince

Grams—and Dad, who's been playing truancy officer from afar—that a shift at the Shave Ice Shack wouldn't interfere with my schoolwork.

But, for as much as Brander and I have seen of each other, our third musketeer has been strangely elusive.

Between keeping up her grades and practicing with Malia for the paddleboard race, Jazz definitely has a good excuse for avoiding me, but a timid part of my heart wonders if she's keeping busy for a different reason.

Probably the same reason I've been avoiding her.

Ever since that day at Ruby's our friendship has seemed stronger than ever—but, at the same time, more tenuous. As though we both know the moments we share are fleeting. Sometimes being apart, as lonely as that is, is more appealing than spending all day with Jazz, wondering how much more time we have left before we say goodbye.

After all, if this last week could fly by so fast, who knows how quickly the rest of my days on the island will go by?

Hopefully not as fast as Jazz is paddling right now.

Brander, Macie, Grams, and I whoop and holler as Jazz draws near, Malia just strokes ahead of her. The two girls are leading the pack. They're followed by another girl maybe a year or two younger, or older—I'm terrible with age—who's wearing a determined scowl.

I take a breath and hold it in for a long moment as Jazz and Malia pass by, their eyes firmly fixed on the finish line at the other end of the beach. The other girl paddles furiously, eyes set on the finish line. She's gaining on them.

"Come on." Brander swings Macie down as the rest of the paddleboarders skim across the water, some of them moving more slowly now that the clear frontrunners have been established. "If we take the path, we can make it to the finish line at the same time as they do."

"Let's go." I hand Macie my poster and make my way out of the throng with Brander close behind me. Once we reach the path above the beach, we break into a run.

"She's doing great!" Brander throws the words over his shoulder, his long legs carrying him faster than I can manage.

"Yeah." My breath comes in short puffs as we jog along the deserted path—everyone must be watching the race, because there isn't a soul up here. "Do you think she can pull ahead of Malia?"

"Maybe."

God, help her do it.

Jazz needs this victory as much as I need Dad to order up a miracle from the powers-that-be at Harvard. Not only for her own sake, but to show her mom exactly what she can do.

"Come on." Brander waves at me as he rounds a bend. I follow him, and we find ourselves on a grassy knoll above the finish line.

"What's going on? Can you see?" I dodge a woman pushing a double stroller and trail after Brander as the crowd thickens. Cheers come up from the beach as the contestants draw nearer, but I can't see a thing. Too bad I'm not Macie-sized or I'd make Brander put me up on his shoulders.

"They're dead even." Brander ducks in front of a few girls, all of whom give him second—and third glances. His cheeks flush pink, and he gives them a quick, *shaka*-fisted wave before turning back to me. "Malia doesn't look happy about it either."

I almost laugh, but a tiny part of my heart hurts for Malia. She'd been so hoping to get that money for her family. But Jazz needs this win to show her mom—to show everyone—that she's as much a real person with one leg as she was with two.

If only they both could win.

Another cheer goes up from the crowd, and my heart

kicks at my throat. "What's *happening*?" Good grief, this being-short business is a pain.

"Can't you see?" Brander peers down at me, as though noticing how much taller he is for the first time. He hesitates for a second, nibbling his lower lip, then bends down. "Come on, get up."

"No way." I take a step back. "I'm too heavy. I'll crush you."

"Do you want to watch your best friend win the race or not?"

"Win? I thought she was behind."

"Not any more. Hurry!"

I don't have to be told twice. Brander hoists me onto his back, and my breath catches in my throat as the ocean comes into view. Sure enough, Jazz has pulled slightly ahead of Malia.

Come on Jazz. You can do it. Go! Though my brain is shouting words of encouragement, my mouth stays strangely shut. I grip Brander's shoulders, and we stand as one silent island amid a sea of excited spectators.

"I hope her mom has a good view of this." Brander's voice is low as Jazz closes in on the finish line.

"Jazz said her mom wasn't coming."

"I bet she's here."

"She'd better be. I can't imagine missing this for the world." My own heart is so full of pride it nearly bursts as Jazz draws nearer and nearer to the finish line. Her tanned, toned arms move in perfect, rhythmic strokes, and her brow is knit in concentration.

And then, with only a few feet to go before she reaches the finish line, Jazz stops.

"Oh, no." I gasp and watch as Malia closes in on Jazz. "What are you doing?" I yell the words as loud as I can, but Jazz doesn't seem to hear me. "Go!"

"Olive." Brander shushes me.

"What's wrong with her? Why isn't she going?" Could it be a phantom pain?

Not now, God. Please not now.

Malia continues to shorten Jazz's lead, and she's about to retake her number one position when Jazz finally dips her paddle into the surf again.

"Go, Jazz!" Brander cheers and I join in as Jazz paddles with renewed vigor. She must hear us this time, because she raises her head and looks right at us before flashing a *shaka.* Then she drops her paddle, unfastens her board leash, and...

"Jazz?" It comes out in a whisper.

I watch, heart pounding in my ears, as Jazz jumps into the water and swims—actually swims—the last few yards to the finish line.

She ducks underwater right before she reaches the hanging blue-and-white bunting that marks the finish line, then pops up on the other side and lets out a whoop. "Thank you, Jesus!"

I'm laughing and then suddenly I'm crying as Brander lowers me to the ground and takes my hand. Together, we race down to the beach to congratulate her right as Malia crosses the finish line. A stray wave pushes Jazz's board across too.

Brander and I reach her first, barely ahead of that oily reporter who bombarded Brander at the airport. I tackle Jazz in a hug the second she emerges from the water, dripping wet and grinning wider than three Cheshire cats put together. "That was amazing," I whisper in her ear before letting go.

Jazz's face is drenched in saltwater, so it's impossible for me to tell if she's crying or not, but her eyes are suspiciously shiny. "I didn't do it for me, you know. I did it for you. And your mom. And Brander too."

"Huh?" I'm about to ask Jazz what on earth she means

when that reporter cuts in front of me and sticks a recording device in Jazz's face.

"Well, little lady, today's your lucky day. What do you have to say about that remarkable performance?"

"It's all Jesus." Jazz brushes wet hair out of her eyes and leans in to speak into the recorder. "He was the one to give me the courage to even enter the race, and He was the one who saw me through."

"Surely you must've had more support than that, though. What about these friends of yours? I see you and Mr. Delacroix seem pretty close." The man waggles his eyebrows as Brander gives Jazz a quick side hug.

"Whoa, hey!" Brander backs away. "Jazz and I have been friends since Sunday school, and I've had enough articles written about me to last a lifetime. Why don't you make this one about her?"

"Fair enough." The man steps closer to Jazz as more people crowd around to offer their congratulations. "Tell me this, young lady—why did you swim those last few yards? This is a paddleboard competition after all. You could be disqualified for a stunt like that."

My blood boils beneath my skin. How can this guy be so insensitive and still expect people to answer his nosy questions? It's not like her jumping into the water was any accident. Jazz could've made it across as easily on her board. They wouldn't disqualify her.

They *can't.*

Thankfully, despite my bottled-up annoyance, Jazz doesn't seem to share my irritation. She flashes a bright, shiny smile, then opens her mouth to answer. "Before the amputation, swim team was my life. I haven't been in the water—really *in* it—for months. I guess I wanted to prove that I could still do it. And if I'm disqualified...well, I'm proud of what I did, and I know why I did it. That's all that matters."

"Wonderful!" The reporter grins like a greedy old gold miner, and I can almost see him spinning the story into more of a sensation than it already is.

Before he can ask Jazz any more questions, though, a loudspeaker crackles. "Would Jazz Whitaker, Malia Akina, and Kaela Almond join us at the podium please? Thank you."

"Go get your prize." I shoot Jazz a thumbs-up, and the crowd surrounding us parts as Jazz makes her way to the podium.

Brander and I follow at a slower pace, sharing a smile. My phone buzzes in my pocket, and half of me is tempted to pull it out right then and there. It could be Dad, calling with news.

My chest quivers at the thought, but I let it ring. I can't let anything tear my attention away from Jazz's big win.

Brander and I end up right in front of the winner's podium, and my chest swells with pride as Malia and the other runner-up help Jazz clamber onto the top platform. A few people make brief speeches, then a man with three medals hooked over his arm steps forward.

But before he can do the honors, a petite older woman wearing an official-looking lanyard and badge hurries over, waving a handful of papers. "Wait!" Her voice warbles out across the beach, and my eyes connect with Brander's. I know what we're both thinking.

Uh-oh.

The woman confers with the other officials before taking the microphone for herself. "It has been brought to my attention by one of our esteemed supervisors that, according to the rules and statutes imposed by the founders of this race, there has been an infraction.

"As it says in the official contest rules, the winner of the Lahaina Youth Paddleboard Race is the contestant whose *board* first crosses the finish line."

"This means, unfortunately, that although Jazz Whitaker crossed the finish line first, her board came in second. In accordance with the rules, she will not be named the winner of today's competition."

"Are you kidding?" I snort. "What a bunch of old coots."

Brander shushes me again, though there's a smile on his face.

Onstage, Jazz and Malia share a quick smile as they trade places and Malia accepts her gold medal, as well as a check and gift card to the Hula Grill.

Typical Jazz—she beams as wide as ever as she receives her silver medal and another, much smaller check. She reaches down to hug Malia, then the other girl.

The second the formalities have concluded, Brander and I race over to the podium. "I can't believe they did that to you!" My hands clench into fists. "I have half a mind to throttle whoever came up with that rule."

"Calm down." Jazz's expression doesn't waver as she reaches out to grasp my arm. "This wasn't about winning medals. It was about proving to myself that I could do it— and I did."

"That's for sure!" The girl with the bronze medal turns to Jazz with a wide-eyed, admiring gaze. "I paddleboard all the time with my older brothers, but I think you're faster than all of them put together."

Jazz's cheeks turn pink, and she ducks her head. "Thanks, Kaela."

"You're welcome." Kaela flashes a huge grin, then runs over to show off her medal to a group of boys I'm guessing are her brothers.

"If you're so good, then you should've won." I kick at a clump of sand.

"Olive's right." Malia walks over. "You lost on a technicality. And I bet you knew it."

Jazz just shrugs.

"I think we both know this is yours." Malia removes the gold medal from her neck and hands it to Jazz, who slips it on and hands Malia the silver one.

"What do you mean? I—"

"Save it for the press. You've always been too nice for your own good." Malia's tone softens. "And I appreciate it. This money is going right into my family's house fund. Thank you, Jazz."

Malia sashays away without another word, and I practically have to hold my jaw in place to keep my mouth from falling open. "You *knew* they wouldn't count your win? And you gave it up anyway?"

"Maybe." Jazz's grin narrows into a small, almost-sneaky smile that tells me all I need to know. "But who cares? Let's go celebrate." She hooks one arm around me and the other around Brander, pulling us toward Gramma's picnic blanket. I start to follow along, but then my pocket buzzes again.

"I'll catch up with you guys in a few." Without waiting for an answer, I duck off the path and lean on a warped palm trunk before answering the call.

"Hello?"

"Oh, good. I caught you." Dad's voice booms in my ear, and I scramble to turn down the volume before I burst an eardrum. "I wanted to let you know that I heard from my friend on the board."

A shiver starts at the nape of my neck and runs all the way down my spine. "What'd they say?"

Chapter Forty

"I HAVE SOME NEWS." I STAND up and rap my fork on Gramma's polished wooden table. We all decided to gather at her place for dinner—Pirate Pete's Pizza, of all things— after the closing festivities of the race, and it's a full house.

Jazz invited her mom and Ruby, and Brander's parents are here too. Even Malia and her family decided to drop by. She claimed it was for her whole family to thank Jazz, but my bet is it's for the pizza. For someone who usually turns up her nose at all things greasy, Malia has been chowing down like a hungry wolf. Guess she figures she earned it after all that paddleboarding.

"I hope it's not bad news." Macie's lower lip slips out, and she pushes away her plate of pizza. "It usually is when we have Pirate Pete's."

"Not this time, squirt." I tug on one of Macie's curls— maybe a little too hard, if the glare she shoots me is anything to go by—before addressing the rest of our guests. "For those of you who don't know I got a full-ride scholarship to Harvard...well, now you know."

Brander's parents murmur their approval, and I toss them a grateful smile before I continue. "Honestly, it was a hard step for me to even send in the scholarship application. Going to Harvard was a dream of mine ever since I was a little kid, but then I came here and I...sorry. I'm rambling.

"The point is, after I sent in my application, I realized that God wanted me somewhere else. Right here."

"Wait." Jazz pushes to her feet too, brushing still-damp bangs from her eyes. "Does that mean you're not going to

Boston after all? I thought you said—"

"I'm still going to Harvard."

Jazz's face droops, and I work to keep my tone sober, crossing my fingers that my eyes won't twinkle and give everything away. "And I still don't know how I feel about it. It'll be super hard to leave this place...for a semester."

"Huh?" Everyone at the table echoes Jazz. And *that's* when I let the smile burst onto my face, along with a laugh I can't possibly hold back.

"After I got the scholarship, I realized I couldn't leave Maui for all four years of school. It was too late for me to un-enroll, but my dad got in touch with the people at the online learning department. I only need to take a semester's worth of classes on-campus this summer. After that I'll come home, and Jazz and I can do school together like we planned. I can get the rest of my degree online"

There's one moment of beautiful, blissful stunned silence, and then Jazz starts clapping. The rest of our guests join in too, but Jazz, Gramma, and Brander clap the loudest.

And somewhere, amid the din of clapping hands and congratulations, I can almost hear Mom's voice coming from somewhere off in the distance. Telling me how proud she is. How proud she'll always be. How she can't wait to tell me that in person one day.

And the very best part?

I know she will.

Chapter Forty-One

Three Months Later

"I CAN'T BELIEVE YOU'RE LEAVING US." Jazz pooches out her lip until her expression mirrors the same sad stare Zuzu gave me when I said my goodbyes to Gramma and Macie earlier this evening.

"Only for summer term. Then I'll be right here where I belong, ready to start school with the rest of you." I say it as much for my own good as I do for Jazz's sake, and my chest gives a nervous kick as I climb out of the backseat of Brander's Porsche. Last time I flew to Boston, I had Macie with me. This time I'm on my own.

"It'll be okay." Brander flashes me a smile as he hoists my suitcase out of his trunk. "I'll keep Jazz busy making shave ice, and you'll be so busy writing papers you'll practically forget you're even gone." Brander convinced Jazz to take my place—the job I finally got back—at the Shave Ice Shack while I'm gone, and I know the two of them will have a blast working together.

"I hope you're right." I return Brander's smile, though it feels bittersweet, as we all walk toward the airport. My heart nearly buckles under the realization that tomorrow I won't be going on a snorkeling trip to Molokini Crater like the calendar Brander got me says. Instead, I'll be settling into Dad's apartment and trying to remember what it's like to live on the mainland.

"Hey, don't go all sad on us." Jazz squeezes my arm as I make a quick stop to grab my boarding passes. "It'll be okay.

You'll see."

"It really does go by fast." Brander leads the way to the security checkpoint. "Even when you're not getting hounded by the paparazzi."

At that, I can't help but smile. Besides, I'll have over twelve hours of travel time to cry any tears that I need to. I might as well enjoy these last few minutes with my friends.

We come to a stop right before reaching the TSA checkpoint, all of us growing strangely quiet. Brander scuttles off with some excuse about using the bathroom, and then it's only me and Jazz.

"Take care of yourself." The words—cheesy and melodramatic as they are—slip out before I can think twice. It's not like I'm going off to war or anything.

"I will." Jazz nudges me. "You're not going to go all sappy on me now. Are you?"

"Not a chance." I flash a smile, but a lump forms in my throat anyway. I push the tears away and focus on my friend. "Thanks for always being here for me, Jazz. You don't know how much it means to me."

"Yes, I do." Jazz's laughing silvery eyes are deadly serious. "I know because you mean that much to me. Maybe even more." At that, she puts her arms around me, wrapping me up in a hug so sweet I never want to leave her warm embrace.

All too soon, she lets me go and steps aside before waving at Brander as he reappears around a corner. "I'll let Brander do his thing now."

"Um, okay." My heart yelps as Jazz melts into the crowd of sunburned tourists on their way home. I have half a mind to run after her and give her another squeeze, but Brander stops me with a warm, bergamot-scented hug of his own.

When he pulls away, his chocolate-covered almond eyes have turned to glass, and he stares at me. Dead serious.

"Whoa, what's wrong?"

"Wrong?" He laughs, but he doesn't sound happy. "Nothing's wrong. You're getting ready to fly five thousand miles across the globe is all."

"It'll go by quick. Like you said."

He shrugs, then takes me in his arms once more and holds me tight before pulling away. "I guess I'd better let you go, huh?"

"Yeah. The security line's getting pretty long."

"Okay." He shuffles his feet. Clears his throat. I give him one last wave and take a step toward the line. Not exactly the goodbye I'd pictured, but maybe it's easier this way.

I turn to catch one last glimpse of him, but a beefy surfer-dude guy falls into line behind me, blocking my view.

Oh well.

Tears rise again, and this time I let them come.

I almost laugh at myself. I'll barely be away for a few months. But still, after everything I've gone through on this island, a few months sounds like an eternity. I shuffle forward in line, a little bit at a time, until it's almost my turn.

I'm fumbling in my backpack for my boarding pass and ID when a familiar shout sends my head shooting up.

"Olive! Wait. Jazz—"

"Brander?" I crane my neck to see around the people in line behind me.

"Olive!" He cuts through the line to reach me, ignoring the serious stink eye the guy behind me is giving him. "Do you have—one last second?"

"What's wrong? Did Jazz's leg give out on her or something?"

"No, nothing like that. But she..." Brander keeps his voice low as he pulls me out of the line and into a quiet alcove. "She said I should do this. So there aren't any regrets later."

"Do what?"

"Olive…" Brander lowers his head. "Oh, man this is a dumb idea."

"Brander." I clasp my hands together to resist the urge to shove my watch in his face. "I've got a flight to catch. Talk to me."

"Here's the thing." He clears his throat. "When you get back would you like to go get dinner together sometime?"

"We get dinner all the time. Why would you drag me all the way out of the line to ask me that?" I tap my foot. Not much time left. The line's getting longer every minute, and this is only making it harder to want to leave.

"No, no." Brander shakes his head. "Not like that. Like, on a date."

"What? Come on, be serious."

Brander's mouth twitches, and I can't tell whether he's about to smile or sob. Maybe both. "I *am* being serious."

"You and me." I point to myself. "On a date. Like with flowers and chocolate and fancy clothes and everything?"

"Not if you don't want to. We could go pig out on malasadas for all I care."

"But we already do that. Why change things?"

"I *knew* I wasn't going to be able to do this right." Brander rolls his head back and breathes in deep, as though asking for help from Above. "What I'm trying to say, I guess, is… Olive, will you wait for me?"

At that, everything but Brander seems to fall away. The rush of conversation filling the terminal building, the hordes of people crushing around us, and the sticky humidity of the air—all of it is lost as Brander's words sink in. "You mean—"

"Shh." Brander places his finger over my lips. "I should've known better than to ask you here. Now. We can talk about it later, when there's less pressure."

"No! Wait. I get it." I'd give anything to be able to tell him how *well* I get it, but now my heart is in my throat. Choking me.

And then it doesn't matter because he's leaning in, bowing his head, and letting his lips rest on mine for one feathery, magical second. My breath catches in my throat, but he pulls away before I can kiss him back. Because—unless I'm hallucinating—that's what happened.

Brander kissed me. Not on the forehead. Not on the cheek. On the lips.

His smile is sheepish as he tucks one hand in his pocket. "*Aloha*, Olive."

"*Aloha*, Brander."

He walks backwards, waving goodbye as he goes, his big, beautiful heart spilling from his smile in a way that makes it hurt to tear my eyes from his.

Because something in my heart tells me that our *alohas* mean a lot more than goodbye.

They're everything—goodbye, hello, *and* love.

Goodbye. *For now.*

Hello. *For later.*

Love. *For always.*

And then, even at the risk of looking like someone in one of those lovey-dovey Hallmark movies, I bring my fingers to my lips, as if pretending I can still feel his gentle kiss—taste it. Because, whether he realizes it or not, Brander's kiss tastes a little bit like shave ice. And saltwater.

And home.

As I step into the security line, a curiously giddy laugh bubbles up in my chest.

Brander and me? Together? Like, *together* together?

After all, he always said he didn't want to date until he found the girl he wanted to...

Marry.

Tossing my purse and shoes onto the conveyer belt, I wait my turn at the metal detector, my heart pounding almost as fast as my brain is spinning.

Brander wants to...whoa.

I step through the metal detector and grab my stuff, letting the thought roll around in my mind a moment longer.

Brander thinks I'm the person he wants to marry? And, like, spend the rest of his life with?

I guess I can see that.

As soon as I think it, I snort out loud. A girl walking by shoots me a *look*, but I ignore her.

Of course I can see it.

I've been able to see it for a long time. Longer than I'd ever admit to myself. Probably ever since his bozo guard dog scared the living daylights out of me when we first met.

But now...knowing he feels the same way.

Wow.

I've never thought much about growing up and getting married before, but now that I'm about to start college I guess it's time to start thinking about the future. And a future with Brander Delacroix in it wouldn't be a bad thing.

Not at all.

Maybe *that's* the reason why God's been pushing for me to stay in Maui all this time.

And that's why, when I get ready to board the plane an hour later, I'm not at all surprised when I feel as though a small piece of my heart chips off and lands in the boarding area at Gate Seven—why I have no doubt it'll be waiting there for me when I come home.

What on earth would you think of all this, Mom? I clutch my necklace, twirling the shell between my fingers, as I stand in line amid a mass of sunburned tourists, soaking in the feeling of standing on Hawaiian ground for the last time.

And then, even later, when the plane is taxiing down the runway and the rose-gold light has begun to fade from the evening sky, I hear it.

I'm so happy for you, sweet girl.

Mom's answer comes to me so clearly that, for a second, I'm sure I must be right up in heaven with her. I snap to attention, head whipping around, eyes straining in the darkened cabin as the airplane takes to the skies. "Who said that?" I whisper, but of course no one is listening.

Instead of trying to figure it out, I lean my chair back, tilt my head to gaze out over the shrinking outline of the island I love, and dream of the future that awaits me.

I don't know exactly what it holds, but I know *God* knows.

And maybe, for right now, that's enough.

Author's Note

Well, friends. We did it. *Barefoot Memories*—and therefore the entire *Tradewinds* series—is complete. Are you still here reading? If so, thank you from the bottom of my heart. You are my most faithful supporters, and I couldn't be more grateful for you.

When, at the age of fifteen, I set out to tell the story of a lonely girl on a porch swing, I had no idea I'd end up here. With Olive, Brander, Jazz, and a whole slew of others who have become like family over the last four years. With three books and a novella spanning one remarkable year in the lives of these beloved characters. With a very empty hole in my heart at the realization that their story is complete.

Or is it?

Because you know as well as I do that God never stops writing our own stories. He doesn't simply walk us through a trial, then pat us on the back and slip out the door.

He stays with us in trial and in triumph, through hope and heartbreak. And though the world tries to turn these beautiful truths into platitudes—trite little sayings that get oh-so-easily tossed around—the fact of the matter is that *it's true.*

God is with us—*always* with us. He will never leave us nor forsake us.

Though Olive has made it through one of the most challenging years of her life, I know in my heart that she hasn't seen the last of God's help and provision in her life.

And maybe...just maybe...she hasn't seen the last of me, either. *winks*

Until I Write Again,
Taylor Bennett

PS—If you enjoyed *Barefoot Memories*, or any of the other books in the *Tradewinds* trilogy, I'd love to connect with you! You can send me an email at taylor.bennett.author@gmail.com or connect with me on Instagram @taylor.bennett.author.

And, if by chance my books have made you laugh, cry, or grow closer to the Lord, I would so appreciate it if you would leave a short review on Amazon or Goodreads…those of you who do will receive *allll* the hugs and an extra slice of (virtual!) key lime pie. *Aloha!*

Discussion Questions

1. Olive is determined to start the New Year off by letting go of the heartache of the past year. Do you think this is a realistic "resolution" or do you feel that healing takes time?

2. Jazz tells Olive she should be grateful to *have* a dad, since Jazz has always longed for a father figure in her own life, even though Olive and her dad struggle to connect. Are there people in your family that you have trouble getting along with? How can you work to see them as a blessing instead of a bother?

3. Olive has dreamt of going to school at Harvard ever since she was a little girl. What dreams have you had for a long time? What are some of your new dreams? If forced to choose, would you rather chase one of your old dreams or a new one? Have you ever realized an old dream is no longer alive? Did you let it go, or did circumstances cause it to disappear?

4. Olive has a hard time deciding whether or not to give Brander a valentine. What would you have done if you were in her shoes? Have you ever given a guy-who's-a-friend a valentine? How was it received?

5. Olive decides seeing her sister smile is worth bringing a dog into the house. Did you expect this kind of selfless decision from her? How has Olive grown throughout this series?

6. If you were Brander, would you have accepted the record deal or stayed in Maui? Why do you think Brander ended up turning it down?

7. Do you think Olive's dad had the right to expedite Olive's college enrollment process? When he tells Olive it's "too late" to back out, do you think he's being completely honest or trying to save face as a faculty member?

8. Do you think Jazz's mom really sees her daughter as a failure, or is she trying to prepare her for the harsh unfairness of the world? Do you think there's hope for a relationship between Jazz and her mom? Have you had to deal with people like this? How could you be a go-between?

9. Jazz gave up her chance to win first place in the paddleboard competition to help a friend *and* prove something to herself. Which do you think came first—her decision to swim the last few yards, or her eagerness to help Malia in a time of need?

10. Brander asks Olive to "wait for him." Do you think they'll end up as boyfriend and girlfriend? Getting married? How do you see their more-than-a-friendship playing out? Were you bothered or intrigued by his decision to not date unless he could see himself marrying that person?

Jazz's Favorite Key Lime Pie

From the kitchen of Tutu Bonnie

This pie, complete with a white chocolate-studded crust and rich, creamy filling, is one of Tutu Bonnie's specialties. It also happens to be Jazz's favorite dessert, perhaps because the decadent filling is a delicious balance between sweet and sour. Some bites may seem a bit tart, but the more one eats of this delicious pie, the more they'll notice the inherent sweetness that prevails through each piece—just like we can always find a way to look on the bright side when we go through trials in our own lives. It's the perfect treat for an optimist like Jazz!

WHAT YOU NEED:
1 cup graham cracker crumbs
1 tablespoon brown sugar
1/8 teaspoon salt
1 ounce white chocolate, finely chopped
2 tablespoons butter, melted and cooled
1/2 cup plain Greek yogurt
1/2 cup Key lime juice (regular lime juice works fine too!)
1/2 teaspoon grated lime rind (plus more for topping)
3 large egg yolks
1 (14oz) can sweetened condensed milk
Whipped cream (for topping)

HOW TO MAKE IT:
    1. Preheat oven to 350°.
    2. Combine crumbs, sugar, salt, and chocolate in a bowl, stirring well to combine. Add butter and toss with a fork until moist. Press crumb mixture into a 9" pie plate.

Bake at 350° for 8–10 minutes or until beginning to brown. Cool completely.

3. Place yogurt and next 4 ingredients (through milk) in a bowl and beat with a mixer at medium speed for 2 minutes. Pour mixture into crust and bake at 350° for 14 minutes or until set. Cool pie completely, then cover loosely and chill at least 2 hours. Serve with whipped cream and an extra sprinkle of lime zest, if you'd like.

4. Enjoy!!

www.ingramcontent.com/pod-product-compliance
Lightning Source LLC
Chambersburg PA
CBHW070456170726
48291CB00005B/1777